This is a work of fiction. All of the characters, organizations, and events portrayed in this novel are products of the author's imagination or are used fictitiously.

Books may be purchased in quantity and/or special sales by contacting the publisher, Arbor Bay Publishing, by email at arborbaypublishing@gmail.com.

Published by: Arbor Bay Publishing LLC
Cover design and logo by: Angela Fristoe
Editing by: Frankie Sutton
Format Design by: K.M. Debro

ISBN: 978-0-9984782-2-7

HER SIDE OF THE FENCE

By

CHRISTINA LUND

ONE

The rain hit the windshield mirroring the sound of tiny pins being dropped on marble flooring. The sound echoed up from the back seat as my young daughter swung her thin little legs, tapping her stiff crinkly rain boots gently against the seat.

The murky sky had a single razor beam of sunlight peeking through the thick charcoal clouds, and the rich smell of earth seeped inside my SUV.

The concrete sidewalk leading up to the elementary school was speckled with children, while a rainbow of tiny umbrellas bounced and floated in the hazy rain around them. The usually bright and bold flowers along the sidewalk were depressingly hunched over, sad, and wet.

"Bye, Mommy!" Julia yelled, as she stretched between the front seats and gave me a kiss on my cheek before she slid out of the SUV, the crinkling of her raincoat bustling while she closed the door. I smiled at her before looking out the window at the scowls on the parents' faces, many desperate not to get wet.

Regardless of the dull atmosphere, I always found something calming about the rain. I usually liked sitting in a vehicle surrounded only by the sound and smell of rain, while the world outside moved in a brisk chaos. Lately, there has been no calming effect for me, just the realization that my dull life reflected the morose weather outside.

I wasn't sure what had happened to my identity, my desires, or me. I thought about this, as I often had been lately, while staring at my reflection in the rearview mirror. The almost unrecognizable image seemed to answer my desperate question; I was gone, or worse yet, invisible.

I looked in the mirror at my tired eyes and I attempted not to think of the past, or the regrets I had, not for any big mistake I had made, but for the little ones that didn't seem to make a difference at the time. I tried not to think about taking my youth for granted, which was now nothing more than a distant memory, covered by the doldrums of present day life. Life had gone by too quickly, the roller coaster wouldn't stop, and by the time I grew up and moved into our large house, there was almost nothing left of my young vibrant self.
I had become insignificant.

After marriage, the house and a child, there was a massive shift in life. I had an overwhelming pressure, mainly self-inflicted, to take on the "Wifestyle." I had an image to maintain and a house to keep perfectly beautiful, but all that never seemed to matter, as those stupid Joneses were always one step ahead of my image and me.

In the short existence of my high-end, cookie-cutter life, there was one thing in my world that exceeded even the highest of expectations, and that was Kyle. He housed a wonderful jaw line, straight white teeth, thick dark hair, and broad shoulders, what you would refer to as "classically" handsome. Perhaps something out of a black and white French or Spanish film.

I continued to look at my reflection in the rearview mirror, noting how I swore that my hair was getting thinner, as my skin looked old and tired. I thought about Kyle and my growing resentment towards him. I was rational enough to know it was not truly any of his doing, but that knowledge did nothing to ease my soul.

Kyle was handsome and smart, hardworking and compassionate, but I felt left behind, and below his level. I resented the fact that women smiled and laughed at every small joke he made at a restaurant, even if he was completely oblivious to their hopeful advances, and regardless of the fact that I was by his side. I resented the fact that he took his shoes off upstairs in the bedroom, even though the closet by the front door had a shoe rack, which I personally purchased just so dirt wouldn't be tracked through the house. Petty? Maybe. It drove me insane and I was resentful for playing musical shoes for the last eight years. Above all, the largest growth of resentment was for the fact that he was so oblivious … to me. Oblivious to my leading questions, my advances, my desires, my need for him, or even to be present. It had become torturous, even agonizing for me to feel alone, even if I was in the same house with my own husband.

Kyle had goals to achieve, and he did so with such intense ambition that there was hardly any room left for the needs of those around him. The repetition of letting him push toward his goals because of my desire to avoid a possible fight, or to play the role of the good supportive wife, lead me down a path where I just gave in and sacrificed for whatever he wanted.

I stared at the hair thin lines around my eyes, wondering if other people could see the lines I saw, and if others could see my youth fading as I could. I thought about that youth with Kyle, and I remembered how in the beginning, his drive and motivation pulled and attracted me to him, even impressed me with his determination, finding it both strong and inspiring. After all, I had landed a 'catch', and everyone knew it.

I missed Kyle. I missed our relationship that we had in the beginning, when his eyes locked with mine and nothing else mattered around him, only me. I missed the fact that there once had been laughter and fun, and I felt as if I were interesting and special to him. It's what women want to feel, and what women *need* to feel. I longed for those nights when he was in law school, I would just walk by his desk, and moments later, he would wrap me in his arms and smile at me. Many times, we never even made it to the bedroom. Now, those nights had been replaced with my subtle advances for his affection as I walked into his study, gently running my fingers on top of his hand while he poured over files. Then I would softly ask if there was anything I could get him. I waited and hoped that the memories of the past would become real again and he would look up at me, smile, and make it to the bedroom. However, that doesn't happen anymore, and it hasn't happened for a long time. Now I get a polite, "No thank you, Dear, I'm coming to bed as soon as I'm done." As usual, I go to bed alone with nothing more than the warmth of my tears, as I wish to have the man I fell in love with back.

I think about how I routinely drift into a sleep remembering those nights of the past, full of passion and life. Those were the good memories, the ones I tried to keep and hold onto, finding it harder than ever to do so, afraid that even the best of memories might fade to the point of being forgotten.

My eyes start to warm with tears as I continue to look at my face, while the trickle of rain softens, hitting the SUV with a whisper of droplets. I live with the truth that while my husband was beyond extraordinary, I, on the other hand, was not. Almost everything about me was average and ordinary. Almost the entirety of my physical appearance from head to toe was average. Even my hair was such a dirty, murky blonde, sticking me in between a blonde and a brunette. The only positive was the freedom to pull off either color if desired, which I had on various occasions. I had been fortunate enough to be gifted with a single noteworthy quality, a strikingly pleasant smile. Everything else took a great deal of effort to enhance through cosmetics and Pilates classes.

It was in all reality that the primary thing about me that wasn't average, was my world and life that existed around me. I was only a tiny, ordinary person in a vast sea of an extraordinarily perfect world.

I took a break from my self-indulgence of pity as I took my eyes off my reflection in the rearview mirror, focusing my attention to the long row of luxury sedans and SUVs with their windshield wipers flicking back and forth. The usually quick moving drop off in front of the school was painfully slow. I searched through the speckled children until I found Julia's purple umbrella and matching raincoat. She was barely taller than my waist, but felt that she had keen fashion sense and insisted every shoe matched every coat. I reached up my hand and waved frantically in preparation for her to do her last turn around to see if I was watching her, and like I expected, she quickly spun and smiled as she disappeared beyond the entrance.

Mrs. Nolan, Julia's teacher, stood just inside the doorway with her frail, wrinkled arms crossed tightly to her chest. She watched the kids with a placid look as they carefully scurried up the steps. I always found it odd that Mrs. Nolan seemed disturbingly fond of gaudy sweater vests with pictures of whatever holiday was the closest, and always accompanied with a long, straight denim skirt that hit right above her ankle.

Finally, after several agonizing minutes of waiting, the row of vehicles began to creep forward and fan out into the street, leaving behind the long prestigious drive of the school.

I slid my SUV into the pack among the other wealthy ants and headed toward my house. Every house I passed was larger and more beautiful than the last one. Each lawn had expensive landscaping, complete with the expected white picket fence. They were all the picture of desire, each one appearing as if it had graced at least one month's issue of Better Homes and Gardens. Each illusion fit the mold.

I knew that there was only one thing I needed to do in order to get out of my mood and away from the mundane was to run my errands as quickly as possible and make the near thirty-minute trek across town for a visit.

I found that if I skipped breakfast (that was a lie, I had an iced mocha latte and muffin) and ran my errands in record time, I could arrive fashionably early. The weather did a turn around and cleared only minutes after I dropped Julia off at school. As I got out of my SUV, there was the illusion I had traveled to a different state all together. The sun was shining and the bright blue sky was streaked with wispy white clouds.

I walked around the path of the enormous residence of my best friend, Abby. Her place was a massive and beautiful six thousand square foot luxury home, which caused me teasingly to refer to it as the "little palace." As I stepped from the path onto the cement, I saw the wet imprints of feet. The foot trail eventually led me to a table next to the pool. A second later, I heard the loud voice of Abby as she yelled in my direction.

"Hey, Vi! Do you want some lunch?" Abby stood next to the table with a glass of iced tea in one hand and her large brim hat in the other. The sunlight bounced off her glossy, honey blonde hair, creating a virtual halo effect, and her skin was a natural golden hue. The combination of her skin and hair gave her the coloring of a Swedish swimsuit model. Abby's best feature was her eyes, a vibrant crystal blue.

Her appearance mattered none, compared to her personality.

She was pushing thirty-two but didn't look a day past twenty-four. Abby was one of those friends that you wake up one day and realize she's so much like you, only the better and more sophisticated version of you.

"Sure, I'll have some iced tea." Abby's lips curled up into a wide smile under the shade of her brim hat as she lifted the glass pitcher, the ice cubes clinking together like rusty wind chimes, while she poured tea into another glass.

"Do you mind if we eat lunch inside? I've already been out here in the sun for thirty minutes." She owed that paranoia to the fact that she was the daughter of an avid sun worshiper who had many negative experiences due to her UV obsession, so Abby learned never to spend excessive amounts of time soaking in the sun.

"Yeah, that's good. I can't wait to eat. I'm starving," I said with a half-turned smile. We both loved to eat, although you couldn't tell by looking at her.

Abby flung open the French doors at the rear of the house, and we were greeted with a cool, fresh breeze. She had one of those places that never ceased to smell clean, probably because she could afford to hire a cleaning service to clean three times a week, and she didn't have children and all the sticky fingerprints that comes along with them.

Our instant friendship started in our freshman year of college, long before her prestigious lifestyle, and it was one of those friendships that happens once in a lifetime. It didn't take long into that first year before we became inseparable, bonding over Ramen noodles and hot chocolate, the cheap kind in little packets without marshmallows.

At that time, neither of us had imagined our lives the way they became. We were far too busy living in the reality of the college experience and digging up change from pockets to scrape together enough to order a pizza. Abby's ideals and character had remained consistent throughout the change around her. Even in her current situation with her lush mansion and twenty pairs of high-end shoes, excitement still hit her when she'd whisk off to the thrift store and find a vintage piece of furniture for an unbeatable steal, even if it was something that her neighbors frowned on.

The seedling of her wealth was while we were in college and her grandmother asked for help with the small cosmetic line she owned. Abby couldn't refuse to help her only living grandmother, and occasionally on her visits home, would lend a hand with the product, packaging, and everything on the ground floor. Abby had valued the little business more for the quality of time with her grandmother than the very moderate commission she received, often being paid by way of baked goods and trinkets. On an early fall morning, Abby was called to the dean's office where she was handed the phone and connected with her family's estate lawyer. She was then told her grandmother had passed on, leaving the cosmetic and skin care line to her, and making Abby the sole benefactor.

However, what her grandmother had not had a chance to tell Abby when she was living, was that she got a contract to sell her line exclusively, as a test run, to over a dozen Macy's Department stores for a fraction under one million dollars. The loss of her grandmother and the information that she was the sole benefactor came at such an intense shock that I had to help her walk back to the dorm.

Perhaps it had been the years of scraping and saving money, and knowing how much her grandmother loved the line that Abby took that line, turning a trial run with those Macy's locations into a contract that extended nationwide. Abby never forgot her roots and the people that were there before the contracts and financial swing.

Her money didn't buy her the thing she longed for the most, a true relationship and children. I was one of the few that saw through her mirage of loving the single life, and quickly admitted that it was nice to have the freedoms that she had.

Only one week before that shocking phone call in the dean's office was when Abby had walked in on her new fiancé and a girl from our dorm. The event altered Abby so tremendously that it sank deep to her spirit and twisted the strongest characteristic she possessed, loyalty. From that day forward, she was beyond skeptical for the loyalty of any man who was remotely interested in her. She was jaded.

"Hellooo, Vi, you okay? You're a little spacey today." I shook my head, trying to focus myself back into the room.

"Sorry, I was just thinking about stuff. Anyway, I think Julia has something in dance in three weeks. Do you want to come? I need to check my calendar first though."

Abby lifted an eyebrow and gave me the best friend stare as she said, "Wait a minute...are you still writing everything down on your pocket calendar? Aren't you using the Calendar App on the smart phone I bought you for Christmas?" Abby couldn't breathe without her phone, and I drove her insane with my resistance to be controlled by a device. I was like an old lady refusing to learn a computer for the first time.

"I'm trying to use it, but you know I'm old school. I still love my pen-and-paper method." I looked at her half-embarrassed, knowing that I did not intend to use the App.

"Well, you can't teach a cat a new tune," she said with a shrug. Abby had a gift for getting sayings mixed up, and her quirky versions seldom made sense, but I always found them amusing.

"What do we have to eat?" I changed the subject and looked over at the small but gorgeous spread on the buffet table next to the dining room. Abby's house was not only fresh and clean, it was also beautifully decorated with imported furniture from around the globe, and secret thrift store finds.

"Couldn't help myself, I got Italian." Her perfect figure glided over to the buffet table. It would be so easy to hate her for her figure if it wasn't for the fact that she had grown up as a chubby kid, giving me yet another reason to believe in karma.

I scanned the pasta and quickly replied, "That sounds great, but I'm only going to have just a little. I think I'm starting to put on some weight." She stepped back and looked at me with such a disapproving stare that I felt embarrassed I had even mentioned it.

"Oh, shut up...you look great. The Pilates is working for you. Besides, do you think Kyle is gonna leave you over a couple of pounds?" She looked at me with an arched eyebrow. The question sounded like it should have been a rhetorical one, but she said it with a tone that indicated she expected an answer of some kind.

"Who knows? He's so oblivious to everything, I don't think he would even notice if I gained a hundred pounds." Abby gave me a half eye roll as she put a heaping scoop of pasta on her plate, gently shaking the spoon to get every last bit onto her plate. I continued speaking, holding nothing back. We had that type of friendship where we could share even the most intimate of thoughts.

"Kyle has been working so hard lately that it feels like an eternity since we've had any real physical intimacy. I'm starting to get scared if this goes on any longer that I'm going to be reclassified as a virgin." Abby chuckled a little and turned to me. She spoke with such an air of confidence as if she was giving a piece of ancient wisdom.

"Don't worry, there's nothing that can't be fixed with a good push-up bra and a slice of pie. Just give him the slice of pie wearing nothing but the push up bra, and I think being oblivious will be a thing of the past." Abby gave me a wink and a joking grin. She then picked up my plate, and gently shook it in her hand like a tambourine. It was easy for her to think a bra and a slice of pie would solve any problem. She had a wonderful body, a fortune, and no husband to ignore her. Even still, I appreciated her attempts to make me feel better and lighten my mood with some of her humor. She continued to wiggle the plate teasingly.

"Why don't you go ahead and give him a little extra something to hold on to. You never know, he might like some junk in your trunk." I couldn't hold back my laughter, as I stuck my butt out and glanced back at it. I had a little bit of a curve back there, but like everything else on me, it was just average. She looked down at the plate and then back up at me, indicating with her eyes that she was waiting for me to tell her how much I wanted. All the laughter aside, I felt a tiny ping of sadness knowing the truth. Kyle was so oblivious that he might not even notice a hundred extra pounds. I decided not to think about the weary state of my marriage, and smiled as I pointed to my plate.

"Yeah, pile it up." We both laughed, and my spirit was soon rejuvenated as I enjoyed the rest of the afternoon.

TWO

"Auuughhh!" I grunted just as the car halted to a stop. I felt my cup of iced coffee tip, spilling onto my beige trousers, with the extra shot of espresso making the dark stain more obvious.

"Mommy! The new teacher said that all parents need to bring the permission slips inside," Julia said, gazing at me with her big brown eyes.

"Okay, okay, let me clean this coffee first. Give Mommy a second." I tried frantically to dab and smudge out the brown coffee, but it was only getting worse considering I had worn dry clean only pants. I just hated meeting someone for the first time after such a catastrophe, but that was how my luck ran. I believed that was the way of the universe letting me know I shouldn't think so highly of myself. Not that I did, but it would be nice to meet someone and shake hands without having droplets of this or that on my clothes, like a five-year-old after Thanksgiving dinner. The new teacher had already been there a week, but this was my first chance to meet him.

In frustration, I tossed the useless napkin aside, leaned over, and grabbed my mid-length French jacket, hoping it would cover the coffee smudged across my right thigh.

As Julia and I walked into the elementary building, the smell of paste and crayons floated through the air, creating a magical world of imagination and nostalgia. Standing near the classroom door, I spotted Beth, the mother of Julia's current best friend. Our daughters were also in the same ballet company, and we occasionally sat together during recitals. I put my hand out, giving a slight wave and softly called out her name.

"Beth." She spun around. Her bone-straight, platinum-blonde hair shifted off her shoulder. I smiled and walked over to her with Julia glued to my hip. I immediately noticed how great she looked. She had on her beautiful Burberry coat that I had only seen her wear to recitals. Her hair had just recently been cut, highlighted, and styled, and if I had known any ritzy salon that opened so early, I would have sworn she had just come from there. Beth was on the pale side and had a petite frame, with small modest curves, trapping her in time as if she never finished late puberty. Her body and mannerisms always gave off a nervous energy. I had observed during the few encounters I had with her husband, who was an excessively tall man that towered over everyone both in height and in attitude that he came off as extremely uptight and negative. Often during those occasions, he would speak to her like a mentally disabled child.

Beth was a very attractive and sweet woman, and I imagined she had her fair share of suitors before she married, but in my opinion, she married a man that had more to offer from his wallet than his heart.

"Did you come to see the new teacher too?" Beth asked me. She seemed fidgety in such a manner that made fidgets almost look like a nervous tick. She repeatedly smoothed the sides of her hair while gliding her finger back and forth across her neck and ear. I was so hypnotized by her anxious movements that I took a moment to respond.

"Yeah, I got the note that the parents should bring in the permission slips so he can introduce himself... So, what's the deal with the teacher?" I made the half-joke as I saw another mother dressed in a knee-high skirt and high heels. I did not predict that my little joke would make Beth so uneasy, but it did, and what little color she had in her face melted away, making her look positively sick with fright. It was as if she were afraid any answer to my question would cause her husband to pop out from behind a door and accuse her of gossiping---or worse, flirting. I quickly changed the subject so her nerves didn't become overly frazzled.

"You look really nice, Beth. Did you get a new haircut?" She gave me a shy smile, reached up, and smoothed out her hair.

"Yes. I was a little overdue for something new. The new teacher seems pretty nice, and he's British." She straightened out her hand with her fingertips against the corner of her mouth, unintentionally mimicking a five year old telling a secret. Then she spoke in a whisper.

"I think men with accents are so attractive, and a British accent is at the top of my list. Not that I'm looking, but it doesn't hurt just to notice, right?" She leaned back and studied my face for some form of approval.

I wasn't sure what to say to her, since I didn't have the power to read her thoughts. I decided to reassure her with the confidence that I could keep her little fantasies a secret.

"Don't worry. I won't breathe a word to anyone," I said in all sincerity. The fact is that the conversation seemed to be borderline strange to me. I really didn't have a feeling one way or another if she thought accents were sexy, as most women usually find them so.

"Oh, thanks. I don't know if you know this, but my husband, well, he gets a little jealous sometimes." Beth's voice became so low I was forced to strain my ears to hear her.

I looked back at her, faking a look of ignorance and surprise about her husband. We both smiled at each other signaling our agreement of confidentiality.

I turned and grabbed Julia's attention as she was practicing ballet moves with Beth's daughter, Ginger. I took her hand and made my way into her class, walking through the small cluster of well-dressed and overly perfumed women. *How handsome is this guy?* I thought to myself.

Julia skipped past me and slid into her seat. There was a bustle in the room with small children chirping and chattering with each other like a coop full of baby chicks. I was slightly disappointed that the mystery man was not in the room. All I saw was pudgy, bald, Mr. Kaufman, the third-grade teacher from down the hall. Mr. Kaufman looked up and greeted me with a goofy smile. On the desk in front of him lay a large stack of permission slips, so I was sure I was one of the last parents to arrive. Mr. Kaufman had a son in Julia's class, and we had casually known each other ever since an incident that landed us both in the principal's office. His son wouldn't stop bullying Julia and yanking her hair, and in return, she retaliated by shutting the desk on his hands. We were lucky enough to resolve the issue and still keep our cool. I was pleased that she did stand up for herself, so that day, I took her out for ice cream –a secret between us.

"Violet. I'm sorry, I should say, Mrs. Taylor." He tipped his head and gave me a quick nod. We had been on a first-name basis since our kids had their schoolyard crush or more like schoolyard smash.

"You know you can call me Violet, Greg. Did we scare the new teacher away already?" I looked around the room expecting him to open the door and make a grand entrance from the supply closet or something of the sort.

Mr. Kaufman, with his pudgy belly, wobbled his way over to me. His dingy white dress shirt was a perfect fit across his chest, but his belly area was a different story. The buttons near the bottom pulled, leaving thin oval gaps between each button, almost enough to see his tank top underneath. His hair had so much gel holding it down to one side that it looked greasy and dirty.

"Oh, no. He had to take a call in the office, something about his move over here from England." I nodded politely and turned around as a few of the mothers in the hallway decided to call it quits and head out. The children were quietly shuffling around and putting pencils in and out of their desks.

Mr. Kaufman took off his thick glasses and began to clean them with a handkerchief from his shirt pocket. He spoke again before I could say anything.

"He'll be back in about ten minutes. You can wait for him if you like, but I think he intends to stay late this whole week to get caught up on lesson plans and whatnot." Mr. Kaufman was definitely a character; the type of character that you never think really exists until you see him in the flesh. Even though he wasn't that far past his early forties, his body and way of speech would easily be paired with a man of a much older age, perhaps a grandfather even. His hygiene left much to be desired, and his superior intelligence made for long and uninteresting conversations, at least to me. Mr. Kaufman and his wife could not have kids, so they had adopted a son roughly six years earlier. The child was promptly spoiled and given everything he ever asked for.

"No, that's okay. I really gotta run. I have some errands to finish up for the day. I'll pop in when I pick Julia up after school. Can you pass that message along?"

He gave me a nod, and I quickly headed for the door, hoping to avoid any long, tedious discussions he might feel like having. I quickly shuffled over to Julia's desk, gave her a little peck on the top of her head and told her I loved her before I dodged my way out of the classroom and into the hall.

I rushed back to the SUV with such a quick pace that it border-lined on a sprint. There was an irrational fear I had that Mr. Kaufman would flag me down to tell me about cold fusion or some other topic along those lines. I shoved in my key and took a big sigh of relief that I avoided what could have no doubt, been an intellectual drain on my morning.

I pulled into my driveway and opened my door, smiling as I took a moment to appreciate the sights that surrounded me. Fall was right around the corner. The thing about fall is that you can always smell the crispness of it first, before any other change. The best part is the aroma of the leaves in the early dewy mornings, right before the first frost of the season.

The start of autumn always invoked a happiness within me. With autumn, it made anything seem possible, like a chance for change. Most people seemed to feel this way about spring, but not me. I was born and raised in the North East, so each year was like a brief return home to my childhood, full of memories with crisp days and bright changing leaves.

I took in a deep breath of air, walked up my steps to the front door, and noticed that it was unlocked. This startled me for a second, as I had clearly remembered locking it. I paused and leaned in, straining to listen for any indication of trouble. I reached in my purse, fishing around for several seconds before I found my pepper spray. It became clear to me that if I was ever attacked, it would not benefit me to have my pepper spray buried at the bottom of my purse. I grabbed the spray, twisted the knob, threw open the door, and cautiously ducked to the side as the police do on reality TV shows when entering a crack house. I was greeted by a voice shouting my name.

"Vi! Can you come help me please?" Kyle's voice trailed down the stairs from his study. *What's he doing back home?* I turned around and looked, but didn't see any sign of his car. I knew Kyle had left first thing that morning, as usual, right before I took Julia to school. I paused for a moment to steady my heart, as it had not received the message yet that we were clear of danger. I walked upstairs and opened the door to the study. My husband was crouched over his desk in his undershirt and going through papers. His dress shirt was crumpled on a chair next to the window.

"What are you looking for?" I asked him as I watched his face change to concern.

"Uh, I had some pictures. The client is coming in today, and I thought I had them with the file, but they're not there. Plus, my shirt got caught on a stupid nail and the cuff ripped."

I held my breath since I knew which pictures he was looking for, and exactly where they were. Kyle was a lawyer who specialized in divorces, expensive ones. He had talked for years about wanting to switch to criminal law, but the business of divorce is sadly lucrative – something I always found ironic, considering how lucrative the business of weddings are. I quickly offered to help.

"I'll grab you a new shirt and I might know where the pictures are." I darted out of the room while Kyle continued to rummage through his drawers. I couldn't prevent the smile on my face when I thought about the pictures he had on file. The pictures were for a client whose wife was having an affair with a clown-- literally the big shoes, red nose, everything. Stuff like that is way too hilarious to be fiction.

I had taken some things into his study when I saw the pictures on his desk. I was glad to have a real laugh with what would have been a usually dull day, which made my stumble on to the pictures a treat. I read over the client's file and the notes that were taken at the meeting and learned that the client's wife, once the school cheerleader, was caught by the PI with a clown. That clown turned out to have been an ex-lover from many years earlier, prior to her marriage. The pictures were so hilarious that I put them in an empty folder and took them over to Abby's so we could have some really good laughs, and we did. I had not really thought that Kyle would have even noticed they were missing. Now, I had to figure out what to say to him. I couldn't tell him I had taken the pictures out of this house, or that I had even shown them to anyone. My mind raced through all the different excuses and reasons I could give. I really hated lying, but this felt like one of those things that would turn into a huge deal for many years if I told the truth.

I could hear his search intensifying, as I hurried downstairs and opened my bag to retrieve the file with the pictures in it of Cirque de Erotica. I couldn't believe I had forgotten to put them back, and next time, I wouldn't be so negligent if say, I found pictures of a wife and a mall Santa. The thought of the ridiculousness of it all brought a wide smile to my face that I hid before I walked back upstairs.

"I got them!" I held up the file, while he looked bewildered.

"Why were they downstairs?" he asked me with curiosity. I could tell by his look that he was reaching all corners of his brain to remember if he had taken them downstairs, or put them in a new folder as well. Kyle was a great lawyer, but he was forgetful. He often worked late and would forget that he had moved files or set records somewhere. Even though it felt slightly wrong, I used his forgetfulness and seized the opportunity.

"Well, I came in here last week and the pictures were on the floor. I wasn't sure which file they went with, so I put them in a new file and took them downstairs to give to you to take to work." I gave quite the convincing performance -- almost Oscar-worthy. However, there was the small sense of guilt that I couldn't shake, and I felt both foolish and annoyed that I lied. I truly wished I could have been forthright and told the truth without the fear of being plagued for the next five years with annoying repercussions.

He looked at the file for a second and then just shrugged it off.

"Oh, okay. Thanks. Did you get my shirt? I gotta go."

I wasn't entirely sure why, but on some small degree, I was angry that he wasn't thankful I rescued his pictures from the floor, even though it was all a complete fabrication. Instead of saying what I thought, I kept my disappointed mouth shut and handed him his shirt.

We both walked down the stairs as he buttoned his cuff. I handed him his briefcase and he leaned in to give me the obligatory goodbye kiss on the cheek, checking his watch as he did so, which was definitely not my idea of romance.

"What's on your pants?" He asked when he tore his eyes away from his wristwatch and finally noticed the brown smudges all over my thigh.

"It happened in the car. I came to a stop and my iced coffee spilled. Now I need to take them to the dry clean--"

"Oh, since you're going to the cleaners, could you take my suit?" He said, cutting me off mid-sentence.

"You know my favorite one that is up in the closet. I have court tomorrow, so if you could drop it off with your pants that'd be great, but make sure that you pick them up tonight. Thanks. Bye." As he spoke, he fiddled with his phone. His eyes didn't look at me once. When he finished talking, he leaned in and gave me another quick peck on my cheek, all the while staring at his phone. A moment later, he was out the door, and I was left standing there, invisible as always.

"Dick," I said after the door was closed. I knew he couldn't hear me, but a tiny piece of me wished he could have. A wave of sadness came over me, and I felt so ignored and unloved, a more familiar emptiness than I would have liked to admit.

I dragged myself upstairs to find something half decent to wear to meet the new teacher. I was more curious about his appearance so I could have something interesting to tell Abby, than I was about having some handsome man to gawk at, and throw the occasional flirtation in his direction. I already knew I had received my fill of a handsome man when I married Kyle, but in reality it turned out to be more loneliness than it was worth. After all, he was one of the most handsome men ever seen, and I saw all too well what that did for me. Maybe if I had to do it over again, I would pick an average-looking geek so I could be the best looking one in the relationship, which is the best advantage for a woman. It wasn't hard to see my husband didn't marry me because I was a trophy wife, but because of my fun wit, charming personality, and maybe my smile.

I sat and stared at my reflection in my dresser mirror. I reached up and ran my fingers through my simple, mediocre, nothing-to-talk-about hair. I wasn't remarkably beautiful like most of the wives in the neighborhood that went jogging in their expensive, skin-tight Capri pants, always in full makeup. I hadn't had the customary breast implants or porcelain veneers, which seemed to be the green card application in this area. I wasn't the wife that a husband would want to take around town to show off her incomparable beauty. No, I was the witty and fun wife, the cute one with the nice smile. At first, I was good with that, but now it never felt like enough. Kyle had stopped paying attention to my wit and he was not only unappreciative of my personality, but he was oblivious to my presence in its entirety. The rate at which things were decaying, I began to ask how long it would take for me to vanish, indefinitely. I frowned at myself in the mirror, and then I stopped looking at myself all together. I was beginning to feel there was nothing to look at, so maybe I couldn't blame him for staring at his phone.

I picked his favorite suit out of the closet and headed out of the door so I could complete the mundane task of taking clothes to the cleaners, not that he would appreciate it, or even notice it for that matter. Most importantly, I had to pick up one of my favorite outfits so I could go and meet with Julia's new teacher.

THREE

I paused in the doorway, staring at the new teacher, his arm stretched, making big sweeping loops as he wrote against the chalk board; Mr. Conway.

At first, I didn't understand what the other mothers were making a fuss over. He was a hair above average, but nothing spectacular. I put him around the same age as me, possibly older, but not by more than a year or two. His hair was thick and soft brown with what looked like a slight wave to it, but the short clean cut made it hard to tell if it was naturally curlier than it appeared. He had a classic prep-school type charm about him, complete with well-pressed and styled clothes. I could picture him standing in the large halls of Oxford with books under one arm and an apple in the opposite hand.

The afternoon light created a thin glowing aura that outlined his back, enhancing the curve of his behind, which was quite stunning. Even as a woman who typically didn't notice men's behinds, I couldn't take my eyes off his.

I continued to watch him for a few seconds longer as the faint smell of a crisp, clean cologne floated to the doorway, which was a far better cry than the musky Old Spice that usually lingered the halls behind the older male teachers. Then, I began to realize that this teacher was like candy for the sweet-toothed housewives looking for something besides their lackluster husbands.

The momentary silence was broken by Julia's voice, as tiny hands pushed me from behind, her little arms just reaching to the lower part of my back as she leaned in with all her weight, giving me a surprising jolt as I lunged forward.

"Go, Mommy! Come see Mr. Conway!" Julia said in a typical shrill of excitement for any younger child.

"Hello." He turned and looked at me, giving me a nice smile, flashing boyish dimples in his cheeks. I smiled back and gave a nod as Julia ran around me, bouncing up to the side of him. Then she continued with her excitement as she spoke.

"Mommy, he is really nice. And he let us have extra art time!" She turned her excitement over to him and continued as she pointed to me.

"This is Mommy, but I'm the only one that calls her Mommy. Daddy calls her Vi, so you should call her that name, and not Mommy." He nodded in agreement and understanding, and then he said,

"That sounds good, I promise to call your Mommy, Vi." He gave her a warm grin, which she quickly returned. He glanced over at me.

"Did you show your mommy the picture you drew today about community?" She dramatically stuck out her bottom lip in a pout.

"Oh, I didn't finish it." Very gently, he crouched down and leaned in as he said in an imitation of a whisper.

"That's okay, you can finish it real quick if you like and I won't tell Mommy...I mean Vi... then you can give it to her." He gave her an exaggerated wink as she nodded her head in agreement to the plan.

She turned to me and in a dramatically sneaky fashion, proclaimed, "I'm going to sit at my desk, Mommy, but I'm not going to tell you that I didn't finish my picture, 'cause it's a surprise." She smiled believing Mr. Conway and she had worked together on a type of covert operation. Julia's little shoes tapped against the floor as she skipped to her seat.

The classroom was empty, except for us and the cartoon like characters gazing at us from the posters on the wall. The overhead lights had been turned off, while streams of pale white sunlight poured into the room from the row of windows across the wall. Mr. Conway stood up from his crouching position and set his chalk down. He walked toward me as I stood next to his desk. His body language was smooth and slightly seductive. It was beginning to look like he might be the kind of man who was used to having women fall all over him, and I, was not one of *those* women.

"It's nice to meet you. You can call me Paul."

I cleared my throat, feeling nervous for an odd reason before I apologized.

"I'm sorry I'm late." There was no need for my introduction, as Julia took care of it for me.

"Not a problem. I'm just reviewing lesson plans from my

predecessor, and I don't like to take stuff home with me anyways, it's such a chore." His charming accent seemed to bring the empty room to life. He fixed his eyes intensely on me, making it easy to notice the pretty sky blue color hiding behind long brown lashes. He half sat on the edge of his desk, one leg outstretched and the other bent at the knee, just inches from my thigh. I cleared my throat again.

I glanced back at Julia who was consumed by her project, her colored pencils lined in a perfect row at the top of her desk, which she preferred over crayons. I looked back at him and he quickly said,

"She's extremely talented at art. I can't believe the detailed and creative things she has shown me. Has anyone ever told you she's gifted?"

My sense of pride stretched a wide smile across my face as I blushed.

"Yeah, I know. She draws all the time. She loves it. She takes after me. I was originally an art major in college." I felt a little ping of guilt as if I was being too boastful and taking from my daughter's compliment, so I quickly stated,

"But she already shows more talent than I had at her age." A look of genuine interest crossed his face.

"That's great, what is your profession? Do you do anything in the art world?"

I regretted I had even mentioned my passion for art, because I didn't know what to say, and I didn't do anything with my talent. The closest I came nowadays to creatively painting was when I painted Julia's room with multiple shades of purple. I didn't even make simple things like crafts anymore. All I had was the memory of my talent by way of paintings and chalk sketches that were housed in a wooden crate in my closet. So I shrugged, and then pretended I was not personally interested in my old dreams.

"No, that was in another life for me. I don't really have the time. You are really good with kids." I decided to change subjects, and the compliment came out so naturally and sincerely. He gave me a similar warm smile that he had given Julia. His eyes sparkled like crystal blue waters when he looked at me. Not past me, or through me, but directly at me, like truly seeing me. I could imagine that beneath his clean shave, well-groomed hair and sharp pressed clothes, there was a mischievous streak in him, a rebel... in a very sexy way.

Instinctively, I glanced down and noticed that he was not wearing a wedding ring on his finger. Embarrassed with myself for even looking, I shook my head, as if the physical act of doing so could erase the reality that I had checked. My face flashed red as his smile widened, aware I had looked at his finger.

"Thank you, I really like children and I enjoy teaching. I hope I can do an adequate job in replacing Mrs. Nolan, as I am told she had been with this establishment for many years." As he finished his sentence, in my nervousness, I began to babble.

"I heard her sister became ill and she decided not to wait to retire. Her husband had passed away several years ago and her sister was the only family she had left, so I suppose she wanted to go take care of her. She was pretty good with the kids but could be a little cranky with parents sometimes." As the words just blurted out of my mouth, I was oddly surprised at how easy it was to talk with him, who was not much more than a stranger. There was a feeling around him that made it comfortable and easy to give him information. I would have considered giving him my social security number if he asked for it. To my relief, my foolish ramblings didn't seem to faze him.

"Yes, that does make sense." He appeared to have the same level of ease speaking to me that I had with him. There was a strong sense of familiarity between us, like an old childhood crush that you lost contact with for two decades. I looked at him and asked coyly,

"Why do I have the feeling I just told you stuff you already knew?" He tilted his head and gave a sly, flirtatious smile, as he brought his finger up to his lips.

"Shhhhhh. Trade secrets of the ever so famous teachers' lounge." He gave me a slow wink that would never have been attached to a wholesome sort of man. I inched back, and ever so slightly gave him a smile and nod, unable or unwilling to go further verbally with the beginning of our flirtation. It was leaving a thick feeling of sexual desire that seemed to appear instantaneously. His body language became more professional and his tone changed.

"Is there anything you'd like to know about me? Maybe my credentials or experiences?" He leaned slightly to the side, picking up a pair of thin glasses, and began cleaning them on a cloth that he picked up from his desk. He glanced up at me while still cleaning them. My throat became dry and I honestly did not have a desire to ask about either his credentials or experience. The scent of his cologne mixed with his fabric softener slowly surrounded me like a warm blanket of alluring bait. I had always been a sucker for a clean, well-scented man. Good cologne was a frequent gift I bought for Kyle.

Between the vision of him and the scent of him, my heartbeat began to increase in rhythm, leaving me almost dizzy. Instinctively, I reclaimed my position moving slightly closer to him. Then, without hesitation, I blurted out,

"Are you married?" I was horrified at my own self and lack of professionalism. My mouth had become disconnected from my brain and all good conscious, all of which was out of character for me.

He placed his glasses back on top of the desk as his mouth curved to a half-frown. I sensed more pity in his expression than sadness, but he took no pause as he spoke openly with me.

"I was engaged back in London, but as it turned out, my fiancée didn't want to get married – at least not to me." I felt I had put my foot in my mouth when I saw the look on his face.

"I'm really sorry, I shouldn't have asked." I broke eye contact with him and glanced back at Julia. She was biting down on her tongue as it stuck a fraction out of her mouth, another trait she got from me. I slowly looked back at him, feeling remorseful that I had asked such a personal question. His voice was soft as he said,

"Don't worry about it, better it happened before we got married than after." Then he cleared his throat and in a serious request asked,

"I would like to ask that you not repeat that. Others don't know about it and I'd like a fresh start over here. Can we keep this little secret just between us?" He reached out and put his hand on my arm. The minute he touched me, my heart skipped a beat. His touch was like a warm, vibrating electricity that tingled as it crept up my arm, and then branched out through my entire body. I could feel the warmth of my face as it became red, and I cautiously took in a deep, slow breath.

"Sure. You got it." I flashed him a smile, and he smiled back at me. I looked away for a moment trying to regain some composure, which was nearly impossible with the warmth of his skin against mine. This urgency and desire I had to talk with him, be flirtatious and even let him touch me, was not my character, it was not who I was. . . I found it alarming. I slowly moved my arm out from under his hand so as not to be offensive to him. His hand was so hot that the minute I removed my arm, I felt a burst of cool air hit my skin.

"Thank you. I really do appreciate that."

"At first, I was going to say we have some single moms... but that might not be for you right now, and I could be inappropriate for suggesting." I said this in an uncharacteristically enticing manner. We smiled at each other and the pull between us was real. There was a laugh in his smile.

"You are really funny, and nice." I waited, and hoped he would reach out again and touch my arm, but the thought of my foolishness made my face burn, along with my body.

"Oh, thanks."

It was not a delusion and there was no mistaking it, there was an obviously strong attraction between us. Like a thick, sexual tension that his intense stare continued to keep lit. My mind filed through my vast memory bank, trying to recall the last time my husband gave me such a feeling. A feeling as if I was a girl about to be kissed for the first time.

I had entered a room where I felt like I had fresh air to breathe for the first time in a long time, and the attraction was so obvious, even an onlooker would not deny it. I could see in his face that he felt it also. I did the only thing I could do, and that was to pretend that the spark in the room did not exist. My conscience compelled me to stay away from the dangerous line and out of trouble.

"Well, I better get going." There was a sense of longing in his face that he tried to hide. I took a step back and he stood up from the desk with the light shining behind him, reminding me of a scene I would picture out of a romance novel, not that I read them.

"I honestly am glad that I met you. I wish we could talk longer but I know you have much to do. I do look forward to seeing you again. I see that you are a chaperone this Friday." He glanced down at a handwritten list sitting on top of his desk next to his glasses. He tilted his head and put his hands deep in the pockets of his trousers, his British accent fitting nice with the whole image of him.

"Oh, yeah, I believe I'll be able to make it." I had forgotten that I was holding the permission slip in my other hand, which had become almost a crumpled ball of paper. I opened it up and smoothed it out as I lay it on top of the stack along with the others.

Even as he pretended to be indifferent and professional in his manner of asking me, the sexual air never lightened. It was more than troubling. It was truly dangerous. I shyly matched his act of professionalism and said,

"It was really great meeting you too, and I hope you like it here."

I slowly reached out my hand in a polite manner and we shook, the heat from his palm pressed against mine, forcing me to hold my breath.

I called back to Julia and she eagerly jumped up from her desk, skipped to the front door as she gave him a wave, and raced out into the hallway, leaving me behind as she typically did.

We gave each other one last smile and I quickly turned on my heels and marched out of the classroom, eager to hurry home and make a couple of calls. I could feel this introduction was dangerously sexy, and if there was one thing I knew, I needed to cancel being a chaperone. Because after all, I just so happened to be married to one of the best divorce lawyers in the county.

FOUR

Big, loose curls of auburn brown hair swept across her peaceful face as she slept. I sat on the edge of her bed, quietly watching her take slow and even breaths. Even though Kyle and I had straight hair, she had inherited her beautiful soft curls from his mother. Sometimes I sat in her room on the edge of her bed, while the light from the hall laid a small shiny sliver against her cheek. It was so peaceful in her room, billowing with love. Julia was an angel to me, fulfilling an emptiness that would exist without her. Along with her peaceful presence, I came into the room to enjoy the faint smell of laundry soap and her lilac candles that smelled so fresh, even though they had never been lit. In all things, her room, her presence, drove me harder to hope for a better marriage and a happier home for her.

Kyle had wanted more kids, but the timing for another child never seemed quite right. In addition, intimacy is required for the making of a baby, and his long hours and burnout of energy rendered our sex life next to nonexistent. When I paired these facts with the modest difficulty for me to conceive, the statistical odds were one in a hundred.

I could hear Kyle let out a sigh from his study down the hall as papers rustled in the background. I slowly got up as Julia snuggled the side of her cheek deeper into her pillow, while a faint smile came upon her face. I closed my eyes partly blocking out the brightness of the hall light as I stepped out of Julia's room. I could see the door to the study down the hall was open just an inch or two.

"Are you going to be working a while longer?" I opened the door and leaned in to ask, bracing half my weight against the doorknob under my hand. He sat at his desk writing down some notes as he flipped through one of his books of law. He was wearing a tank top and basketball shorts, and the shadows cast from the lamp on the table next to the desk revealed the slight chisel of his shoulder muscles.

"Um, no, not much longer. Was there something you needed?" He asked without peeling his eyes up from his book.

Yeah, I was hoping to get laid, was the first thing that crossed my mind, but I decided it was best not to use words. Instead, I walked across the room and sat in the leather wingback chair that was perched directly in front of his desk. I slowly crossed my legs, foolishly doing my best Sharon Stone impression while resting my wrists just off the edge of the arms of the chair.

"Well, I was thinking we could go to bed early?" I said as slowly, deliberately, and seductively as possible. For a moment, he glanced up without lifting his head at first, giving me a half smile before his eyes glanced back down.

"Oh, I see." His smile softly faded as something in his book grabbed his attention before he frantically tried to write it down.

I sat across from him and watched as he began to forget I was even in the room, as I was slowly vanishing before his eyes. I cleared my throat to let him know I was still there.

"Vi, I'm really sorry, but one of my clients has a really good lawyer, and I'm just afraid they're gonna get screwed. This other guy has all kinds of tricks up his sleeve. Would you be mad if I took a rain check for tomorrow? I'm just swamped right now." He looked so sincere, and I knew how he hated to lose when his clients had the possibility of being screwed. My heart sank into sadness because I knew there would be no rain check for tomorrow. I put on a small smile and said gently as I stood up,

"Of course not, I understand," I lied. The fact was that I didn't understand at all. I didn't understand how a divorce lawyer who spent all day hearing about how his clients partners neglected them for years, could come home and not have a clue he was neglecting his own marriage. All that would lull me was just a fraction of his time and affection. I started to walk out of the room when I was instantaneously hit with the urge to ask,

"Do you still care about me?" He looked up surprised by my question. When he looked at me, I was taken back to the memories of the past – the way he had always looked at me with such love. His eyes would light up when he saw me walk into the room, but that seemed so long ago, centuries maybe, or even a different couple. The past haunted me because I could still remember it like it was yesterday. I could even remember the very first time I ever saw him.

I had been visiting Abby's hometown on a long weekend in

February, our sophomore year of college. We went to the local university's lacrosse game just for fun, and there he was, playing on the field. He was so handsome and talented, friendly and encouraging to his teammates. We shared a quick glance with each other for a moment, but I never imagined a boy that handsome would have been interested in me. After an unfortunate clumsy stunt in the parking lot, a spark was lit. In the beginning, it had seemed so promising and hopeful, never changing, and never ending. That time almost became more like a dream with each passing day, making the current state of things seem more and more like a nightmare by comparison. He paused for a second and then replied,

"Of course I do, Vi. I don't know why you would even think I don't care for you. If you want to talk about it more, we can do it tomorrow." I shook my head and gave him a little smile at another promise for tomorrow. I already had a pocket full of his tomorrows, and they weren't doing me a bit of good.

"I was just asking. Don't work too late. You need a little sleep too." I walked to the door, and every step saddened me further. I heard him as I reached the door giving a casual, professional reminder.

"Door." He continued to flip through papers as I closed the door behind me. The moment the door clicked shut, a wave of loneliness overtook me. I walked to the bedroom and got under the extra soft cream colored Egyptian cotton sheets. The bed was king sized but never seemed too big for us in the beginning, but now it always seemed half empty. I pulled the covers up around me, feeling as if I was nothing more than the ghost haunting this large expensive house.

FIVE

"I can't believe it, Vi!" Abby exclaimed as she jumped in the front seat next to me and shut the door.

"Believe what?" I asked looking over at her as she raised her shoulders and pulled her jacket closed, trying to over dramatize the current temperature, as if we were in the North Pole. I didn't understand what she was so agitated about.

"It's sixty-three degrees, Abby. That's called fall, not winter." I gave her a sly smile and a half-eye roll since I had only worn a light jacket on top of my yoga clothes. She looked over, gave me one more dramatic shiver, and smiled.

"I'm just complaining because we could be in my house right now working out. I don't know how you talked me into going to your Pilates class with you. I guess this makes me a really great friend." She gave me a big smile as if she was going to ask me for a huge favor in return. I smiled back at her.

"I just love your company. Besides, if I don't talk to you, who am I going to talk to?" She turned her head quickly in my direction like a puppy that just heard his favorite squeaky toy.

"Talk? Hmm. I know there has to be something going on... spill." Her eyes lit up like a child's on Christmas morning with both her eyebrows raised high enough to touch her hair line.

"Down, girl. Down." I remarked like a dog trainer. Her smile faded and she crossed her arms, giving me a small pout for withholding information from her. I knew she was hoping for another hilarious cheating clown story or something of that nature.

"Well, you know Julia's new teacher? He's very handsome... *And* single." I raised my eyebrows up and down a couple of times so she would get my intent. I didn't know why I hadn't thought of it right off the bat. She was single and he was single. She looked over at me and gave me a thoughtful smile, as if to say she was grateful I was thinking about her, but she wasn't interested.

"Thanks, but I'm kinda seeing someone. I just met him last week so I don't know where it's going. Honestly, I'm not really looking for anything serious, but thanks for keeping an eye out for me." I didn't ask her about her new guy because she always told me when she thought it might be something. She wasn't a stranger to dating, but was one of those girls who had a wall around her heart to save herself from another possible heartbreak.

I rolled to a stop in front of Kyle's building, taking in the sight of the perfect landscaping, and even if it was fall, it still looked great.

"I have to drop off some of Julia's tickets so Kyle can give them to some friends. I'll be just one second." Abby gave me a nod and snuggled her back into the chair as a restful look came over her face, as if she was planning to take a nap.

The office smelled of expensive leather and Xerox paper. The huge windows allowed the faint sun of autumn to creep into the room. I walked through the large cedar doors after pushing them with all my strength. I always hated those doors and how heavy they were. They always reminded me of the tall wooden doors you would see on old church buildings.

I looked up and saw an unfamiliar figure. She stood against the filling cabinet. Her legs were long and lean, and they led down to black high heel shoes . She wore a classic black pencil skirt and lilac blouse. She was stunning, not your typical movie secretary with blonde hair and black glasses, like the characters that are usually played by the Marilyn Monroe types. No, she had beautiful skin with a hint of olive in it, and long, dark hair that was thick and flowing like a Pantene commercial. I immediately felt sick to my stomach with how sultry and sexy she was. I took a deep breath because I had unknowingly been holding all my air in. She was every wife's nightmare. She heard me and twisted her body like a smooth panther.

"Oh, hi, can I help you?" As if it couldn't get any worse, it did, her voice was like a nightclub jazz singer. Low, but sensual. I was really starting to hate this girl. She gave me a huge smile and flashed brilliant white teeth. I did hate her now.

"I'm Mrs. Taylor, Kyle's wife...is he in?" I asked these questions in hopes that this was like an episode of the twilight zone and I had stumbled into another office that just looked identical to my husband's.

It was alarming to think this creature is what he worked with every day, or perhaps even his reason for wanting to stay late. My stomach did another flip as I got a sharp pain in the pit of it.

"He's just finishing up a phone call, but I can go in there and let him know you're out here waiting? Oh, yeah, and it's really great to meet you." She gave me such a diplomatic smile as she turned walking around the corner to his office, swinging her hips ever so slightly like an exotic dancer, while the bottom of her high, high heel shoes flashed a shade of bright red… Expensive slut.

I decided quietly to walk behind her since his office wasn't that far from the front desk. His door was only cracked and she gently creaked it open, gliding across the room. She stood in front of his desk with a passive and patient stance, clasping her hands tightly together in front of her waist, which squeezed her chest together. I could tell she knew exactly what she was doing in this subtle move to enhance her cleavage.

Kyle was leaning back in his chair, talking on the phone and smiling in response to the person on the other end of the line. He looked up and saw Miss Slutty-two-shoes and gave her a kind smile and head nod acknowledging her presence. Seconds later, he ended the call with some professional goodbyes.

I clenched the corner of the wall, hiding half behind it like a seasoned PI, taking in the whole interaction when he hung up the phone and greeted his *sexretary* with a large warm smile. The sharp stabbing pain returned to my stomach. I couldn't remember the last time I had gotten such a greeting. She said something he found funny and they both chuckled like little schoolchildren. I felt even sicker. I wanted to go and push her out the window. She then got a professional look on her face while obviously informing him that I was waiting in the lounge. His smile faded for a second and then was replaced with a smaller thankful smile for her services. I ducked back behind the corner and quietly walked back to where I had been standing. Moments later, they both walked around the corner.

"Vi, is everything okay? Did you want to go to lunch or something?" He asked far too formal to make me believe he was genuinely interested in going to lunch with me.

"Uh, no, I just wanted to drop off those tickets so you can give them to the Lerners." I reached out, handed him the envelope, and then looked back several times toward her as she returned to her filing. His body slightly jerked, realizing he had not introduced me to her.

"Oh, Olivia, could you come over here for a sec? I want to introduce you to my wife." She set down her files on top of the cabinet. As she walked over, her long legs stretched out and her high heels hit the wood floor with precise taps like a runway model. She stopped and gently flipped her hair back with her long neck and perfect jawline sticking out. I imagined for a second what it would feel like to reach out and put my hands around that neck, choking her. My thought replaced my fake smile with a wider, real one. I reached out my hand and shook her long fingers with perfectly manicured nails.

"I'm Vi or Violet, well everyone calls me Vi." We finished shaking hands and then I gave her another smile, the keep-your-hands-off-my-man-or-I-will-cut-you smile that all women understand.

"But you can call me Mrs. Taylor." Her smile half-faded, but she quickly found it again and replied,

"Of course."

I looked at my watch and gave Kyle a kiss on his cheek, letting him know that Abby was out in the parking lot waiting. The heavy cedar doors closed behind me with a long creaking sound and then a thump like something out of a scary movie, I felt sick all over again.

I was so heated from anger it no longer seemed cool outside, as I jumped in and slammed the SUV door shut before I leaned forward, grabbing the wheel in a mock choking move, and wishing it were Miss Slutty two shoes herself.

Abby looked over with a bewildered look on her face, not sure what to say.

"You should see the new girl they have as a secretary. She looks like she just ended her career as a high class call girl." Just saying it out loud forced a lump into my throat and I could barely swallow. Abby sat up, prepared to comfort me.

"Vi, you don't have to worry about Kyle. He's not that kind. Besides, I don't care what she looks like, she's not you, and I'm sure Kyle knows that." I shrugged my shoulders and then shook my head.

"No, you didn't see this girl. She's the kind that turns every man into that kind of guy. And just the way he smiled at her was enough to make me sick. I know we are having some problems right now, but I still care if he would do something behind my back. I just don't want to be made a fool." I took a couple of deep breaths and tried to relax my nerves.

"Vi, I'm sure he was just being nice. I didn't see the smile but it was probably nothing. Don't get yourself worked up. You're a good thing and he knows it. You've been by his side even when you guys had hardly nothing, and he's not the kind of guy to forget that sort of thing. All marriages have their ups and downs. You guys will get connected again. Well, that's what they say on talk shows, but I believe it." She reached out and put her hand on my shoulder. I had to bite my tongue to keep the tears from forming in my eyes. I felt as if suppressed emotions were coming to the surface. The long nights of loneliness and desperation. It was embarrassing to think of me making myself look like a fool trying to impersonate Sharon Stone in order to get my husband to sleep with me.

Abby tried to cheer me up.

"You want to get going to Pilates and burn off some of those feelings?" I looked over to her and saw the sad but helpful look in her face.

"Screw Pilates today! There is a martini with my name on it." She looked down at her watch shaking her head at the morning hour, and then she looked up at me, smiled, and with a 1940's Silver screen goddess voice, she replied,

"Darling, where have you been my whole life?"

SIX

The sound of clinking saucers and the deep hissing from the espresso machine echoed throughout the atmosphere, while the smell of fresh ground coffee floated in the air.

I sat in a brown leather armchair only a few feet from the small, decorative, gas fireplace. I flipped through my book as I sipped on my delicious soy chai tea latte, one of the finer pleasures in life. I really had a soft spot for this coffee shop, it was more of an individual place, and they used great ingredients and had even better prices. It was my secret place. This was the place I would come to when I needed to think, or just be by myself. It often reminded me of home with the wood floors and small fireplace in the middle of the room, all of it surrounded by small wooden tables and matching chairs. My favorite spot was in front of the fireplace, which was lined with deep brown leather armchairs. It felt more like a cozy cottage than a high priced corporate coffee shop.

The little bell on the door rang every time a new pair of shoes walked in. I would get a slightly chilled breeze against the back of my neck as I sat in the path of the fresh air sweeping into the room. I heard the bell ring and continued to read my book. I pulled my knees up to get comfortable, but then I held my breath as I heard the familiar voice of a British accent. I immediately slumped forward and raised my shoulders as if I could evaporate into the chair. It was no use. I was directly in the middle of the main sitting area of the small shop. I could see the back of his jacket while he stood at the counter, which was less than ten feet from my chair. I very gently closed my book and put my feet on the ground, sliding to the edge of the chair ready to switch seats with smooth intentional moves, imagining that I was in a cave with sleeping bears. My mind raced over my rehearsed explanation for canceling as chaperone on Julia's field trip. I wanted to get out of there before temptation was laid before me. The temptation would be like offering a sweet piece of pie to a woman who has decided she no longer wants to be anorexic. I was afraid of what I might say or do.

My stomach once again was stabbed with a sharp pain, as the image of Olivia flashed in my mind. Her long perfect legs, her perfect hair and teeth. *Did my husband feel something for her? Was he attracted to her?* I closed my eyes, took a deep swallow, and thought of the question that I had been trying to forget for two weeks now. *Has he done something with her?* I felt so completely alone. So sad. I kept my eyes closed and thought of all the nights I had been rejected for the sake of his work; the nights that I fell asleep before he even came to bed. The times I would tell him he didn't have to work so much, we had enough money already and everything else was just extra. I felt sad, thinking of the man that I had loved so much. The fun, carefree college boy that smiled at me and made me laugh. I knew he was ambitious even in the beginning, but I had thought that his love for me was stronger than his personal ambitions.

I took some deep breaths, putting those thoughts out of my mind. I didn't want them to ruin what had been such a peaceful day so far. I kept my eyes closed, afraid to open them. I had forgotten for a moment Julia's teacher was just a few feet from me. I squinted one eye open tilting my head toward the counter. I didn't see him there, I sighed some relief, believing he must have left.

“Mrs. Taylor?” I jumped and twisted my body, my heart jumping from my chest. While my mind had gone into deep thoughts, he had silently sat down on the edge of the armchair next to me. I placed my hand against my chest, hoping to push my fast-beating heart back into place.

“Oh, you startled me.” My words came out breathy and intense.

“I didn't mean to, you looked so enchanting with your eyes closed.” He scooted a little further off the chair leaning in even closer into my space. His elegant British accent made his words appear more like music or poetry than anything anyone else could say.

“Enchanting?” I looked at him, not sure what to make of such a sentence.

“Sorry, should I have said peculiar?” He gave me a little chuckle and I smiled back at him. The sharp pain that had been in my stomach quickly changed to nervousness. I felt as if I had been hungry for so long, he was morphing into such a mouthwatering piece of cake. A very dangerous, adulterous cake.

“You probably should have said peculiar. That word would

better describe me. Along with clumsy and sometimes forgetful." I said this with pure sincerity. I was desperately hoping that these were traits he found the most unappealing. Perhaps if I was afraid I could not resist him, I could play my cards right and make him uninterested in me. He leaned even closer to me and lowered his voice.

"There's nothing wrong with a woman with those qualities or quirks. I find them, refreshing." He reached out and placed his hand on my arm, and I once again felt like a teenage schoolgirl. My foot began to twitch as my body tried to find ways to channel my nervous energy. I looked at his face and he smiled, his eyes squinting ever so slightly in the corners. I felt like a moth, trying to get close to the flame, but not catch my wings on fire at the same time. '*How far was too far? How flirty is too flirty?*' I asked these questions to myself.

"I'm really sorry you didn't make it as a chaperone on the field trip. Honestly, I was looking forward to you being there. I feel like we get along pretty well and I don't feel like such a stranger in this country when I'm talking to you." He looked at me with such a boyish charm in his face that I couldn't help but smile. This was going to be even harder than I thought. I felt happy and almost foolish at the same time, being so pleased to hear a compliment. It made me want to tempt fate and get even closer to the flames, but I still tried to watch my wings as I replied.

"Thanks. I'm sorry I couldn't make it. I had to take the ballet costumes to the seamstress so they could be finished for the recital. Like I said earlier, I am forgetful." This was only half the truth. I did have to take the costumes to the seamstress, but not for a few days after. I was also keeping my fingers crossed that disclosing the fact that I was not domestic enough to sew would pinch off a little of the attraction toward me that I could sense.

"I completely understand. My sister is a single mom and I have seen her go through a lot of stuff, so I have an inside understanding as to how much work it is just to be a mom, and a wife." How did his fiancée let him get away? They must have a large supply over there of appreciative men. If this is the case, I wish they'd send some more over here. My curiosity was peaked and I began to forget my nervousness.

"Really? That's not very common for men over here. I can't really speak for men in England, since I have never been there, but I think with your handsome looks and even more fantastic accent, you shouldn't have a problem getting any girl you want." I lowered my voice and leaned in, not wanting to disclose his information.

"And forget your ex, she was a fool."

I leaned back into my chair and shook my head, agreeing with my own statement. For a moment, I was completely astounded at the level of comfort I felt saying such things to him. I was also shocked at the words that just poured out of my mouth. What was I saying? Sometimes, I really just need to learn to shut up.

He looked so pleased and content with my statement and affirmations toward him. Then he paused for a long moment, looking down at the floor. After his moment, he raised his eyes glaring directly into mine and said:

"But what if the girl I want is already married?" He made it crystal clear he was speaking directly to me and about me, as his look was so intense that I could hardly breathe with the realization I had definitely gotten too friendly. Now I was almost sure the flame was going to burn me. My heart raced with excitement, then guilt. I took a moment too, looking away trying to form an answer, trying desperately to figure out what I wanted, and how far I should go. What was I thinking? I knew how far I should go and how far I shouldn't go. I continued to look at the floor, frantically weighing the pros and cons. And why couldn't I get the image of Olivia out of my head? Was it a sign, was something telling me that he got his, so I should get mine? I couldn't control the roller coaster of emotions. I felt almost seasick from bouncing back and forth between excited and guilt. Finally coming to my senses, I paused, and then looked up.

"Mr. Conway, I am so flattered, but please, please don't. There really isn't anything special about me. And I'm just..." I stopped mid-sentence and looked down. I wanted to say so many things. *I'm just sad, I'm lonely, unloved, unwanted, ignored, and invisible.* I just couldn't bring my mouth to utter those things to him. Guilt over took excitement, and then suddenly it was replaced with anger. Why couldn't this be Kyle? Why couldn't Kyle put his hand on my arm and feed my hungry soul with much needed affection? Once again, Olivia walked through my mind. I looked back up, almost unable to speak. He kept silent, letting me speak as he listened to me intensely.

"Things are so complicated for me at the moment, and it would be so, so easy for me to need someone. I just can't, so please, please, don't. Trust me, you don't even *want* me." I let out a long breath, as if giving my final answer on a game show. I had realized that my answer seemed extremely desperate, but even if I tried, I wouldn't have been able to hide the truth of my desperation. Paul leaned his body back, but did not remove his hand from my arm. I could see a look in his eyes as he toiled over the answer I had given him, and when he spoke, it was with so much sincerity.

"I can respect that, but I want you to know that I think you're special. You are, enchanting. The moment you walked into my classroom, I felt a spark I had *never* felt before. I don't know exactly how to say it, but even though there has been such a small amount of time between us, being in your presence makes me feel at home. You are not like the other women around here. You're different. You think you're clumsy and forgetful, and I don't know, maybe you are, but those are not bad things. All I see in front of me is an amazing woman." He took a long pause and bit the bottom part of his lip that spoke volumes of sexiness to me. He looked at my face, obviously contemplating how much of his thoughts he should reveal. I gave him a fraction of a nod letting him know he could continue, and he did.

"I do hope I have not offended you? I would have great remorse if I also have made you uncomfortable. The root of it all is that I really just wanted to get better acquainted with you. I know what I'm about to say is bold, but, in the very short amount of time we have spoken, I've felt a real connection, and that connection has, in a way, made me wish you belonged to me." I sat stunned. I had to glance around the room for a camera since I believed only men in the movies talked like that. My body became so warm and I could feel the heat from my face as I began to blush. His words were so refreshing. I had to fight with my conscience, so it would not forget that I was already currently married. I imagined for a second getting up and walking out the door with this man. This handsome, well-spoken man with his posh accent.

"I want to say one last thing, if you'll permit me. *If* you ask me, I will not talk to you or bother you again. I will leave you alone and respect what you wish, but please don't call me Mr. Conway. Call me, Paul." I had a strong desire to break out in a panic when he offered this suggestion. How could the flame just take itself away from the moth? I had felt so warm and happy to be seen for the first time in ages, and now the possibility that it would end left me terrified. The image of Kyle smiling at Olivia was right in the front of my mind. All the attention she was probably getting should be mine, not hers. I answered quickly so that he wouldn't make the choice himself, vanishing from me completely.

"No, we can talk. I'm always open for a conversation, and you're pretty interesting. Besides, I couldn't let you go and feel homesick, now can I?" I gave him a flirtatious look and I could feel the flame light back up. I told myself there was nothing wrong with a little flirtation and good conversation. Besides, as long as I didn't get to close, there was nothing wrong with this moth keeping herself toasty during the autumn months.

SEVEN

I was beginning to feel helpless and could see so clearly the string hanging from my life. I was worried the smallest tug would unravel everything. I flipped the overhead mirror in my SUV and looked at my skin. I had spent a longer amount of time on my make-up than usual. I just came from the salon and my hair was looking, and smelling good. I opened the door and spun around, putting my foot on the ledge of the SUV, fixing my Gucci thigh high boots. I had spent a small fortune in preparation for today, but I figured it would be worth it, and since I usually didn't spend a lavish amount of money on myself, I didn't have buyer's remorse. The boots were too stunning to feel guilty over anyway. So I walked across the parking lot and took a deep breath, holding my head up high so that my body portrayed confidence.

I could smell the cedar as the elevator door slid opened at the end of the hall. I walked down the hallway that seemed extra-long all of a sudden. The wall sconces let out strips of yellowish light against the floor, which gave the building an old-time charm about it. For fun, I envisioned I was a lioness walking to the opening of the cave to claim my mate. The thought made me grin as I reached for the door. I strained and pulled with great difficulty, hearing the door creak as it usually did when it opened. It shut behind me quickly and gave a deep moaning noise when it finished.

“Oh, hi.” Olivia stood behind the desk and gave me her political fake smile as I had expected. Her eyes moved gradually down my body and rested on my boots. Her smirk faded and was replaced by pure envy. *So far, this day was looking pretty good.* I gave her the most amused smile I had ever given and said,

“Could you get Kyle for me? We're going to lunch today.” I looked down and fumbled around with my purse as she walked around the desk. I waited ‘til she was only a foot away from me and I mumbled, just loud enough for her to hear.

“I'm sure he's really hungry after last night.” I casually glanced at her for a moment, just long enough to catch the disappointed look on her face. I had lied. I knew we hadn't done anything last night, as usual, but I couldn't stand the thought of her being able to sense our lack of intimacy. She reminded me of a starved wolf, looking for the most helpless rabbit. Her hair was pulled up in a French twist and she wore long black trousers and a peach colored blouse. I clearly out dressed her today, as intended. After wrestling with my guilt last night, I made the decision I could do better and try harder. I did not want to step aside and watch Miss. Slutty two shoes seduce her way into my husband's arms. I couldn't help but desire the man that I had loved for all those years, the charming, loving, truly devoted lacrosse player I had kissed so many times. I felt so deceptive. I felt shame for loving the attention another man had given to me, and even more wicked for what I imagined I could do with him. I had tried in the coffee shop to keep my desires to myself, but I knew what all the tempting possibilities could be if I didn't work to regain some control. I also tried to shake the recurring anger I felt toward Kyle, for not being the man that said such wonderful things to me. My mind kept spinning this feeling repeatedly; why didn't Kyle speak like that to me anymore? If Paul saw something special in me after such a short time, then why couldn't Kyle see that after all our time together?

Kyle walked around the corner behind Olivia, still carrying a sullen look on her face. Unable to make eye contact, she looked down at the floor to walk past me.

"Vi, I didn't realize you were coming here today. Was there something I forgot to do? Or something you needed?" He looked puzzled, but a little pleased. I was disappointed that he had not even noticed my dashing new appearance, and he was completely oblivious to my new highlights and lavish thigh high boots. I didn't have to look over to Olivia to sense the small smirk on her face. She would be harder to beat than I thought. I stepped forward and looked him in the eyes, and then I placed my hand on top of his pale blue silk tie, trying so desperately to recapture a distant feeling and memory.

"Honey, I came to take my husband to lunch. You can't blame a girl for wanting to eat with her husband, can you?" The side of his mouth curled up in a crooked smile and I saw a flash of flirtation in his eyes. My heartbeat quickened and I felt a brief moment of connection with him. I wanted to hold him there and never let go of this moment. I was like a rat in a maze who after so many turns of disappointment finally saw some cheese.

"Of course we can go to lunch. Can you give me a few minutes to wrap up a couple of things before we take off?" He softly reached down, putting his hand on top of mine, and keeping eye contact with me. My heart fluttered, and the emotion was becoming almost overwhelming.

"Yes, that would be fine. Do you want me to wait out here?" I looked over to the big soft waiting chairs. He shook his head repeatedly from side to side and gave me a scolding look.

"No, come sit in my office and keep me company. Did you do something with your hair?" I was astonished. I could hardly believe it; keep him company and he noticed my hair? I felt as if I had been a ghost in his life for centuries, and now he was able to see and hear me. I sounded almost giddy and childlike as I responded, and I could barely keep it from my voice.

"Okay. Yeah, I just got it highlighted, nothing big." We walked back to his office and I sat in the chair across from his desk, as I had done so many times before in his home study. He shuffled through his papers and flipped through his notebook, glancing up every minute or two to acknowledge my presence. He made me extremely happy to feel alive. I heard the door creak open and Olivia glided across the room standing directly in front of me. I looked down my boot at my long heel and thought of kicking her right in the back. I wondered if I tilted my body back if I could reach my leg up high enough to kick her across the room. I caught a strong inhale of her thick flowery perfume. I realized it was coming from her thighs. 'What kind of woman puts perfume on the inside of her thigh?' My smile completely fell off my face. I thought of the answer to my question. Perhaps a woman who was getting lucky at the office? I knew my husband was not the only lawyer in this office, but he happened to be the youngest and best-looking one. I clung to the hope that she liked much older, vulnerable men.

"Mr. Taylor, I have Mrs. Stevens on the line and she is asking if she can come in this afternoon to meet instead of tomorrow? She said unexpectedly, she has to go out of town tomorrow and won't be available. I told her I would consult with you and give her a call back." She asked him in the most sympathetic fake tone I ever heard from a woman. I leaned over, pushing her slightly on the thigh to remind her she was standing directly in front of me. I had to keep eye contact with Kyle for fear our momentary spell would be broken.

"Excuse me, Olivia, can my husband and I have a word for a moment. He'll let you know in a second." She let out a sigh and her posture slumped forward ever so slightly.

"Sure, no problem. Just let me know whatever you want, Mr. Taylor." She looked at him the entire time as if I was not in the room. I heard the door shut behind her and waited a moment before I spoke, in case she was listening outside.

"Just let me know what you want to do. I honestly want to go to lunch, but I know that you have clients." He rested his elbows and arms on the desk in front of him. He scrunched his lips together, and then brought the top lip to touch the underpart of his nose. This was a habit he had ever since I knew him. He always got that look on his face when trying to make a decision on a moment's notice. I sat back and waited for him to finish his thought processes. My joy began slowly to fade. It was quickly replaced with anxiety. I knew this situation all too well. If he had to choose between work and me, work won far too many times in my book. I became assertive and sat up. I couldn't let this be another one of those times. I couldn't let the tempting thought of Paul lure its way back into my mind.

"Kyle, I really want to go to lunch with you. We never get to go to lunch and I miss you." He gazed up at me and looked so remorseful for that he even had to make a decision like this, wife or work. He looked down, pressed his finger against his lips, and took in a deep breath before he spoke.

"Vi, I really, really want to go to lunch, but this client has such a crazy schedule and I have been trying to get her in here for two weeks. Believe me, if it were any other client, I would blow them off. Please forgive me. Can you take a rain check?" He gave me the saddest look. Like a small child that was about to bury his favorite pet in the backyard. I hated those rain checks. Millions and trillions of stupid rain checks. At this rate, we were going to be in our sixties before we enjoyed our life together. I knew he was going to pick work. I was so disappointed that he couldn't understand the plea in my voice. I wanted to jump up and choke him. I wanted to yell, "I want you to see me! NO. I *need* you to see me." I felt my words had been useless to this point. I looked at him and finally mumbled,

"Yeah, that's fine. I understand." But I didn't. I stood and didn't wait for him to say anymore to me. I walked out of his office and quickly put a small smile on my face. I didn't want to tip off the wolf that the rabbit was injured. Olivia glanced up from her desk looking slightly amused. I paused just as I reached the door and turning to her, I said,

"We've decided to go to dinner tonight instead. It should be better to have a long romantic evening instead of a quick lunch." I gave her a wink and her face revealed pure resentment on her part. It only lasted a fraction of a second before being replaced with a pleasant farewell, but it was too late, I already caught it. I would have to do something to get her fired. If she hadn't already done something with my husband, it was obvious she wished too, and with her looks, I didn't want to take that chance.

The light was dim as I stepped out on to the parking lot pavement. I could feel the moisture in the air. I hustled across the lot in my boots. Just as I shut the door, the clouds opened up releasing a downpour. The water hit my windshield reminding me of a drive through car wash.

I chuckled and laughed. It looked as if the heavens were giving me a million little rain checks.

EIGHT

The room was dark, and the sound of an older woman coughing in her handkerchief echoed up to my seat. I could hear the faint tapping of shoes and humming of cell phones as they were being put on vibrate. A thin yellow beam draped down the middle aisle from the crack in the exit door and seats creaked as the final small group of people hustled to fill them. The sweet, soft smell of Abby's expensive perfume traveled over with the breeze every time someone walked past our seats. She glanced over at me flashing a smile. She wore a long, white wool trench styled coat, which was absolutely exquisite, and I found myself a tad on the jealous side. I told myself not to be jealous since most likely, it was way out of my price range, and I already blew way too much money on boots that got me nowhere. I reached over to the seat on the other side of me and put my hand on top of Kyle's arm. I sat in the middle of both of them and snuggled my back into my coat that I had hung over the back of the wooden auditorium chair.

The main doors closed and the light disappeared from the aisle. The room became darker and a man squeezed past some people in the row in front of us to claim the open seat across from Kyle. I fished through my purse as I was hit with the familiar smell of fabric softener and cologne. My heart stopped and I peered up to see the back of Paul's head, while he sat in the seat in front of us. I could feel the blood rushing through my body and I could sense my cheeks burning with fire. I couldn't keep myself from continuously gazing at the outline of his head, thinking any moment he would turn and say something flirtatious in front of my husband. Would Kyle be able to tell this man was attracted to me? Would he think something was going on? I heard a whisper and looked over at Kyle.

"Vi, are you okay? You're squeezing the life out of my hand." My hand shot up as I instantly released his hand from my grip. I gave him a clumsy smile and replied,

"Yeah, I'm just excited. I hope people like the costumes I designed." He studied my face for a moment and then remarked,

"Your cheeks are red. Are you blushing?" He looked at me and I searched through my mind frantically to find some explanation.

"I shouldn't have worn a long sleeve shirt. I'm really hot." He opened his mouth to say something just as the music started and the curtain went up. He gave me a quick nod and turned to face the stage where the kids were performing. I took a couple of quiet, deep breaths to calm myself. The music was so calm and relaxing, and I tried to focus my attention toward the stage. I couldn't help but catch a glimpse of Paul through the corner of my eye. I was attempting not to act suspicious. *Suspicious? Why should I feel suspicious? I haven't done anything. People can't read minds. They don't know what you wish you could do, and wishing to do something and actually doing something, are two different things.* I crossed my arms after I finished my mental argument with myself and focused my attention on the stage. I tried with great effort to put the thought of Paul's hand on my arm out of my mind. My efforts were useless as I could still remember the heat from his hand and the electric sensation that followed. The smell of his cologne drifted over to me and danced around me, luring my mind and thoughts to him. I crossed my legs, bouncing my foot up and down rhythmically to channel my energy of excitement. I could sense Abby peering over at me. Having known me for both so long and so well, she knew all my nervous ticks and habits. I felt her breath on my neck as she spoke in a soft, faint whisper.

"What's going on, Vi? You're all twitchy, like you're about to have a panic attack." I looked over to her for a moment trying to decide if I should let her in on my current mental state of mind. I decided against it since I had already told her so much about Paul, and I didn't know what her reaction would be. I wasn't worried about her creating any kind of scene or having a loud opinion, Abby was very calm and cool in these kinds of situations. She had, on a handful of rare occasions, given things away without realizing she had done so. The last thing I needed was one of the best divorce lawyers in the county thinking his wife was being unfaithful. It would be better to confide in her at the right moment, and this was not the right moment.

"Too much caffeine. I'm fine."

I devised a different approach to relax myself and pretended the man in front of us was not Paul, but some random stranger. The deception made it easier to watch Julia on stage. As the little girls danced and twirled, often out of sync, you could literally hear the smiles on parents' faces. I could also hear whispers throughout the crowd as each set of parents remarked to each other how their child was the best one. I slid toward Kyle and faintly said,

"She's doing such a great job. I'm so proud of her, and I'm really glad you could come and see her perform." I reached over and gently set my hand on top of his once again, and he flipped his hand over, grasping my palm against his. He smiled and said,

"I know; me too. I'm glad I made it." I nestled my head into his shoulder and took in the moment, and Paul began to slip further and further from my mind. I closed my eyes and wished for a million moments resembling this one with Kyle. The thought made my anxiety fade and I stopped twitching my foot.

I opened my eyes shortly after relaxing and the girls finished their routine, linked arms together, and took a bow. The audience exploded with applause and many parents jumped to their feet in support of their rising stars. The house lights came up slowly as many people began to pick up purses and jackets. I was jolted back to the reality of the situation. Kyle looked over at me with an apologetic look on his face. I had a feeling I already knew what he was going to tell me.

"Vi, I know we are supposed to go to dinner, but I have to go to court in the morning and have a few things to go over before then. I need to grab some things from the office and then head home." He already had on his jacket and he was fixing the collar. I could tell he was going to leave no matter what case I pleaded before him. Thoughts snapped into my mind, as I wondered if Olivia was at the office, or if she was meeting him there. I was mainly hoping I was just being paranoid. Ever since she started working there, I found myself consumed with paranoia and jealousy. He had revealed to me she had only been there two short months so far, but I didn't understand why she was never mentioned before. Was he attracted to her immediately, so he kept her a secret? Or was she not even a thought to him?

I shook my head and he gave me a quick kiss on my cheek at the same moment he squeezed against me, trying to scoot out of the row. Abby watched him leave and gave him a smile and a wave as he waved back at us, before doing a slow jog to duck behind the stage to give Julia a kiss goodbye. Abby turned to me just as Kyle darted from the stage to the exit and with a disappointed look on her face, she said,

"Julia's gonna be sad that Kyle didn't stay to have dinner." She gave me a little frown. This was most likely more personal for Abby since she had such a difficult relationship with her own father. I almost didn't have the heart to tell her that Julia was most likely used to it by now.

"Yeah, we'll have to give her a little extra ice cream for dessert." She nodded her head and leaned down, picking up an expensive and elegant half-dozen long stem red rose bouquet that was sitting on the chair next to her.

"What are those?" I asked because it was the first time I had noticed them.

"They're for Julia. Come on, you know that the great performers deserve only the best? Besides, I'm Auntie Abby, this is what I do." She held the roses in her arms like a baby with her purse over her shoulder. I shook my head and gave her a sly smile as we stepped out into the aisle. I could see the row in front of us slowly leaking out into the main aisle as well. I knew it would only be a fraction of time before Paul was close enough to recognize me. I spoke quickly to Abby.

"I'm kinda hot. I'm going to go to the hall, get some water, and use the restroom before we leave. Do you want to take little diva her roses and then meet me out in the lobby?" She squinted her eyes giving me a highly suspicious look. She knew me well, and she could tell I was hiding something. While her eyes were still squinted in their suspicious manner, she quickly surveyed the room, and replied,

"Sure, but I hope you tell me later why you are *really* going to the lobby." She gave me a disciplining look and I knew I couldn't pass her off by pretending I didn't understand what she meant.

"Okay, I will." I sighed and shrugged my shoulders like a small child that was caught in the cookie jar. She turned and weaved through the crowed to make her way to the back stage. I wasted no time and weaved through the crowd heading to the lobby. I knew if I could avoid seeing him I wouldn't have to worry about being presented with the temptation all over again. I wouldn't be able to avoid him forever, but at least I could try, while I knew my defenses were low with the desire to be touched and wanted by someone. I knew the edge of that cliff would be particularly slippery for me now.

While in the bathroom, I got a paper towel and dabbed the tiny beads of sweat from my hairline, all the anxiety was making me perspire. I opened the bathroom door and stepped to the drinking fountain in front of the restroom. I hunched over taking a few small sips of the metallic tasting water. I stuck my tongue out trying to catch a breeze on it, trying to wipe off the nasty taste. I looked up and Paul stood right in front of me, grinning like a Cheshire cat. He couldn't help but laugh a little when he spoke.

"Cat got your tongue? Or is the water really that bad here?" I smiled and couldn't help but like his witty charm. I put my tongue back in my mouth.

"It's pretty bad. We don't have that Grade A London water here." I was maybe being a bit flirtatious, but I seemed unable to control myself since he made such interaction so easy. Still not completely able to resist myself, I took a step closer to him, as if I had been physically pushed to do so. His amused smile faded for a moment and he got a serious, inquisitive look on his face.

"Is your husband here?" He surveyed the room trying to figure out which of the men could belong to me. I wasn't sure why, but for some odd reason, I waited a moment before I replied to keep him in suspense.

"No, he just left to go to his office." I wasn't sure why I had told the truth. What would have happened if I had said he was there? Would Paul walk away? And why was he here anyway? Did he know I would be here? His presence seemed odd since the dance studio is not connected with the school.

He had a most interesting look on his face, and I couldn't figure it out. Was it assurance? Was it hopefulness? I asked him a question.

"Do you know someone in the class? Or, are teachers required to go to functions like this?" My tone was almost protective, as if he belonged to me and I was checking up on him. I had not intended for my tone to be similar to sounding like a jealous lover. His smile became one of satisfaction and belonging. I took a step back for fear that the other parents would begin to wonder why we were talking for such a lengthy amount of time. I took a glance around the room to see if anyone had noticed me talking with him, but no one seemed to notice, or most likely care for that matter. Little girls in dance costumes began slowly to sprinkle out into the lobby. He looked at me and answered my question.

"A couple of my students invited me in front of their parents... so I kind of had to say yes. Besides, I don't know very many people and this beats sitting alone at my flat." He gave me almost a pleading look, silently asking me to help him with his loneliness. I wasn't sure what to say, the reality was that I was probably lonelier than he was. Taking a step back, he put even more distance between us. He shoved his hands in his pockets and used his head to motion to me to follow him around the hall to the corridor, away from everyone else. He walked around the corner and I scanned the room to see if Julia had come out into the lobby. I knew that between her and Abby, they would be the last ones to get out. Julia was the type of girl who would have to show Abby every switch and extra costume backstage before they came out to get me.

I walked around the corner and my legs felt slightly wobbly. I rested my back against the wall to help give my body stability since it seemed to have a mind of its own. We could hear the bustle of the lobby, but were completely out of sight. He leaned in and placed his hand on my shoulder running it down my arm, and stopped it as his fingers curled around my hand. My heart was racing so fast that I thought I might faint. I struggled to catch my breath. This felt dangerous, as if someone had just asked me to rob a bank. He looked at me so affectionately as he declared his feelings to me.

"I know I have been pretentious at times, but I cannot help it. You are not like any other woman I have met. I think of you constantly. I even dream about you when I sleep. I know I have been bold and forward, but I feel as if I am in agony when I don't see you." He looked down at the floor and a boyish charm filled him, he spoke like a schoolchild trying to get his crush to take a flower he had picked. Still looking at the floor shyly, he continued:

"I know it is foolish and childish to feel such a way for someone who I've only shared brief conversations with, but I do." He looked up gazing into my eyes as he ran his finger slowly down my cheek. This sent a shock wave through my body and my legs almost completely gave out. His flame was so bright and beautiful that I felt once again like a completely mesmerized moth. I tried to control myself... in body... mind... and soul, but it was useless. I, as the moth, could not resist such a flame. My life had been black for so long that Paul had become a light in my dark world. I was certain I didn't *want* to betray Kyle, but my paranoia of Olivia had become a constant thought in my mind. I could picture her as clearly as if she was standing right behind him. I wanted to be kissed, desired, appreciated, and above all, I needed to know that someone loved me so passionately that he couldn't live without me. I wanted my husband to feel and do these things for me, but instead, it was coming from a practical stranger who stood in front of me. Paul was so charming and affectionate that with his words and the pull from his presence, he effortlessly lured me into him.

Once again, Olivia flashed in my mind, and for a brief second, I imagined her sitting on top of Kyle's desk as he passionately kissed her. I closed my eyes and envisioned them pulling back from each other as they laughed, sharing an inside joke about how foolish and naive I was not to suspect them being together. I opened my eyes as Paul gazed at me, intensely wanting me to give him some kind of reply to his declaration. Even though I knew we could not be heard, I lowered my voice and spoke softly and deliberately.

"Paul, even if my marriage is hard right now and even if I want you, I still can't betray my husband." The words flowed from my lips and I was amazed at my blunt honesty. I knew immediately that I should not have conveyed my marriage in a negative way, but my brain became disconnected from my mouth and the gates of honesty slid open. I continued to confess, knowing I had already said more than I should have, so I didn't care anymore.

"It's true...I can't seem to stop thinking about you. About the way you make me feel, how you look at me... But no matter what, I can't do anything with you. I just can't. I'm married." I had been invisible for so long that my words were a huge relief from myself. I had not spoken words like that to a man that was actually listening to me for a long, long time.

I felt his body gently press close to mine. I tried to sink farther into the wall, but it was no use. His cheek was now only a fraction of an inch from mine, and the smell from his shirt collar was intoxicating. Once again, I felt weak as my legs trembled. Guilt started to override my mind and a shameful feeling of responsibility came over me for being so honest, which may have progressed the situation I was in. I couldn't think straight as his warm breath grazed against my ear, smelling of peppermint.

"I loathe your husband. He doesn't deserve you." I was revitalized and amazed at his intense passion and affection for me. I thought it must take such passion in order to hate a person you have not met because they have something you want with all your being. His statement made me feel hopeful and loved, truly needed and truly wanted.

The side of his mouth was now gently pressed against my cheek near my ear. Guilt no longer existed in me at that moment. I no longer thought of Kyle or Olivia, as they slipped from my mind. I was utterly consumed in the whole essence of the moment, nothing else existed. All I wanted was for him to kiss me. Every molecule in my body yearned for him to touch his lips to me. My mind became like a record player silently pleading, *kiss me, kiss me, kiss me*, repeatedly.

"Mommy?"

"Vi?" The voices of Julia and Abby startled me and I jumped up, not realizing I had managed to sink down into the wall, becoming almost one with it. He leaned back and looked at me with pleading eyes as if saying, just give me a few more minutes, please. Paul was still holding my hand as he raised it slowly to his lips and kissed the back of it. A cloud of disappointment covered over my misfortune. Deep inside me however, I knew I might have just been saved from a grave mistake. I looked at him sadly. I slowly released his grip and walked out into the lobby.

NINE

Distance is the key to so many things. Distance is the key to winning a long race. Being able to have the stamina and go the distance with someone helps to determine the life of relationships. For me, keeping a little distance or a lot would be the key in preventing an affair. My mind pondered these ideas as sweat rolled down my neck, trickling down my back. The air was thick and hot, a big cloud of steam hung around us. Abby and I sat in her sauna that was next to her own personal fitness room. I tried to take in a deep breath as I felt the warm steam fill my lungs. I sat against the wood paneled wall, as she stretched out across the bench next to me. We both relaxed in towels wrapped around our bodies as they slowly became damp with perspiration. Abby's arm laid across her eyes. She was calm and relaxed. A large devilish smile came across her face. With her eyes still resting under her arm, she spoke.

"I have a little something for you when we're finished, but we'll get to that later."

Abby removed her arm from across her eyes and strained her

neck to glance over at me. A more pressing look came across her face and she was inquisitive as she asked,

"So, are you going to tell me what was going on with you the other night or what?" I instantly knew what she was referring to, but thought I might try my luck at playing ignorant.

"What do you mean? There wasn't anything going on." She sat up and crossed her legs while putting her hands behind her head. She gave me a knowing smile and said,

"Oh, Vi, you know that I know you really well, right? Are you going to tell me or am I gonna have to beg you?" She was almost transformed into a teenage girl wanting to play truth or dare. She was right. She did know me all too well and I was bound to tell her eventually anyway.

"You remember what I had told you so far about Paul. Well, he was there and we talked for a few minutes." Truth be told, I had told her very little about Paul, just the basics, and that I thought he might have a thing for me and he was handsome.

Abby sat up and scooted to the edge of the bench. Her mouth curled into a little 'O'. She studied my face with such intensity while she nodded her head slightly up and down, knowing I had more to share.

"And?" She gazed at me with impatience.

"Abby, he kinda, almost, but not really...kissed me." I let out a breath, feeling as if I had just confessed a major crime to the cop sitting in front of me. Abby had been in love with her fiancé and she never got over the fact that he had cheated on her back in college. She had put up a wall around her from that point on, creating trust issues in every romantic relationship she had been in since. I knew her feelings on matters of infidelity and such. I did not have to guess. She would be against any type of adultery.

"Vi! What are you gonna do? What about Kyle? I know you guys are having your problems now, but wait a minute. Was that all that happened?" I could tell by the look on her face she was expecting something more profound, but was not really prepared for the words that might come out of my mouth. I continued to explain, hoping to put her nerves at ease just a little.

"I know. Things have been so...I don't know, cold with Kyle. I know he's not doing it on purpose, but the way Paul looks at me just makes me feel awake, alive. I don't know how to explain it." She was giving me such a disapproving look that I continued to try to redeem myself a little.

"Abby, I haven't done anything with this guy, but honestly, for a minute, I almost didn't care if we did do something. After seeing Olivia slutting around Kyle's office and everything." I looked at her while having difficulty trying to read her face. I knew my words sounded borderline desperate, even if she wasn't going to approve of my desires. I at least wanted her to understand why I was having these temptations.

A little glimpse of softness and understanding came over her face and I felt a moment of relief. Abby's face quickly changed to a disapproving look.

"Vi, I love you like a sister. You have been like my only family. I don't mean to judge, I really, really don't. I've just known you and Kyle from the very beginning and I know *you*. I really, really know you, Vi, and if you take that leap into this thing with this guy, who you *don't* know, you're going to regret it. You will, big time, because you can't just do something like that and not feel bad about it. That's not who you are. I just don't want to see you tormented and then see Kyle crushed. I'm just being real with you... Are you thinking about a divorce?" She looked at me almost tearfully and I knew my answer without hesitation.

"No, I mean I am so unhappy right now. It's miserable, lonely, sad, depressing, but I just can't help that I love him. I love Kyle and always have. I'm miserable but not able to get a divorce, I don't feel it in my conscience. I don't know. I don't know what to do." She looked at me almost lost for advice. She had spent a lifetime of dodging any kind of serious relationship just to make sure she never ended up like this. I knew even though she had never been married or woken up next to a man on a daily basis, the odds were favorable she was a lot less lonely than I was. Sweat continued to roll down my back as the steamy cloud seemed to suck the moisture from my mouth as we talked.

"Oh, Vi, I don't know. Just be careful not to do something you will regret, whatever you do." She laid back down staring up at the ceiling. Her face revealed she was in deep thought over my dilemma. I always knew I had lucked out in the friendship department with Abby. I felt a wave of remorse come over me, as I knew she would take this to her heart, most likely losing sleep over it. I scooted to the edge of the bench and spoke to her warmly, trying to ease her mind.

"Don't worry about it, Abby. I'm sure I won't do anything, and I have a feeling Kyle will come around soon and this guy Paul will meet someone better than me and we won't have to worry about having another talk like this again." I gave her a passive smile and reassured her as I gave her a gentle motherly pat on the leg. She looked at me and gave me a weak smile.

"I know, Vi, I know you'll do the right thing. I'm always here for you. I'll always have your back." I felt slightly relieved she was not as tense about it, but there was still a guilt of possibilities. What if I didn't do the right thing? I knew I couldn't explain to her the allure and intoxication of being around Paul. The pull I felt when he was near me. The intense desire just to throw caution to the wind and free myself of this ghostly state of being. For the first time ever, I was somewhat sad that I didn't have more married female friends. In truth, I knew that perhaps I only felt that way because the chances would be higher I would receive validation and approval for what I desired.

We sat quietly for a minute or two while we soaked in our own perspiration. I grew fearful to open my mouth, afraid the thick steamy air would siphon my thoughts and I might let out all my secrets and all the fantasies that had begun to build up in my head. The day dreaming of sipping wine by a fireplace as Paul stroked my hair and told me wonderful, lovely things with his beautiful accent. No, I couldn't risk letting it all out, so I stayed silent.

Abby sat up, stretched out her arms, and rolled her neck around. She stood up clenching her towel, speaking.

"You ready to get out? Or do you have some more cooking to do?" She gave me a sweet little chuckle and then opened the door. I felt at ease now that our conversation about Paul was over.

"I'm ready to get out. This turkey has popped." We both

laughed. Stepping out, the air felt much colder than it was, as the cool air slid off our skin like gentle fingertips that pulled up the hairs on our arms.

"I have something for you." She walked in front of me and her flip-flops clapped against the floor in a rhythmic pattern.

"What is it? I hope it's something good to eat." My words were said with complete sincerity since I could feel and hear the hunger pains in my stomach.

"No, it's not something to eat. It's not a big deal, just more like a little favor." She smiled her devious smile again, and I thought hard about if I had asked her for any favors recently. I was not a person prone to asking for things, so I knew this was something she took an initiative on.

"Hmmm, okay, let me just rinse off in the shower and then I can see what this favor is."

I picked up my clothes bag, and went to the extra shower room just a few feet down the hall from the sauna. I showered and dressed quickly, surprised how much motivation suspense could be.

"Okay, what's the surprise?" I repeatedly fluffed my wet hair with the towel. I bent over and tightly wrapped the towel around my head. I saw Abby walk around the corner with a manila envelope in her hand. I was completely baffled as to what was in the envelope.

"Okay, so I know how stressed you were about Olivia and wanting to know a little something about her. So, one of my regular lawyers that handles all my legal stuff about the business has this little law school assistant, whose family happens to owns a private investigative service. Well, I paid him to do some research on her. The basics... I haven't seen any of it yet." Abby was biting her bottom lip and pulling on her ear lobe, a personal nervous habit of hers. Her body language said to me that she was nervous that I would be mad that she did this for me. I couldn't fault her for wanting to be a good friend and help me get rid of some of my stress. I looked at her warmly and said:

"Great! Let's see what we got?" I was hit with the thought that what if a private investigator was called and there are photos of my husband in there? I was no longer hungry, but instead, wanted to vomit all over the table, which I might have done if the sauna hadn't drained me of all fluids.

She opened the large manila envelope and pulled out roughly six pages. I couldn't see any photos. She flipped through the pages while very quietly humming. Then she stopped scanning through a page and traced her fingertips along some information printed on the paper. I stood there, not knowing what to expect. I felt almost frozen, unable to reach my hand out and pick up the papers myself. This must be what wives felt when they sit across from an investigator who is about to reveal if her husband has been cheating or not. I paused as a thought of hopeful possibilities covered me. What if there was something in there that could have her fired? Better yet, what if she has some outstanding warrants and I could not only get her fired, but put in jail. A sly, devilish smile overcame me, it faded quickly the moment Abby opened her mouth.

"Oh, this isn't good." Her tone indicated it wasn't looking good for me, which made me feel sick as the anticipation choked me.

"What. What? What! Come on, Abby, just spill! You're killing me over here."

"Okay, she's divorced." I looked at her with disbelief. Was this the worst thing? That wasn't any kind of news. I shot her a disappointed look and she continued.

"She moved here about a year ago from the West Coast. She's just had her fourth divorce. That's right; numeral four." She held up her hand with her four fingers sticking out. I was taken aback. I hadn't really prepared myself for something like that. She looked too young to have had four husbands. My mind was turning over all the different scenarios for snatching four husbands.

"Does it say anything about the guys?" It was as if I had a few puzzle pieces and no picture on the box. She kept reading, flipping through the pages trying to gather as much information as possible before saying anything else.

"Okay, she doesn't have any kind of criminal record. According to her birth date, she is twenty-four years old. Her first marriage was at age nineteen, only lasting eight months. The second marriage by the looks of the date, happened two months after her first ended." She looked up from the paper giving me a look as if we were in high school and just found out the head cheerleader had just slept with the whole football team. With a coy look, she said,

"I guess we know what that means. The secretary, little Mrs. Slutty two shoes *is* really slutty." I nodded my head in agreement with her. She took a few seconds trying to find more dates and information, going back and forth trying to connect a few of the pieces. I was torn between oddly disappointed and relieved at the same time. So far, there didn't seem to be anything that I could really use to get her out of there, but I was happy that a group of photos with my husband and her didn't fall out on the table. Even if there were no photos, it still wasn't iron clad proof she wasn't looking to make Kyle a new man in her life.

"Her divorce went through about two years after her marriage. So, the second one only lasted two years. Her third husband lasted less than two years, umm, about eight months, and she just divorced her fourth husband last year." Abby looked up at me and shook her head. I couldn't hardly keep all my jokes to myself.

"So basically, you're telling me my husband's office hired Elizabeth Taylor?" I chuckled a little and she laughed back replying,

"Yeah, but the younger, slutty version of Elizabeth Taylor." We both laughed and then a more serious look came over Abby's face.

"This girl is collecting husbands like a habit. You need to find a way to get her out of there. I mean, Kyle doesn't seem like the type but still…" She stopped herself obviously not wanting to put any serious doubts in my head after my confession about Paul, and possibly drive her best friend into the arms of another man. I quickly said with strong conviction,

"I know what you mean. I need to get her out of there. Problem is, Kyle isn't the only lawyer that works there and he doesn't make the decisions on whom to hire as a receptionist. I don't know how to do it." Abby's face was contemplative with her reply.

"We'll think of something." I looked down at my watch and realized I had stayed longer than intended.

"Abby, I gotta get going. Thanks for doing this for me. You're the best. Don't know what I'd do without you." I picked up my small bag and took the towel off my head. We walked to the door and she gave me a hug, squeezing me like there was no tomorrow.

"You know I got your back, Vi. Don't do anything crazy, okay?" As a reply, I gave her a warm smile, not wanting verbally to make any sort of promises I might not keep.

I walked out the door hurrying to my SUV. I sat behind the wheel and flipped down the mirror. My face and hair were a mess. I needed to get home as quickly as possible to change and clean up my appearance so I could go to school and pick up my daughter.

TEN

My Gucci boots clinked against the cement steps as I walked up toward the school opening. The old-fashioned style cast iron rails were cold to the touch, so I forfeited the safety of them to protect my fingers. I walked through the doorway and was instantly greeted with the warm familiar smell of glue and crayons. Beth stood a few feet from the classroom as Julia and Ginger laughed and twirled. Julia put her hands on her hips and stuck out her butt pretending to fart. Both girls shrieked with laughter and jumped up and down. Beth looked up with a huge smile on her face. Her presence was cheerful and relaxed, demeanors I was not familiar seeing her possess, particularly at the same time.

"Vi, come over here and see this. Julia and Ginger are having so much fun." She was rejuvenated and somewhat, bouncy. I couldn't hide the puzzled look I was carrying on my face. Her skin was glowing, her hair was shiny, and it looked as if she had just gotten her nails done.

"Mommy, we're making up new moves for the class." Julia touched the top of her head with her fingertips of both hands, sticking out her butt and pretending to fart again. Both girls once again shrieked and then threw their arms around each other, jumping up and down.

"Vi, would you mind if Julia came over to play for a couple of hours? Better still, can she spend the night? I know it's such short notice, but they're having so much fun, and it's Friday." I was almost taken aback by her offer. Not that she had ever been the kind of woman who didn't want her daughter to have friends over, but Beth was the kind of woman who always worried about what her husband thought of friends coming over.

Beth stood there pleasantly looking back at me and patiently waiting for my reply.

"I don't mind, but is it going to be okay with your husband? I don't want to impose on any family plans for the evening." Her lips curled up almost touching her ears, speaking in a sweet and relaxed voice.

"My husband is on a vacation. He needed a little get away to the Cayman Islands. I told him he should go because of how stressed he's been at work." She could hardly keep from smiling. I had a feeling she told him he should go so she could have less stress of her own.

"Well, okay, if you want to go ahead and take Julia now so they can ride home together, I can swing by later tonight with a bag of her sleeping stuff." Beth bobbed her head up and down reminding me of a bobble head you might find in someone's car. Julia danced around Ginger as they now pretended to be fairies. I bent down looking at her big brown eyes, as her large soft curls fell from her shoulder.

"Julia, I'm going to let you sleep over at Ginger's house tonight. I will come and drop off your sleep things later this evening, but you must be a good girl. I want you to listen to what Ginger's mom tells you, okay?" Julia was a bundle of energy smiling and shaking her head so fast it was more like a vibration. I gave her a gentle kiss on her forehead and hugged her good bye.

"Thanks, Vi. I'll see you later tonight. I still have your number in my phone if I need to call." Beth stopped for a moment and then asked on the fly,

"Oh, by the way, we missed seeing you at the recital. I looked for you and didn't see you anywhere. I hope everything was okay?" She looked sad for a moment. I couldn't control feeling nervous, thinking sporadically of what to say.

"Oh, I was with my friend Abby. We didn't hang around too long because we were going to go out to dinner and Abby had a few things she had to get done. Sorry I missed you; we'll have to arrange it next time so we can sit together." Once again, Beth nodded like a bobble head doll.

"Okay, we'll do that. Let's go girls."

Both girls held hands and skipped behind Beth as she walked out the door.

I turned and walked a couple of feet making my way to the class. I figured I might as well let Paul know that I was here for Julia, but I honestly just wanted to see him, even if for only a moment to recapture the thrill of the other night. I tried to reassure myself that I wasn't completely abandoning my resolve to put distance between us. What was a quick harmless hello?

I bent forward fixing my boots and skirt. I had figured since I spent all the money on my boots that it was not fiscally responsible to let them go unworn.

I heard the sharp annoying sound of a man clearing his throat repetitively. As I walked through the threshold, I saw Mr. Kaufman cleaning the board. My heart dropped and I felt dismayed. He looked over and gave me a goofy smile. I didn't have the energy to portray excitement and have any kind of long conversation with him. I looked around and the classroom was empty as usual, since I was late. He walked over to me with more of a hobble than steps. I started to feel sick as I wondered what had happened. Did he quit and leave the country? Would I see him again? Did he have an accident? I was looking at one of the desks as Mr. Kaufman approached me.

"Mrs. Taylor! I'm sorry, Mrs. Violet." He still carried the goofy smirk on his face, as if he just made a joke, which I'm sure I would not have understood.

"Hi, Mr. Kaufman. What happened to Mr. Conway? Is everything all right?" I used my energy to seem somewhat concerned, not giving away my real feelings about his absence.

"Oh, he just has a cold, called in today. The substitute had to leave early so I was able to come over for the last twenty minutes. I'm sure he'll be better by Monday." He looked at me with his big thick glasses and the same goofy smile plastered on his face. I started to fix my coat to leave, hoping to avoid any strange and long conversations that Kaufman usually dragged me through. He sensed my urgency and abruptly started talking.

"Mrs. Taylor, could you do me a favor? Or truthfully, it would be more for Mr. Conway." I could feel my whole disposition change as my ears perked up and my curiosity was peeked.

"I'm not sure, what is it?" He rocked his short, stubby body back and forth while he talked, almost afraid to ask.

"Well, he had asked me to bring in some information about some programs in the community that are happening this weekend, which he adamantly wanted to be a part of. I tried to call to give him the information, but he's not answering, and he doesn't seem to have his answering machine set up, so I was wondering if you would please be willing to drop them off in his mailbox? Just pop it in his box. You wouldn't have to trouble yourself any further than that." He made a goofy hand gesture and sound effect as if he was popping something in a mailbox. He looked up at me, hopeful that I would cooperate. With a guilty look, he quickly added, "I would do it myself, but unfortunately, I have an appointment on the other end of town." I waited for a second before giving my reply. I felt a mixture of excitement and apprehension to do this favor. I pictured myself just opening the mailbox and sliding in the envelope. That would be simple, wouldn't it? You're just doing a favor and you don't even have to see his face. I convinced myself there would be no harm in helping out Mr. Kaufman.

"I don't have anywhere to be right away, so sure, it's not a problem. I can do it for you." He jumped up like a little pudgy rabbit and grasped his hands together with one big clap.

"Oh, thank you, thank you, Mrs. Violet. I really do appreciate this. This isn't something that teachers usually ask any parent to do, but I know we know each other and I really do appreciate this. As I said, this isn't really school policy, so it does mean a lot…"

"Do you have the information on you?" I cut him off mid-sentence, because I could see we might be standing there for a long time. He reached his hand down the side of his brown leather briefcase that looked a hundred years old and slid out a thin manila envelope.

"Does it have his address on it for my GPS?" The grin was still stuck on his face as he replied.

"Yeppers, it sure does, I got it from the office and wrote it on there this morning."

I gently took the thin envelope from his hand and smiled wide as I turned and walked out of the room.

The GPS system guided me toward his house. The closer I got to my destination, the more hesitant I felt. *Maybe I shouldn't have offered to bring the information. I'll just drop it in the box, just drop it in the box.* I kept repeating my plan out loud to myself while I drove. I tapped my hands on the wheel trying to calm myself. I spoke aloud into the air.

"Okay, Vi, all you gotta do is drop it in his box and not worry about a thing. Then just get home, get Julia's stuff. Just drop it in his box. In… the… box." I paused, realizing I was now having a full blown conversation out loud with myself. I laughed at myself a little, amused by my own behavior. He was sick, so he would probably be asleep. *Should I get him soup? No!* My mind became jumbled with thoughts that made me ever so thankful for GPS.

I pulled up to the apartment complex. I passed the large

clubhouse that had the pool, now covered for the fall weather. The apartments resembled townhouses, and looked new and well cared for with short, white picket fences lining the sidewalks. I spotted his building and quickly got out of the SUV after I parked next to the mailboxes. I stared at the mailboxes and sighed out of frustration as a sense of distress came over me. The massive cluster of boxes were for several buildings and each box had a letter-number code that was intended for privacy purposes. I stood there, biting down hard on my lip, knowing that my whole plan had just gone out of the window.

"Augh!" I grunted because I knew I had no choice but to find a way to slide the information under his door. I thought for a moment of laying it by the door and then knocking while I made a run for my car, but what if he didn't answer the door and someone else picked it up?

After a quick search and locating the correct building, I walked through the archway to the hallway where the four doors were next to each other. Two on the left side of the hall and two on the right. I could tell the apartments were arranged with one door belonging to the bottom floor and the next door leading to the top apartment. Each door had the owner's names below the doorbell belonging to that apartment. I looked for Conway and found it, reading number four. I raised my hand to knock, stopping as if some force was physically preventing me from knocking. I felt butterflies in my stomach and my legs were becoming weak. The voice of Abby was in my head, asking me not to do something crazy, but I felt I had already crossed over into crazy for even coming to his apartment in the first place.

I decided to squat down to see if I could stuff it under the door.

The threshold and door flap were so tight together that all my force began to wrinkle the manila envelope. I worked the envelope back and forth along the bottom 'til I found an area not as tight. I wiggled it through the spot 'til I barely saw a fraction of the tan color sticking out. I felt satisfied with my work as I used my fingertips and shoved the last piece under the door.

"Vi?" I was startled so severely that I lost my balance as I fell, twisting my knee to keep from hitting my side. I looked up with my heart racing. Paul stood behind me with a brown paper bag of groceries in his hand, looking both curious and delighted to see me. My face turned red as I imagined how foolish and childish I looked squatting down on the ground and now kneeling. He didn't seem to mind as he fondly looked down at me.

"Did you come to see me, Vi?" There was a tone of affection in his voice.

He set the bag down and then slipped his hands under my arms, and with slight effort, he lifted me quickly to my feet. I brushed off the dirt from my knees and continued brushing upwards to keep my hands busy and divert my attention away from him to allow myself time to think. My mind and heart were racing since this was not part of my plan. What I really wondered was if I could just walk away from him? This had all been a mistake, a terrible mistake that I couldn't seem to stop myself from doing.

The smell of his leather rider's jacket softly swept across me. Despite the chilly autumn day, my body became suddenly warm and feverish. I was afraid and alarmed because I could feel all control leak from me like a bucket with a hole. I looked into his eyes trying so desperately to take my feelings from my face as I spoke in a professional tone.

"Mr. Kaufman just asked me to drop off that information you had asked him to bring today. He said you were sick." Paul's face looked a little sad and embarrassed, revealing he was disappointed that I had not come just to see him.

"I was sick in the morning, but I feel a lot better now. I just came from the market since I had nothing to bloody eat." I was at a loss for words and stood there frozen, waiting for a sign of some kind, some cosmic force telling me to leave.

"So you were just dropping off information as a favor for Mr. Kaufman?" He searched my face. I willed myself to stay professional even though what little control I had continued to drain.

"Yep," I said casually. Paul nodded his head slowly and his mouth turned into a slight pout. He stepped next to me turning the key to his door. He opened the door and stepped inside flicking on the switch. I saw the manila envelope on the floor in front of me, bent down, and picked it up.

"Here. I see you have your hands full." I stepped into his apartment as he took a few steps in, setting his bag on a side table. My heart pounded furiously and my throat began to tighten. I knew I shouldn't even had walked in. *Just go, just go, just leave*! My conscience was screaming, and the little voice in my head was almost strained. There was no protection of any kind. There was no one to snatch me away from him or his place or from my own horrible choices.

There was a terror that I would have to rely completely on my own good conscience, faltering as it was.

I took in a quick survey from where I stood, noticing his apartment was clean and organized and it smelled just like him, fabric softener, cologne, and leather. The living room had a dark green sofa set with rustic pine wood tables, giving it a manly bachelor feel to it, but in a comfortable way. I quickly noticed he had a large bookshelf that housed old leather bound books that sat a few feet from a small gas fireplace.

However, what really caught my attention was the phone that sat on one of the tables. It was modeled after a vintage nineteen-twenty design, complete with the large receiver that rested on the cradle. That single phone gave off most of the charm for the entire room. He turned to face me as I finished surveying the living room.

"Would you like to see the rest of my flat?" He asked hopefully. I felt intoxicated just standing a few feet inside his apartment, and that feeling of intoxication made me nervous. I knew I couldn't stay any longer. I thought of Kyle and felt disgraceful feeling this way, just standing in another man's living room. More importantly, Paul was not just any man, but a man that I was greatly attracted to, a man that I shared a mutual intense chemistry with. He was a dangerously sexy man.

I pressed my lips together and clenched my teeth down as my stomach did cartwheels. I pulled together the last remaining amount of decency I could manage and looked down while I shook my head no, unable to say it. I could not manage to raise my head, but barely was able to bring my eyes up, looking at his disappointed face.

"I see." Paul looked at me once again with pleading eyes as he gently spoke.

"I should apologize for the other night at the ballet. I'm terribly sorry. I came on strong and now I have upset you. I'm sorry. What a wanker you must think I am." I looked at him and had a strong urge to reach out and grab hold of him. My reply was quiet, practically inaudible.

"It's okay. Don't worry about it." He exhaled slowly and his shoulders slumped forward.

"Vi, I don't know what to say. I can't stop how I feel for you. I do know this, I don't want to be the guy that sat back and never told the girl he loved her." The word love was a shock to hear. He looked at me with his long brown lashes and continued.

"I will say this. I respect you and I won't take anything further than you want, and if you want me to leave you alone, I will, but I had to tell you how I felt first." I looked at him, as he appeared to be in agony as the words flowed from his lips. This was the second time he offered to leave me alone, and I felt even more terrified he would keep his word than I did the first time he made the offer.

I didn't want him to stop, I didn't want the way he made me feel to end, and I couldn't go back to feeling invisible, ordinary. I was being chased, pursued, and desired by a charming man. I wasn't having to beg him for conversation or even worry that he was paying attention to me when I spoke. When Paul looked at me, I felt exceptional, meaningful, and I needed that. I had been *starving* for exactly what he was offering to give me, and now I was getting a declaration of more, even love.

Kyle was right there in my thoughts. Olivia was a close second. I pictured Olivia leaning in to show something to Kyle while wearing a low cut blouse. I could imagine the devilish seductress look on her face as she "accidentally" kissed Kyle. What if they were already having an affair? I thought of all the long hours he spent away from home. The information Abby provided did little to nothing to subdue the theory of possibilities of Kyle and Olivia.

I thought of all the lonely nights I cried myself to sleep. Didn't I deserve to be happy too? I thought of Kyle back all those years ago on the lacrosse field. I was angry Paul was saying to me what my husband should have been, but even though resentment was growing towards Kyle, I couldn't ignore the fact that I still had love in there too. I could see Kyle's face and his large boyish smile. I looked up at Paul as he stood there wanting me to say something.

"Paul, I just can't. I love talking to you so much, and yes, I'm even drawn to you, but I just can't. I can't cross that line, I just can't. Please understand. Please don't hate me." I gazed at him, overcome with anguish and sorrow. I knew I was making the right decision but it felt so painful. I felt as if I was going to mourn the loss of my life and go back to being nothing. Paul looked intensely at me, his eyes glistened as tears started to form.

"I would never hate you, Vi." My body was shaking to the core and I decided to turn and head to the door before I got sick from regret, unable to make it to the car.

I could feel the chill of the metal doorknob as I turned it with haste and stepped out into the hall. Crisp air instantly breezed past my legs and I took a deep breath knowing I had made the right choice. The safe choice. Still, my heart ached as if I had given permission for something to die inside me.

I took a few more steps towards the sunlight at the end of the hall before I realized I didn't have my car keys in my hands. Unintentionally, I must have left them on the hall table next to where I stood. My throat felt tight and my heart raced as I turned around to walk back in and snatch them up as quickly as humanly possible, before something could alter my moral stance.

The door was still cracked making it easy for me to slide in. I immediately saw my large mess of tangled silver keys lying on his table. Paul stood in the same position and he had not moved since I walked out. I glanced at him quickly, fearful to lock eyes with him, knowing that would be the riskiest move of all. I mumbled just as I slid the keys off the table and quickly turned back to the door and put my hand on the edge of the doorknob again.

"Forgot my keys, bye."

I felt his hand grab my arm, spinning me around. His body was so close to me I could feel the heat of it through my clothes. My legs felt weak and my whole body began to tremble more vigorously. He looked me deep in the eyes.

"I just want to say one more thing. If you ever change your mind, I will be here. I know you think I don't know you very well, but I want you to know that I see you, Vi. I *see* you." A title wave of desire swept over me and my legs became like Jell-O. With wobbly legs, I lost my balance, fell a few steps sideways into his apartment, and I then braced myself with my body against the wall, trying to keep myself on my feet. The voice of reason insisted that I leave, not forgetting my keys again, telling me to leave over and over again, but I had nothing left, no control, no will power, nothing. In front of me stood a drug that I wanted, and that I had to have. I was on the edge of the cliff and I knew this was it, the moment. I had to leave. I was only a few steps from the door, but I just could not move.

I looked up at him as tears filled my eyes. The fear of losing this moment, this possibility or him entirely was so powerful that I couldn't think of anything else at that moment. The possible loss of the intense excitement was unbearable.

"Would you kiss me? Please?" The words came out of my mouth before I even recognized them. It was as if someone else was speaking from my mouth. My voice was so faint and quiet that I could hardly hear myself. Even though quiet, hardly more than a whisper, the plea to him was passionate, as if his kiss could save my life. Paul looked at me and let out a long breath of air inches from my lips.

"Absolutely."

I closed my eyes while my heart raced, as the touch of his lips pushed against mine it erased all the desire I had to leave his place. His lips were soft and his mouth tasted of sweet mint. I felt his fingers run through my hair and I had been consumed by his presence. Intoxicated by him, as I felt alive and fulfilled. He pulled back slowly.

"I want you, Vi. Let me have you." I couldn't think of anything else but him, and at the moment, my mind would no longer let me. I had emotionally reached the point of no return. I pushed every other part of my life to the back of my thoughts as the answer just fell from my mouth.

"Yes." He kissed me again. I gave in to him completely, and with that kiss, I no longer had to push any thoughts back, because everything went black. All morality was gone, the voice of conscience was silent, neither Kyle nor Olivia lived in my thoughts and the voice of Abby was silent. Nothing would prevent me from having what I wanted.

I closed my eyes once more as everything else in the world faded away.

Just like that moth, my wings caught fire and were consumed by the flames.

ELEVEN

The clinking of the forks against the plate seemed almost in unison. The room was quieter than usual in an uncomfortable way. Kyle sat across the table from me concentrating ever so intently on his knife strokes as he cut his lamb. His precision with the knife would have belonged more to a surgeon than a lawyer. I sat, unobserved while attempting to avoid eye contact with him. For the first time ever in our marriage, I wanted to be invisible. The difficulty even to bring my eyes to look at Kyle was unimaginable, and I began to wonder if he would look at me and just know. If he could just know what I had done. Possibly sense it in some way.

Julia sat to the left of me. Her body bounced up and down indicating she was swinging her legs back and forth underneath the table. She flipped her fresh green beans around on her plate and crinkled her nose. I had spent time in the kitchen making a gourmet meal as soon as Kyle said he was sure he didn't have any work tonight. It had seemed so long since I actually cooked a full meal and we were able to sit down together as a family. My original dream when we first got married was to sit down at the table and eat a meal every night, but reality set in while Kyle spent so many hours away from home. I had come to the realization that my hope was more of a fantasy.

I cut off tiny slivers of lamb and put them in my mouth, feeling uneasy and nauseous. I looked down at my plate, painfully unable to force conversation or beg for his attention, as I normally would have done. Guilt sat on me. I could actually feel its presence on my shoulders, and my mind started to drift. I could feel Paul's warm breath on my neck and his soft lips as they touched my skin. Paul's hair was so soft when I ran my fingers through it. The smell of his clothes and his apartment never seemed to leave me.

I closed my eyes to fight back the beginning of tears. What had I done? I crossed a line that I could not step back across. What would Kyle think if he found out? Would he still love me? I felt a small flicker of sadness while thinking the same question I have been thinking for a while. Does Kyle even love me now? I couldn't help but remember the feeling of belonging to someone, being alive. Now I sat here at the table feeling like a ghost once again, but the difference was that I wanted to be a ghost.

"Can I have pizza?" I opened my eyes and looked over at Julia. She looked up at me with her long eyelashes, her eyes pleading with me to take away her plate. Kyle looked up from his plate and said in a soft but stern voice,

"Julia, Mommy has made a very nice dinner and it is really good. You haven't even tried it. Look at Daddy's plate. He's almost done." He looked down at his plate and then pretended to be a monster as he made a fast eating motion. Julia laughed and giggled. Covering her mouth with her hand, she pointed over at Kyle.

"Look! Daddy's a hungry monster!" She giggled some more, and then put a piece of lamb in her mouth too, chomping down on it and laughing at the same time. Kyle smiled and leaned back looking at me. I felt disgraceful or criminal even. I glared down at my plate pretending to have difficulty cutting some lamb so I wouldn't have to make eye contact with him.

"That was really fantastic, Vi. Thank you." I glanced at him quickly, giving him a small smile. Just as quickly, I looked back down.

"You're welcome, not a problem." I could just barely see his outline from the corner of my eye as I was looking down. I saw him shift his body to the other side of his chair. My heart dropped because I had seen him lean like that on so many occasions, right before he started asking questions.

"I know what's going on, Vi." My heart stopped completely for a moment. I could hear the clock ticking so loudly that it was almost deafening. My hands started to shake slightly so I put down my fork and knife and laid them on my lap, out of sight. My stomach did flips and nausea was intense as my focus remained on my plate. I couldn't believe it. The years I spent being ignored and with one indiscretion, my husband finally sees me? I tried desperately to think of what to say. Should I deny it? I slowly looked up at him and saw a soft sad look on his face. My heart ached and I once again fought back tears. He spoke to me so remorsefully

"You're angry at me for lunch the other week, aren't you? I

know you really wanted to go and I worked instead. This is why you are hardly talking to me, I know. I can tell you're angry." I exhaled slow and steady as relief gradually floated over me. I sat staring at him for a moment in disbelief. I had wanted for so long for us to talk like this, have dinners like this. Again, I felt angry that I put myself in another man's arms for affection, as if it were life itself. I nodded my head gently, letting him think he was right about his theory and my silence.

"Yeah, I'm mad about lunch." I felt honest with my answer since it was said with all sincerity. Kyle stood, walked around the table, pulled out the chair across from Julia, and just on the other side of me. He slid the chair closer to me. Sitting down, he placed his hand on top of mine. My heart trembled, filling with shame. He looked into my eyes. His were full of love, and mine were full of shame.

"Vi, I'm sorry for that other day at the office. I know I have been working so much. I get so focused on work and I can't see anything else. I hope you're not really angry with me. I'm sorry." Kyle slid my hand off the table and placed it in between both hands. I wanted to cry, reach out and grab him, pulling him into my arms to bury my head into his chest. I wanted every day and every evening to be like this. The way at this moment how he looked at me, talked to me, and took my hands, letting me know that I exist.

However, the complete feeling of resentment couldn't be fully alleviated. It started to come to the surface again. I resented the hours he spent at work. I resented Olivia working so close to him. I resented even the thoughts of Olivia and him in my mind. Above all, I resented the amount of infatuation and desire that consistently came from Paul, when they should have been coming from Kyle this whole time.

"That's what real love is, right? Forgiving someone." I said this in the hopes that if the time came where I might need forgiveness, he would hopefully remember this statement. He lifted his hand and gently tucked a piece of hair behind my ear. Julia looked up as a strange look came across her face. She was confused as to the amount of attention Kyle was giving, as it was not what she had been seeing commonly.

The puzzled look on her face served as a reminder to me of the rarity of his actions. I knew most other children didn't get strange and puzzling looks on their face when their parents held hands or kissed. It was probably something they witnessed on a daily basis. I imagined how content my life would be to receive such attention and affection on a daily basis. How my defenses would have been strong and I most likely would not have felt so drawn to Paul. Kyle spoke while my mind was racing through all the thoughts.

"Yes, that's a big part of love. Vi, I will make more time for you." He leaned back and looked over at Julia rubbing his belly as he said,

"Yummy. Monster is full." He made a low, deep silly voice and Julia giggled.

"Thank you, Vi, dinner was great. I'm going to go up to my study to do just a few things and we can relax together tonight, if you're not still mad." Julia looked back and forth at us then looked down at her plate. She had a sense of easiness around her indicating this was a statement from Kyle she was more familiar with, him saying he was going to his study.

"Yeah, I'll just get these dishes done and we can spend some time together." My heart sank, as this was unfortunately the statement I was too familiar with. I fought back tears again and wanted to reach out and grab his arm as he stood up from the table. I wanted to confess betrayal and beg him to sit and stay, beg him to love me. I sat there feeling both guilty and resentful as he walked away from the table.

Julia put down her fork, gave me a little smile, and jumped up from the table.

"Thanks Mommy!" I heard her run up the steps to go to the bathroom. I got up and put the dishes in the sink. I stood at the sink and stared down at the pile of dirty dishes stacked on top of each other. I closed my eyes and could almost smell Paul's cologne as if he was standing right next to me. I was taken back to him pressing his hand against my back and then flipping me over on the carpet. My lips curled in a slow smile as a feeling of warmth and excitement rushed through me. I opened my eyes while shaking my head. My smile melted and my lips curled down as a frown formed on my face. Once again, remorse sat on me, pushing me down. The guilt was so strong and pungent, like rancid trash that was left in a room.

Having finished the dishes, I walked upstairs and opened Julia's door as she finished pulling the covers to her chin.

"Good night, Julia. Did you remember to brush your teeth?" She pulled back her lips, clenching her teeth together showing me that she had. I turned off her light and closed the door as it made a slight creaking sound. I gently walked over toward Kyle's study as not to disturb him. I moved just peering in through the crack of his door as he looked through his papers. He stopped, putting his hands over his face. He had a look of distress that touched my heart, and I reached out to grab the doorknob to let myself in. I paused as I heard the buzzing sound of his cell phone vibrating. I gently stepped to the side of the door putting me out of view in case he looked up. I slowed my breathing and leaned against the wall, listening.

"Hello? Ah, no, I'm sorry, I can't tonight. Will I see you at the office tomorrow?" I clenched my stomach and felt my legs grow weak. As hypocritical as I knew it was, I still couldn't help the jealous and betrayed feeling that choked me. I heard him mumble a quick and polite good bye as he hung up the phone. My eyes filled with tears and I fought to control myself. Was that Olivia? Was I being paranoid and that was nothing? Why was he so nice and loving at dinner? Was he guilty of something also? I bit my lip and clutching my stomach, I made my way to the bedroom. I laid on the bed and wrapped my arms around a pillow. Putting my face into it, I let out my tears and anguish. I cried for all that I had done. I cried for the guilt I felt. I cried for the pain and loneliness I knew every day. I cried for the thoughts of Kyle and Olivia. I cried for the desire I had for Paul. I stopped crying and wiped my eyes. A tidal wave of exhaustion swept over me as if I was on the shore in the middle of a hurricane. After a while, my muscles ached and I had no tears left to cry. I gave in and closed my eyes as I fell asleep to the sound of Kyle shuffling papers in his study.

TWELVE

I laid on the floor with my back pressed firmly against my thin, lime green rubber mat. My hand slowly fell to my side just off the mat and rested against the cool glossy wood floor. I closed my eyes and tried to focus my breathing and movements with the voice of the Pilates instructor. My mind constantly drifted in and out of thoughts and seductive memories. The smell of rubber mats and metal exercise equipment dominated the atmosphere, yet also struggled to overpower the subtle hint of chlorine from the pool that drifted in the air.

My mind continually played the memory of Paul taking his finger and slowly tracing it up my arm. I felt a faint smile settle on my face as I kept my eyes closed. The smell of rubber and chorine no longer seemed to exist, as the memory of his smell became vivid, practically real and fresh.

The instructor's high pitch cartoon like voice startled me back into reality. I felt unable to move as I continued to lie on my back, listening to the soft clamor of the other members as they cheerfully got up from the sea of rainbow mats and rolled them up.

"Okay, ladies, don't forget that next week we are going to increase our intensity, and as always, try to work on some of the moves at home." I tilted my head to look at the tall, rail thin instructor who was being ignored by the women in the class, as they quickly chatted with each other to collect the freshest gossip and latest trend ideas, sounding more like a pen full of clucking chickens. The instructor plastered her smile on her face and shook her head in delusion as if everyone was listening to her. She finally closed her mouth and the cartoon like voice trailed off in the air as she left the room, shutting the door behind her. I sat up and crossed my legs before rolling my neck around. The women continued to talk and chat with each other. I had only been coming to this class for a few sessions, so I didn't have the connection with anyone that they apparently had already established with each other. This gym was close to the other side of town, which was a major attraction for me.

On this side of town, it would be a rare occurrence that I might run into other parents or an associate of my husband. I also liked being in a place where I didn't feel the pressure to be one Gucci step above the Joneses, because on this side of town, I was already below them, so it didn't matter. Even though my section of town was on the higher end scale, some might say, this side was where the rich of the rich lived and played. It would be easy for any outsider to recognize this fact, just listening to all the shallow and designer conversations. Lastly, the instructor, minus her high pitch mousy voice, was one of the best Pilates instructors within a thirty-mile radius, turning out to be my final selling point.

I rolled up my mat and tucked it under my arm heading for the door. The smell of chlorine became stronger as I swung open the door and stepped out into the hall. I could hear the rhythm of the music for the aerobics class next door. I had been late, as usual, and left my water bottle outside. I walked to the closest water fountain and crossed my fingers as I leaned down to take a drink, hoping it didn't taste like iron.

"Vi?" I stopped drinking and looked up as Beth looked down at me with a happy and surprised look on her face. She had her expensively cut hair pulled back into a tight ponytail, as she wore a designer brown and pink active gear that was fit snug against her body. I took a quick glance around to see if there were going to be any more familiar faces surprising me today. Luckily, there was not. As I looked at Beth, I noticed she had a huge smile and was glowing even more than the last time I saw her. She spoke so soft, but elegantly.

"I'm so surprised to see you here, Vi. I don't know anyone at this gym, which is why I like it. Well, that and I have a fantastic trainer." Her cheeks blushed slightly as she spoke. She paused for a brief moment and then continued:

"Do you come here often? We could always come together?" She looked at me with a childish hopeful look on her face. I cautiously searched for the right let down so she would not be offended. I figured she already had a husband that treated her badly enough as it was. I really liked Beth, but I really didn't want a workout partner.

"I'm so glad to see you, Beth. That would be nice, but I really don't come here that often. I mainly prefer to work out at home." I gave her the half-truth, since I would prefer to work out at Abby's home rather than meet up with Beth a few times a week. Beth looked down and then nodded her head, with her blonde ponytail bouncing behind her. I was relieved when she looked satisfied and understanding of my answer. Her skin glowed and she still lacked her usual nervousness that I had come to expect ever since the first time I met her. All this led me to believe her husband was still in the Cayman Islands.

"Is your husband still on vacation, Beth?" Before she spoke, her wide enthusiastic smile gave her answer away.

"Why, yes he is. He was only going to go for two weeks but decided he needed a little more time down there." She lowered her voice and leaned in. I didn't bother leaning in to meet her half way since this was not a place where I cared what the members there thought, besides, they were really more interested in themselves than anything else.

"I think he's been gambling down there, and he must have hit a losing streak, or a winning one." She leaned back, put her hands on her hips, and rolled her eyes, the same way most mothers do if their child does something both foolish and funny. Her whole demeanor was soft and relaxed and I couldn't help but try to satisfy my curiosity.

"Beth, you don't care that he is taking this long vacation without you? What if he loses lots of money?" She looked at me and tilted her head to the side as if pondering these questions for the first time, or perhaps searching for the answer. I knew that was not really a valid question because they had enough money, and any losing streak was pennies to them.

"Honestly? No, I don't care at all that he's on vacation. I don't even care if he loses some money. He's got enough of it anyway, and we both know that's not a secret." Beth paused for a long second as she brought her finger to her mouth, pressing it against her bottom lip. I could tell she was deciding how much information to release to me. Beth took her finger away from her mouth and continued talking in a low voice, almost a whisper.

"To keep being honest, I wouldn't even care if he had a mistress down there with him. I know most people think I married him for his money, but I didn't. I thought he was such a nice, loving guy. He's not. He is mean and cold and I just don't think I feel the same about him anymore. I would divorce him except he has a really good pre-nup, and I wouldn't be able to take care of Ginger. He would have me penniless. Well, that's what he keeps telling me anyway. It's kinda funny, I married a man for love, but now I'm staying with him for money." She gave a little low chuckle and shook her head. My curiosity was intrigued even more and I had so many questions to ask. I could now sense that her new glow and demeanor was from more than just an absent husband on vacation. Or was he really that mean and cold that his absence was all it took to bring out this confident glowing woman? I looked around the gym at what most women would consider perfectly good eye candy, sprinkles of young, good looking muscular men, most of them trainers in skintight black shirts that enhanced their muscles. It almost reminded me of something you might see on National Geographic where you have herds of lions and the few males strut around, trying to be the leader or Alpha male. I wondered which one was her personal trainer. I looked back at Beth, trying to figure out the right way to ask a question about her husband and my new theory on her current situation.

"If I didn't know any better, Beth, I'd think that you may have found someone, or something else?" She flashed me a mysterious and secretive smile. Still smiling, she changed the subject, dashing any hopes I had for an exciting revelation.

"Julia and Ginger had such a great time last week at my house. I just love having Ginger's friends come over to play. You should have Julia come over again, if you want." She looked at me with a genuine offer of sincerity in her voice. I could not prevent my mind from immediately thinking of the opportunity this would give me to be with Paul. Guilt bubbled up inside me as I thought of Kyle, and remorseful that he was not my first thought. What if I arranged to spend that time with Kyle? Would Kyle spend that time with me or would he be working? I halted my thinking for a second and gave her my answer.

"That would be great. I know Julia had a great time. That's all she talked about for a week." A wide pleasant smile swooped across her face and she clasped her hands together in pure delight. It was easy for one to tell she enjoyed playing games with children and being the all American Mom. I had wondered on several occasions why she had not had more children. I had a sneaky suspicion that perhaps her husband feared his wife would gain weight and was extremely disapproving of the possibility. I felt so strongly about my conclusion that I never had the heart to ask. Matter of fact, I hadn't asked her many questions because of the assumptions and conclusions I had drawn on my own. There was a trickle of regret that began to grow and spread inside of me for making all the assumptions about her. Beth was such a stunningly beautiful woman, and it was painfully obvious that she was clueless to this fact. Her skin was so clear and smooth, barely a wrinkle to be found, giving her the skin of a twenty year old. It was as if she was getting younger, so whatever this new thing was she had going on, I hoped it came in a bottle. I asked her as she waited for me to set up a sleep over.

"I think this Friday would work for Julia if that is good for you and Ginger?" With a wide smile, she nodded her head up and down as her blonde ponytail once again bounced behind her head. Then she said so enthusiastically out of character for her, changing her from a timid little book mouse to a hyperactive cheerleader,

"Fantastic!" I nodded back in return and clenched my mat closer to my body preparing to leave. We waved and I turned to walk away. I paused for a moment and spun around as she was fiddling with the zipper on her suit jacket.

"By the way, Beth, you look amazing. Whatever it is that has turned on your light, keep it up." Even though I knew nothing, I still gave her a knowing wink and smile. She smiled so coyly in return. In a cheerful tone, she said softly,

"Thank you."

I climbed in my SUV and slammed the door shut quickly, hoping to lock out the cold. I sat and looked at my wheel before getting ready to head home. Why did Beth have such a glow? Did she really not care if her husband had a mistress? I shrugged these thoughts out of my mind for the time being and started the engine, pulling out of the gym parking lot.

I bent my knee and pulled with all my might as I shifted my

weight to my back leg. I let out a small grunt, as I was able to get myself through the large cedar door.

"I keep telling them they should get different doors," Olivia said in a smooth, somewhat arrogant voice as she sat behind the large office desk barely looking in my direction. She slowly looked up at me and once again put her rehearsed smile across her face. I gave her my most overly exaggerated beaming smile, as I replied,

"I love those doors! They give the office such character and keep you in shape. Besides, character is so important these days. Anyone can buy a cheap good looking door, but it's the ones with character that give it class." I raised my eyebrows slightly just to give a hint of my purposeful metaphor, but also allowing myself to plead ignorance if confronted. Her face twitched as she struggled to retain her fake rehearsed smile, and for a brief moment, a snarl crossed her lips. Olivia's eyes glazed over and a faint, forced smile took over her face. She stood from behind her desk and slowly glided around it as she spoke.

"May I get Mr. Taylor for you? Would you like to follow me to his office? He's on a call at the moment." As she walked around the tall desk, I noticed the black skirt she was wearing was much shorter than the other skirt. Her red blouse was also tighter than the other was and dipped low in the front, not giving her much in the way of discretion. I was beginning to think by the next time I came to the office, she would be in nothing more than a bikini since her clothes seemed to be slowly dwindling away.

"No, that's okay. I'll sit right here 'til he's finished. Go ahead and let him know I'm here if you like." I plopped down in the large brown leather waiting chairs and crossed my legs resting my hands on top of my knees. I heard Kyle's door creak open and then a few moments later, creak back shut. Olivia walked around the corner with a large glowing smile on her face that quickly dissipated as she caught a glimpse of me.

"He'll be done with his call in a couple of minutes." I shook my head and sat in the chairs bouncing my foot up and down. I looked around the room for a moment and then settled my eyes on Olivia, and stared as she pretended to organize papers and work, desperately trying to look busy to avoid a conversation. I decided to try to sweat her a little, mainly for my pure satisfaction. I was able to hide the sarcasm and personal insight rather well.

"So, Olivia, are you married?" She swallowed and pressed her lips tightly together as a faint nauseous look came across her face. I could tell she was trying to figure out what to say as she frantically moved papers around the desk before she spoke. The smile on my face was genuine, as I already knew all the answers to my question and future questions.

"Umm, no, I'm not married right now." She glanced up at me for a brief moment and then looked back down squinting her eyes as if she was concentrating on something very important. She put the end of a pen in her mouth and continued to stare at a paper, which was probably nothing more than a newspaper comic strip. My smile got even bigger and I continued to talk pretending to be oblivious to the fact that she was pretending to work.

"Really? I don't believe a woman of your attractiveness has *never* been married! So you've *never* snagged a man?" I put my hand to my chest and dropped open my mouth. I was satisfied with my acting as I made my comment, deliberately using the word never. She became fidgety and nervous and I could not help the small smile that crept across my face, even though I was trying to portray a look of shock.

"I was married before, but it didn't end to well. We are sadly divorced now." She looked sick for a moment and then a small expression of satisfaction crept across her face, as she believed this would stop my questioning. I faked a look of sympathy and continued.

"Really? I'm sorry to hear that. I can't believe you've been divorced *once*. Well, the good thing is you're young, and now you've made that one mistake that you can learn from. You know what they say. The *second* time is a charm... or is that the *third* time is a charm? I can never remember." I nodded my head as I spoke the way an elderly mentor would give advice to a young lady. Olivia's face changed to a light shade of red, as she immediately looked both sick and angry. Even across from the room, I could see tiny beads of sweat forming along her hairline.

Olivia's demeanor made me wonder if Abby and I were the only two who knew about her past on this side of the country. I contemplated stopping my remarks and questions for a moment, until an image of Olivia leaning into Kyle crossed my mind. I continued.

"I think it is the second time is the charm when it comes to marriage, so you'll find someone, don't worry about it." She clearly could hear me as she swallowed again, straining to avoid eye contact with me. I curled my fingers together leaning forward slightly as they rested on my knee. I glared at her intently, pulling her into further uneasiness. She quietly spoke just glancing at me for a flicker of a moment.

"Oh really? That's good to know... Thanks." I sat back and crossed my arms and a small pout came across my face. I hid it in case she looked up from her desk and saw my pout. I guess the fun would have to end since she was going to pretend about how many times she had been married. I shrugged my shoulders as I thought to myself, *oh, well, I will save some for next time*. I smiled a little and began to dig through my purse for some gum. I glanced up and saw the color return to Olivia's face as she walked around the desk while she spoke.

"I'll be right back. Can I get you a water, Mrs. Taylor?" I shook my head no as she vanished around the corner. I waited for a few minutes longer, and then I heard a seductive and breathy chuckle come from Kyle's office. I stood and walked slowly, almost creeping to the edge of the hall. I leaned, peering around the corner. I was able to see straight to his desk, as his door was a quarter open. Olivia stood at his far side. She was bent at the waist with her hands resting just above her knees, almost in a spanking position. I could feel radiating heat fume off my face. I felt nauseous and sick looking at her as she cocked her head while they both looked at his laptop screen. Kyle pointed to something and they chuckled again. This time, she flashed him a large sexy smile and put her hand on his shoulder. My knees became weak and I felt the need to sit. I pressed myself against the wall for support to keep myself from tumbling to the floor as I watched them, feeling even sicker by the minute. I stopped to think for a moment. *Should I feel this way? It would only be fair if he also had an affair, right?* I immediately became angry with myself for even thinking for a moment that his circumstances were anything like mine. After all, I practically had to throw myself at him to get any form of attention.

I continued to watch as I now felt growing resentment that caused both a sharp and queasy feeling in my stomach. Olivia stood up for a second and mumbled something to him as she slightly brought her hand back up to his shoulder once again. He seemed to be completely oblivious to the fact that her hand was resting on his shoulder. Was it because he was now so comfortable with her touching him? I squinted my eyes and imagined walking in there and using all my strength to slap her across the face, then slowly turning to Kyle and letting him know what I had done with Paul.

My anger and resentment softened a little, and my heart sank, as I wondered why he couldn't let me in. Why is he so distant and oblivious all the time toward me? I wanted things to be as they once were in the beginning when we first met. I continued to watch as Olivia took her hand off his shoulder, standing, and putting her hands behind her back, trying desperately to pose herself as if she was a model in a magazine. I really wanted to kick in her teeth. The phone rang and I nearly jumped out of my skin. My heart raced and I slid back around the wall and tried to make my way back to the chair as quietly as possible. I could hear Olivia's heels as she was making quick speed with her long legs. I stopped at the desk and pretended to get a mint out of the jar since I knew I was not going to make it to the chair in time. Olivia rushed around the corner over exaggerating her hip swing as she shuffled to the phone. I didn't seem to be able to stop myself so I turned my back to her quickly to get in a good eye roll. She yanked the phone up while I took a few steps and grabbed my bag making my way back to Kyle's office. I didn't give Olivia a chance to say anything to me.

I walked through the doorway still feeling the pain in my stomach. I took a deep breath and smiled at him as he looked up from his desk. He smiled at me surprisingly

"Vi! What are you doing here? Is everything okay?" I took a step backwards spinning around to close the door behind me. I didn't want to allow Olivia the same opportunity I usually had to peep in the room. His smile faded and he now looked alarmed.

"Vi, what's going on? Is Julia okay? Why did you shut the door?" Kyle started to stand and I motioned for him to sit back down before I spoke.

"Nothing's going on. I just shut the door so we didn't have to hear the phone ring. I stopped by because I was on my way home from Pilates and wanted to see if you were busy this Friday?" He let out a sigh of relief and sat back down. Kyle looked down on his desk calendar while pressing his finger to his lip.

"Well, I'm not really sure. Can we kinda play it by ear?" I was sad and disappointed that I was seemingly being brushed off, yet again. I sat down in the chair, slumped back into it, and crossed my arms. I didn't have the physical energy to pretend I would be fine with this. To my amazement, Kyle immediately read my face and stood up, walking around his desk and sitting in the chair next to me.

"I'm sorry, Vi, let me have Olivia confirm appointments and see if anything can be moved and I'll really try to get my calendar free for Friday afternoon. Matter of fact, I'll try to get the whole day off, and how about I don't work the weekend too?" He reached out, put his hand on top of mine and my heart melted, as I gave him a small smile. Unfortunately, his words stirred little hope since I knew he was a perpetual workaholic. I did smile with genuine sincerity for the fact that he honestly believed he was going to take time off. My opinion changed rapidly and for the first time in a long time, I thought it might even be possible. I widened my smile and I put my other hand over his as I spoke.

"That would be great." My memory had subsided for a few brief moments and I almost forgot about Olivia laughing and touching him. It came back to me so I casually asked,

"I heard lots of laughing. What was so funny?" Kyle shook his head as if saying so silly and pointed to his laptop.

"This e-mail from one of the partners. He meant to send a business video attachment, but sent a silly video instead. So you get this serious business e-mail and then open up a funny, stupid video." He chuckled and his shoulders shrugged up and down while he shook his head. He looked over at me and asked,

"Did you want to see it?" I shook my head no since I had neither the mood nor the stomach to pretend to laugh at a silly video at this time and place. I pondered for a moment about Olivia using that opportunity to try to lure Kyle into her web, like a creepy slutty spider.

"I'm going to take off. I'll see you later at home." I stood and he stood next to me, leaning in to give me a kiss. Kyle placed both hands on my arms pulling me gently to him and kissing me on the lips. I stood baffled and stunned for a moment. His kiss was loving and purposeful, not his usual peck on my cheek. I also wondered for a brief moment if he would be able to sense the presence of another man's mouth on my lips. I quickly put that thought behind me as I was also desperately trying to convince myself Paul was a one-time mistake. Yes, Paul was a one-time mistake that would never happen again.

I gave him a warm, blushing smile in return and headed for the door. I turned as I opened his office door looking at him as he stood with his hands in his pockets and his back to the large picture window, a soft look on his face, he smiled and said,

"I love you." Warm tears started to form in my face for a moment and I sincerely replied,

"I love you too." I fought back the tears looking at him with his dark blue tie against his crisp white dress shirt and a happy look on his face, seemingly unaware his wife had been in the arms of another man.

I regained composure and as I walked past Olivia, I gave her a sneaky, suspicious look. Olivia looked back at me as I went for the door. She had a small snarl that crept across her lip that she was unable to hide. I got to the door and turned quickly as I said in a bright and joyous voice,

"Have a good day, and enjoy the weather. Fall is so great on the East Coast." I gave her a wink and her face became as pale as a ghost. She stared for a moment trying to figure out if what I had said was just a coincidence, or if I actually knew about her. I let the door shut behind me and I let out a little laugh. I felt much better and my mood was now lifted. I walked down the hall, barely able to wait for Friday to get here

THIRTEEN

The window housed dark curtains and a small thread of sunlight peeped through the slit as it flickered. Laying a small line across the floor, it climbed up the bed and across my arm. My cheek was deep in the pillow and the cool covers felt refreshing on my bare skin. I could hear the crisp autumn wind rushing outside the window and I pulled the sheets closer around me, feeling thankful for the toasty warm house. I shivered for a moment and felt the warmth of his body as he wrapped his arm around me and pulled me closer into him, covering me like a warm blanket. I took his hand and brought it to my cheek, sliding it down to my mouth and gently kissing the back of his hand with my lips. He slipped his hand out of mine and softly swept the hair from my neck, kissing the back of my neck in return. I smiled as a wave of excitement overcame me. I felt as if it had been so long. As if I had been lost at sea and no one was managing the lighthouse to guide me home, safely and securely. He leaned up and kissed my bare shoulder before he spoke:

"I'm gonna jump in the shower real quick. You're more than

welcome to join me." I rocked my body back, tilting my head to catch the boyish, yet devilish look on his face. I smiled back at him and was unable to prevent a childish giggle from leaving my mouth. His face became softer and more serious as he drifted in toward me and set his lips on my forehead. Then he pulled back slightly and whispered.

"Vi, you've changed my whole world and I love you. This feels so right." Paul looked into my eyes and his accent and smooth words intoxicated me all over again. I was safe and loved. I flipped over, pulling the sheets up tighter to my bare chest to face him. Paul slid down on his side where we were now face to face. He reached out and gently moved my hair out of my face while touching my cheek. He looked into my eyes, straight to my soul and smiled so tenderly. My body became warm immediately, and I knew I would not hold out long before I wanted to ravish him again, an anorexic that fell off the wagon, standing in line at a buffet. I had been so starved for love, for touch, for conversation. I had been so starved for just the privilege of existing to someone else, anyone else. He sat up and scooted off the bed. His bare, perfect glutes walked across the room as strings of sunlight danced across his body like fingertips caressing him. The smell of his cologne and fabric softener lingered on the sheets.

As he disappeared around the corner to the bathroom and the sound of water from the shower started, I became drenched with guilt. The image of Kyle standing in his office, telling me he loved me, unaware of what I was doing, what I had become, a cheater.

In my mind, I could so clearly see Kyle, like different snapshots from our life. I saw him sitting at his desk. I saw him holding Julia and hugging her and I saw the young man on the lacrosse field as he looked over at me with his dashing smile.

I pulled the pillow that lay next to my face and buried my head in it while I began to cry. Large sobs came from my mouth and I could feel the pillow around my face dampen with tears.

As I continued to cry, I could see Kyle smiling at Olivia in my mind. I imagined them walking through a park holding hands and laughing at me behind my back. I remembered the feeling in my stomach listening to Kyle on the phone in his study. My mind swirled with thoughts and my heart ached with emotions. I took my face out of the hot pillow and the cool air brushed against my wet cheeks. I could still hear the shower running so I scooped up the sheets around me and slid off the edge of the bed.

Shuffling my feet, I made my way to his small desk in the corner of the room and plucked a few tissues from the box sitting on top. I wiped my face, cheeks, and under my eyes trying to erase any evidence that I had been crying. I could hear the high pitch squeak of the faucet in the shower as he turned off the water. I quickly shuffled back to the bed and sat on the edge, pulling the sheet close to my body, at the same time bunching it together in my hands across my chest. Paul walked into the bedroom smelling fresh and clean, his towel giving off the now familiar scent of his fabric softener. He had his towel tied around his waist, just inches above his now familiar areas as well. I watched him as he walked over to the closet. He was not as handsome as Kyle was, but he was more adorable with a type of boyish charm.

My eyes began to swell up with tears again and I stared at the floor fighting them back.

"Are you okay?" I shook my head slowly and decided to be honest with him.

"I don't know. I just feel, weird. I've never done anything like this before. The whole affair thing." I bit my bottom lip immediately after I spoke, trying to keep it from quivering, as I wanted to burst out crying. The word affair passing my lips gave me an enormous rush of guilt and sharp pain. I had gotten so caught up in the seduction, fire, and the excitement that I never placed the word on it. I had not really owned it and what it was. Now I could see that's what this obviously was; an affair. I let out a long heavy breath, as if I was an addict admitting for the first time I had a problem. *What was I doing? What would happen if Kyle found out? Would he even care?*

Paul walked over to me and traced his finger along my cheek as had become so familiar from him. I looked up into his eyes. He could read my face. He peered deep into my eyes that I thought for a moment that he was reading my thoughts.

"Vi, when we talked that night at the school, I felt something I had never felt before. I know you don't want to be unfaithful behind his back, but don't you deserve to be happy? How long do you want to go without love? I know I don't have the salary he has, but I really do care for you. I can make you happy. I *want* to make you happy." He slid his hand down my hair, stroking it as he pushed some strands back behind my shoulders. He leaned in and kissed me so softly on the cheek. His lips were even softer than his kiss. He pulled back and gave me a smile. I turned my head, placing my cheek against his bare chest. His skin was warm and I could smell the fresh soap on his flesh. I let go of the sheet and it stayed bunched and clenched to my body. I wrapped my arms around him and just breathed. I wanted to let go and be happy. I loved being touched. I loved being heard. I loved being looked at, not just looked at, but also seen. I was under his spell. I pulled back and looked at him.

"I shouldn't be doing this. I know Kyle's not doing it on purpose and he doesn't deserve what I'm doing to him. I just didn't think this would ever happen to me. I'm a bad person for what I'm doing." I threw my hands up to my face, covering my eyes as tiny tears fell down my face, making the palm of my hands wet. I could feel his warm hand as his fingers wrapped around my wrists, gently pulling my hands down. I couldn't look up at him. Fear started to creep in as I began to wonder if my tears and guilt would drive him away. I was afraid he would decide it is too much to deal with this psychotic, sporadic housewife, and pluck me out of his life like an annoying splinter.

"Vi, this is one of the reasons I like you. You have a soul and a conscience. I'm not going to lie though, I'm terribly jealous of your husband. I wish I could call myself your husband. I wish we didn't have to be so bloody secretive. I wish we could wake up Sunday mornings and have breakfast together. If I were as lucky as your husband is to have you, *I* would never forget it." He took my hand from my face and kissed the palm of my wet hand. I stood just looking at him, unable to reply for a moment. I tried to relax and ease myself by thinking, *well, I've already had the affair, I might as well enjoy it.* However, these thoughts were little to no comfort to me. Paul turned and went to the closet. Picking out his clothes, he slipped them on, and I took that opportunity to sneak off to the bathroom.

I shut the door behind me and looked into the mirror. My mascara had run, giving me smudges under my eyes. Even after my attempts to clean my eyes, it was hardly of any use. I turned on the shower and jumped in washing off the scent of my adultery. The water helped to erase the scent of my adultery, but could not do anything to erase my guilt.

As I pulled my shirt over my head, I could not settle my mind. I knew I was not designed to have affairs. I was the kind of person that felt guilty at the slightest of indiscretions. I also knew without a doubt that I loved Kyle. I had been so lonely and miserable for so long, and had on many occasions, looked at him, hating him out of anger, but always to return to my feeling of love for him. *Did other women feel like this when they had affairs? Or do I feel like this because I'm still in love with my husband?* I couldn't help but think these questions repeatedly in my mind. I also couldn't stop thinking about Olivia. Even though I had no proof, I couldn't help but imagine them sneaking off to take long lunches at the hotel together. Images of them doing things together never ever left me, they haunted me, teased me, and my conscience would pluck them out when needed as an excuse to drive me close to Paul.

There was nothing that I could even do now since I was still at the house of my lover. I was here, all the thinking and justifying couldn't turn back the clock. I walked out and saw Paul sitting at the table next to his small kitchen. On the table sat two plates. The food and white plates were arranged on the smooth cloth in a cultured manner, like a hotel, not what you would expect from the typical single guy or a bachelor. Paul was looking through a book, slowly gliding his finger along the edge of the page as he turned it. He sat leaning into the book, one hand flipping, and the other resting underneath the table on his knee. He was now dressed in a handsome knit sweater and jeans, his hair neatly combed and his face freshly shaven. He looked up at me as I walked over, sitting down in the chair next to him.

"I was afraid you weren't going to come out of the bathroom. Is everything okay?" He reached over placing his hand on top of mine. I smiled and nodded. His hand was warm to the touch as usual. I looked down at the plate.

"This looks very nice. What did you make?" I raised my eyebrows, amazed at his thoughtfulness.

"I toasted some baguette bread and put in some fresh spinach and cream, topping it with both Asiago and a little Gouda. And thin tomato slices, of course." One corner side of his mouth curled up in a little half, charming smile. Almost acting in a sarcastic way as if this was not a big deal at all.

"So all you British fellows just throw stuff together on a whim, huh?" I gave a little chuckle as he gave me a little laugh.

"That's what I love about you, Vi, you're so witty and clever." His charming British accent could make just about anything he said sound pleasant. He watched me as if I was a seasoned food critic while I brought my first bite to my lips. It was delicious and my opinion was conveyed on my face as he started beaming with delight at my reaction.

"I'm so glad you like it. I would love to cook for you all the time." An awkward silence fell into the room. I was not sure what he wanted me to say, or where that statement was headed. I gazed into his eyes trying to read his face, wondering for a moment, and then I asked,

"Are you asking me to leave my husband for you?" Sadness came across his face. He looked like a lost boy without his dog. When he answered, there was a sadness in his voice.

"I wish you would. Oh, Vi, how I wish you would." I looked down at my plate, thinking and imagining what life would be like with him. *Would we really wake up on Sunday mornings and have breakfast together? What would it be like to sit down and eat with someone more often than twice a month? Would we make love all the time? Would we take picnics on the weekends and long drives through the countryside? Would we talk through all hours of the night and I would never tire of his stories about England?* Still looking down at my plate, I imagined each of these things in detail. I could see myself waking up next to him, eating in the park on a sunny afternoon, and most of all, I could imagine having someone talk to me and listen to me on a daily basis. My heart became warm. *Could I leave Kyle for Paul? What if I got on a plane and we ran off to London? Would his family welcome me with open arms?*

Then, I pictured Julia's face looking at me with her big brown eyes. What would happen to her if I divorced Kyle? Would we share custody of Julia and take part in the weekend routines you see other divorced parents do when they pick up their kids from each other at

McDonalds? Would she even be resilient if we got divorced? She already spent most of her time seeing Kyle and me apart more than we were together.

For all the wonderful thoughts I could imagine, with all the loving visions that danced in my mind of Paul and me, I just couldn't stomach the thoughts of Julia and her sad face. My happiness in exchange for Julia's sadness was no competition. So with the last thought of Julia's sad face, I dismissed my daydream of picnics in the park and long drives in the countryside. At least for now.

I looked back up at him and could see in his eyes that he also knew this moment was too early for us even to consider such a bold suggestion.

"Paul, I really have feelings for you, but I just don't think I'm at the point yet where I can turn my world upside down and leave everything I know. We haven't known each other long, and that's probably a conversation for the future." He shook his head, his face revealing his understanding of the present situation and that he needed to stop moving things so fast. I gave myself an uneasy feeling. Why did I use the word yet? Was I subconsciously already planning for it to happen in the future?

I took a breath and spoke, quickly changing the subject to end the dry gloomy atmosphere in the room.

"What's that you're reading?" I pointed to his book on the table next to him. It was in a faded black leather bound casing. I could smell the old antique like leather.

"It's a collection of Shakespeare's Sonnets. I like to go through and read them from time to time." I looked down at the plate of delicious cuisine style food then over to the old leather bound book of sonnets, and almost felt as if I was in British movie cliché. I had never seen a man so romantic to whip up a snack, then sit and read sonnets. I also was not forgetting the fact that his apartment was both clean and smelled good.

This situation seemed nothing like the affairs that were portrayed in the movies, where couples sneaked off to dirty hotels and rich women ran off with the local car mechanic. He closed his book and in a thankful tone said to me,

"By the way, I wanted to thank you for asking me to spend today with you. I was more than happy to be sick today." A flirtatious look swept across his face so strongly that I felt my cheeks become hot from blushing. I stopped for a moment, thinking of Kyle and how I had hoped he would take today off work. How sad and disappointed I had been when he didn't, yet how excited I had been thinking of the moment when I would be with Paul again.

Kyle just kept creeping in my mind. He wouldn't leave, and there was nothing I could think of to make him go away. No matter how hard I tried to force out the image and memory of Kyle standing in his office and telling me he loved me, I couldn't. It wouldn't budge. It was like an iron mallet ready to lay into me with more guilt and self-loathing.

I looked into Paul's eyes, enticed again by his spell. There was nothing left to do but lie on the fence and roll over to Paul's side regardless of how hard the mallet hit me.

"I'm so glad you were able to take today off. I hope you don't get into trouble with the school for taking a sick day." He shook his head and did not show the slightest hint of concern as he spoke.

"No, absolutely not. I have great credentials. " He gave me a mischievous look, like a small boy might get before pulling the fire alarm, but knowing he wouldn't be punished because his parents gave large donations. I shot him a quick, sarcastically disapproving look. We both relaxed and enjoyed the moment as we finished our food.

Paul got up and went over to the cabinet, reached up, and brought down a bottle of red wine. He gazed at me ambitiously. His eyes did the talking as they asked if I would like a glass or two. I knew I had already fallen from the path of fidelity, but I also knew that alcohol could lead me to a degree of danger. His presence was alluring and intoxicating, even now that I had already had sex with him, I still was being pulled into him. I kept thinking about the moths, how in the summer you see them, the ones that constantly get so close to the flame and their wings start to burn, but yet, they return over and over again. Why couldn't I stop myself? I was becoming nervous and terrified that I too would continue to struggle to be near the flame, even if I was inches from death.

FOURTEEN

The soft sound of metal rubbing together as the hangers glided across the top of the rack was almost hypnotic. At the very least, it was soothing. I stood there in the perfectly controlled climate and flipped through the rack. I knew I needed some good shop therapy to clear my head. To be honest, even though I had been raised in working middle class America, there were many times both off and on that my parents struggled financially. Secretly, I did get comfort in the fact that I did not have to worry about living paycheck to paycheck. Kyle and I had worked to save money and be smart when we first started off. A small smile crept onto my face as I thought back to the beginning with Kyle. Our small one bedroom apartment we lived in, me trying to get him nice looking suits at the lowest price possible, even driving to another town to go to the thrift stores to see what I could find. My smile slowly faded and my hand stopped midair, and I couldn't help but remember the strong feeling of happiness that I once had. The memories of getting take-out and staying up all night talking 'til we passed out on the living room floor. The memories of him never missing any holiday, birthday, or any small event I had asked him to attend. I couldn't keep myself from wondering if I would be willing to trade this financial assurance for attention and love from my husband. Why couldn't we have both? Didn't other families that lived well spend lots of time together? A sadness overwhelmed me and I finally took my hand down from midair and rested it on top of a blouse.

I had not even known I was crying until a single tear pooled at the bottom of my chin. I quickly stroked the back of my hand across my chin wiping away my tear. I took a deep breath and started flipping through the clothes once more, putting me back in a soothing trance. I took another deep breath and let the sweet smell of fresh new things empower me.

“What do you think of this?” I heard Abby's excited voice as I peered over the rack. She stood, her face beaming with excitement as her arm was outstretched. In her hand was a beautiful coat. She placed her free hand on her hip and glared at me wide eyed, eagerly waiting my opinion.

“It's great! It would look so good on you. Get it.” Abby nodded her head and looked down at the price tag. She opened her mouth while taking a few steps towards me, putting us with in a foot of each other. She spoke in a low voice,

“This price is way too high. I think I'm going to try to get them to take something off.” I couldn't resist a good chuckle as I shook my head at her. The average person that knew about Abby's means would think she was making a joke. But I knew Abby far too well to know she wasn't making a joke. She was dead serious. Abby loved a deal. No, that's wrong. Abby liked a deal, she just loved a steal. I looked at her and in almost a relaxing therapist voice said,

"Abby, Honey, you can afford it. It's okay to spend a little money on yourself every once in a while. Don't feel guilty." She looked down at the coat and scrunched her eyebrows together as her bottom lip puffed out in a small pout. She looked up at me and excitement came back to her face as she spoke.

"You know, I bet it's on sale." I nodded my head.

"It probably is. That's great, now life can be restored to its rightful harmony." I couldn't help but laugh a little as she looked up at me rolling her eyes at my humor. She couldn't help but have a little smile at my joke. She tried her best to look cross with me as she put her hand on her hip.

"Smart." We both smiled and she turned and practically bounced away to check on her sale.

I looked back down at the rack as I continued the rhythmic motion of flipping through the clothes. I was looking for a dress, but not just any dress, the sexiest dress I could find. My mind was now drifting over to Paul, and the sudden feeling of life I now felt. Different images of Paul and Kyle competed with each other as a refreshed memory of Kyle started to crowd my mind. I could remember Kyle sitting on the living room in our old apartment floor as he worked so hard as a new young lawyer, his tank top showing off his firm arms and his basketball shorts. Those were the thoughts that pushed against the new thoughts I was having of Paul. The history of an old love and the excitement of my new affair were in constant competition with each other. It was constant and starting to become exhausting. I let out another huge sigh of frustration from the constant battle within my head.

I looked up and saw Abby with an excited look on her face, which meant her coat *was* on sale. Another wave of exhaustion came over me and I wanted just to lie down and close my eyes, while everything would just naturally work itself out. I knew what I really wanted was to break down and tell Abby about Paul, but I knew I couldn't. I knew what I did was wrong and I could feel it to my core. I had become addicted now like an addict. I just couldn't stop seeing him even though Kyle didn't deserve what I was doing behind his back. I couldn't just give him up with a snap of my fingers, cut myself off cold turkey. Could I? No, I knew I couldn't. I couldn't endure going back to the long lonely days, being invisible, turning back into a ghost.

My eyes started to swell with tears and I choked them back as best I could. I caught a glimpse of a gorgeous black dress hanging up. I quickly made a beeline straight to it so I could do a further examination. I wiped the tears from my eyes and tried to focus on the dress and the whole shopping experience. I heard Abby's voice behind me as she spoke.

"Killer dress, you should definitely get that." I patted my cheek quickly to erase any evidence of crying. I had a sudden change of heart and turned to confess everything to Abby. The weight was too much to bear alone, but before I could force my mouth to utter my confession, Abby spoke.

"Vi, that dress is hot. Looks like someone is spicing things up."

She smiled and did a little salsa shoulder shimmy. Abby looked so relieved to have the thought that Kyle and I were working on our marriage that I bit my tongue. I couldn't bear to see the look on her face when she found out what I had done with Paul. I knew she would not be too harsh on me, but the painful thought was the harshness I was going to give to myself after I saw the sadness in her face. I quickly changed my demeanor and replied,

"You think so? I saw some great heels over here that would look great with it." She became almost euphoric as her eyes lit up, and I knew at that moment, I had awakened her inner shopping monster. Abby looked at me and put her hand on her hip, taking a stance like Superwoman.

"Don't stop there. I'm sure there's some lacy panties with your name on 'em." She clicked her tongue twice on the inside of her cheek and gave me a wink. Abby and I headed over to the lingerie while she became practically air lifted off the ground. She was relaxed and happy, like a marriage counselor that just got an invite to the renewal of vows. I couldn't blame her for being happy, thinking that things were getting better for Kyle and me. Abby had been there since the beginning. Back then, Kyle was unlike many boyfriends that I had seen with other girls. He actually got along with the best friend. Kyle always treated Abby with courtesy and respect. Abby wasn't a fool, even though she knew that married couples fought and there were times I was really frustrated, she never encouraged me to do things I would regret. I have always been appreciative toward her for that. The truth was that she thought Kyle, while nowhere near perfect, was still a pretty good husband, and I knew to my core, she was right.

As we walked across the store carpet, under the dim store lights, I could hear Abby softly talking. I realized I hadn't been listening to a word she had been saying as I was caught up in my own thoughts.

"I missed what you just said." She turned just a few steps short of the beginning rack in the lingerie section. Abby spoke fondly,

"Do you remember when we would do all that shopping at K-mart and Walmart? Trying to get the best and cheapest deal? I thought I'd never get you to shop in a store like *this*." She smiled as my mouth dropped open. I knew she was being sarcastic but I still couldn't keep my comment in.

"What! Me? As I remember correctly, it was *me* that had to drag *you* out of those stores. Oh yes, it was me that introduced you to high end department stores like this." I opened my hand, palm up and glided it through the air like a car model might do for a luxury sedan. She laughed a little and rolled her eyes.

"I know, I know. I'm just joking. Sometimes it's hard to take a fish out of water." She shrugged her shoulders as she said another one of her quirky sayings that didn't really make much sense. I was just about to point out that you *can't* take a fish out of water because it would die, when her face became more serious. She lowered her voice to a whisper.

"But seriously, there are so many times I don't feel like I belong in this store. Or places like this." I looked at her eyes as they shifted back and forth, as if she was an escaped convict waiting for the police to jump out. There were occasions, such as this that Abby almost felt unworthy of having money. Even though she worked hard to get where she was, and made wise business moves for her grandmother's line, she still didn't really believe she had deserved it.

I looked her directly in the eye as I spoke from the heart.

"Abby, you have every right to be in this store. There is nothing wrong with having money. Don't you think you deserve to have something after all those years of having nothing? I mean, what about those rich women who grew up in rich houses and married even richer men. Do you think they deserve more than you?" She nodded her head in agreement. As far as my opinion was concerned, Abby deserved everything she had and more. I knew this is why we became such fast friends our freshman year of college. We both came from families that struggled from time to time financially. We both were never the best looking or the most popular people in high school. We both valued personality and loyalty above money and possessions, and we both understood the reality of life and other people's pretend friendships.

I looked at Abby's face and could see her expression change, as she understood the truth of what I had just said. While slowly and rhythmically nodding her head up and down, she said,

"You're right, you're right. Okay, sometimes I just feel...guilty for some reason, and I shouldn't feel guilty. It's not like I committed a crime." Very slowly, a large, long smile spilled across her face and I could tell she was back to her old self as she spoke in a humorous tone.

"Unless being this hot is a crime? Then I guess *I am* guilty." We both burst out in laughter, covering our mouths with our hands in unison, like two schoolgirls. Turning, we started looking through all the seductive lingerie, perfectly hung and aligned. I opened my mouth as a thought just came out.

"I bet Olivia has a whole closet full of stuff just like this." Without intending too, the words oozed with disgust and hatred. Abby replied so suddenly I imagined she was waiting for the opportunity to say something about Olivia.

"Probably, but I bet she doesn't have what really counts. Female friends and good relationships." I nodded my head in agreement because I knew Abby was most likely right. Olivia was the type of woman that was really easy for other women to hate. I couldn't, no matter how hard I tried, picture her going out to lunch with a girlfriend, or even hanging out with any female friends. Especially if those other women she knew were married. I definitely could not see any women inviting her over to their house with a husband lurking around. For a small, brief speck of a moment, I almost felt sorry for her, but it passed as quickly as it came.

"You're right, Abby. I bet she doesn't." I tried to cut the conversation short because I honestly wished I had not brought up Olivia. I was mad at myself because she was the last person I wanted floating in and out of my mind while I felt guilty over cheating on Kyle. Cheating. I had to stop for a moment to think about the fact that's what I was doing to him, I was cheating. I was a cheater.

My shoulders slumped down as guilt and remorse sat on top of them. I heard Abby's voice just a few steps from me.

"We should go to that little pub deli thing that we haven't been to in a while." The suggestion instantly lightened my mood. No matter how hard Abby tried, she never remembered the name of the restaurant we both liked so much. We both referred to it so often as the 'little pub deli thing' that I always immediately knew what place she was talking about. It was also a favorite of the lawyers in Kyle's office and they ate there almost once a week.

"Sure, that sounds great." I picked out a few sexy lace bras and panties and we headed to the checkout. I knew if Abby was getting hungry, we wouldn't be shopping much longer.

The car was in complete silence as I focused all my attention to the task of parallel parking. I hated parallel parking. Abby sat perfectly still not moving a muscle, becoming the perfect mannequin. I pulled as carefully as possible into the open spot and exhaled a long steady breath. Abby quickly turned to me to break the silence.

"I hate parallel parking. No one should have to do it." I looked over at Abby noticing how tense she looked, as if she was the one doing the driving.

"I couldn't agree more." I flipped down the visor and gave myself a quick glance to make sure that my small tearful episodes in the store hadn't done any damage to my appearance.

The air was still and breeze free and the bright sun almost gave the illusion of a warm spring day. We managed to squeeze a spot just in front of the little pub deli. I rambled through my purse to put on some lip-gloss as I heard Abby's voice.

"I didn't know Kyle was eating here today?" I quickly snapped my head up, almost giving myself whiplash as I gawked in the same direction as Abby. The bright sun bounced off the wall-to-wall windows but there was just enough shadow to see Kyle sitting at a table. I could see the side of his face as he was clearly talking to other people or a person. But there was too much of a glare on the other section of the window to see the rest of the table. Abby looked over at me and was really quiet for a second before she spoke.

"Is he meeting us here for lunch?" She asked the question so calmly and deliberately that I could tell she wanted to ask what was going on, but was afraid of what the answer might be. I could feel in the atmosphere that she was treading around me, trying not to stir something up. I shook my head no to answer her question and leaned closer to the window, squinting my eyes and focusing on the other part of the table, as if trying to will the sun to go away for a brief moment.

Abby sat still and quiet. I could sense from the corner of my eye that she was not entirely sure what to do in this situation. My mouth dropped open for a moment and I took a sudden sharp breath as I saw the silhouette of Olivia's figure walk past the table, most likely on her way to the restroom. Abby saw her as well and pressed her finger tight against her lip, holding back all she wanted to say. She finally gave in.

"Was that Olivia?" I couldn't find the words to reply since my mind was now beginning to spin wild stories and scenarios. The familiar sick feeling started to grow in my stomach again. I looked at her unable to speak as the worst of possibilities began to grow in my head. Abby looked me in the eyes and then she searched my face, reading my question.

"I'm going to go in there, and do a little surveillance and see what the situation looks like... Okay?" She knew exactly what I wanted, so I nodded my head and watched as she slipped out of the car. Abby walked calmly and smoothly to the door. I watched Kyle closely to make sure he didn't look over toward the door and spot Abby. He kept glancing up and down from his menu as if trying to follow some conversation or something in that area.

I couldn't see Abby from where I was parked, so I just focused all my attention on Kyle. Olivia glided back to the table and disappeared out of sight behind the glare on the glass. The soft pleasant look on his face never faded. Time was moving extraordinary slow as I waited for Abby to tell me something. Fear rose inside me with the thoughts of what she might reveal to me, causing my stomach to lurch forward in a sharp stabbing pain. What if she came back and said, "They're holding hands and sharing a sandwich as she laughs." My imagination didn't stop there, as I pictured Kyle talking Olivia into taking a sick day so they could go to the deli and then back to her place. I could feel the heat as it came off my face. I thought about all the lunches I had eaten with Kyle at this little place. Would he turn around and start giving her my jewelry if they were sleeping together? I couldn't control this but I knew that I didn't really have the right to be angry, or did I?

I paused my thoughts, and for that small moment, I thought about how I would truly feel if Kyle was actually having an affair. Would that alleviate some of my own guilt? I shook my head because I knew it would not. I knew I would still feel guilty no matter how slightly it had been lessened.

What if it's not romantic but they are just eating alone? Should that be a big deal? Yes, it should, considering I can't seem to get him to take a lunch with me, and I'm his wife.

I started shuffling my gaze from Kyle to the door, impatiently waiting for Abby to get out here and tell me something. My stomach hurt worse and worse by the second. Finally, the door swung open and Abby came walking out as she propped up her coat collar as if she was a real spy. I glanced back at Kyle who obviously had not noticed Abby's presence inside.

Abby shut the door tight as a quick burst of cool air came rushing in. She turned her body to face me as I waited for some form of information.

"That was extortion I tell ya!" I gazed at her wide eyed and brought my fingertips together mimicking a choking motion if she didn't spill the news. She looked at me, then down at my hands, and continued.

"Sorry, important stuff first. They are not eating alone." I put my hands down and let out a sigh of relief. My stomach began to regain its strength and I sat back into the seat, obviously more relaxed than before.

"What's going on in there then?"

"Kyle and that slutty girl are in there with a bunch of old guys. I tried to get as much info as possible so I gave the host a hundred dollar bill and all he knew was they were celebrating something." She brought her fingers up to make the gesture of quotations as she imitated the host in an annoying teenage West Coast surfer voice. My mind became at ease since they usually celebrated huge case winnings. Abby continued to talk as I could tell she was pumped up from her spy work.

"Olivia is something else. I can't believe she wears such clothes to work. What I really can't believe is that one of those old guys hasn't had a heart attack yet." Abby spoke with such sincerity and conviction it made me wonder why one of the other partners hadn't had a heart attack either. I looked up at Kyle as he rested his chin on his knuckles as his two hands were folded together. I had seen him do that many times when he was bored. I watched him and loathed myself even more for my recent choices. The loathing of myself didn't stop since I knew in honesty, I would make those choices again in the near future.

In that moment, a large cloud passed over the sun and the brilliant glare disappeared from the window of the deli, and as if the revelation of a joke had just been given, I could see the table filled with his coworkers.

FIFTEEN

I stood humming as I flipped through my clothes in my walk-in closet. The sky light illuminated everything in the closet making the colors pop. Before we bought our house, I had never seen a closet with a skylight. I wasn't sure why I was so intent on having one put in, but every time I stood in the closet, I couldn't help but feel proud of the pure genius of it.

I was relaxed and happy as a small bead of water trickled down my neck. I reached up, took a corner of the towel on my head, and patted around my hairline. I was happy to be taking Julia to the apple orchard and pumpkin patch today. We had gone last year and she couldn't wait to go again this year. Julia had been asking me for weeks and I finally decided this was the weekend. I began to make additional plans for the day with Julia, perhaps we would stop at the art supply store and she could get a new set of colored pencils, or maybe we'd go to my favorite coffee shop and she could get a hot chocolate.

That idea made me pause. I ran a scenario through my head, since Paul was a visitor of the same shop. What would happen if Paul also decided to go to the coffee shop and Julia couldn't wait to tell Daddy that she saw her teacher today? Would that make Kyle suspicious? I quickly decided we would be skipping hot chocolate at the coffee shop. I started thinking of all the other things we could do. I didn't have any doubts about the one thing I *wasn't* going to do today. I was not going to think about Kyle or Paul today, or the awful position I had put myself in. I picked out an orchard kind of outfit and dressed quickly, as I could hear Julia downstairs, and only knew far too well the kind of trouble she could get herself into.

I walked around the corner into the kitchen as I tried to fluff my hair with the towel and smelled sweet dough and coffee. My arm dropped to the side as I continued to clutch the towel. I stood stunned as Kyle stood behind Julia, pouring a little more milk in her glass.

"Mommy! Look, Daddy made blueberry pancakes!" She sat straight up and shoved both her hands in her lap as she squealed with excitement in a high pitch voice. Still in a state of disbelief, I watched Kyle as he walked back and forth, putting pancakes on plates. Kyle had on a black ribbed tank top and a dishtowel flung over his shoulder. Most importantly, he was not wearing anything that made me assume he would be going to the office today.

"Are you working today?" I walked slowly over to the counter, as if I was in the presence of an alien. Kyle looked over at me and took a sip of coffee before he spoke.

"Nope, Julia told me last week you guys were going to get apples and pumpkins and she kept asking me to come. I just finished a big case and I don't have to do anything today. So how could I tell this angel no?" He leaned down and stroked her hair. She moved her head along with his hand like a small kitten might do. I took a second to collect myself, thinking I might be in an episode of the twilight zone. I looked down and saw a cup of what appeared to be a chai tea latte sitting on the counter.

"What's this?" I leaned down and took in a deep breath of the magical smell of chai. A smile formed on my face and I looked up at Kyle as he stood with a satisfied look on his face.

"Yeah, that's right. Chai Tea Latte. Like I use to make for you back in college." I glanced back down at the cup and stared for a moment. I had almost completely forgotten how he used to make these for me. It seemed so long ago now. The steam floated off the surface as I wrapped my hands around the mug, feeling its warmth. I heard Kyle speak with concern in his voice.

"Are you okay, Vi?" I looked up at him and nodded as I softly replied.

"Yes, just remembering, that's all." Julia was tapping her fork on the side of her plate as she bounced up and down in her seat while chewing her pancakes. Kyle walked around the table and sat next to her. I watched for a moment, as Julia was high on happiness. I grabbed the plate of pancakes and my mug with the other hand and sat down across from Kyle. Julia continued to bounce up and down as her feet swung back and forth under the table. I looked over at Kyle as he put a fork full of pancakes in his mouth. He looked refreshed and handsome while his shoulder muscles stuck out from his tank top. The kitchen was brightly illuminated from the French doors and the pure white morning sun shined against the side of his face. I stared at him, I had almost forgotten how truly handsome he was. Kyle was not like Paul. Paul was just a notch above average in everything, but Kyle was classically handsome, like an old movie star or a model you might see on the cover of a men's magazine. He looked over at me and smiled as a small drop of syrup pooled at the side of his mouth. I chuckled and pointed to the side of my mouth indicating he had a spot to wipe clean. Julia looked over and laughed with glee. I took a long sip of my heavenly chai before I spoke.

"So are you up for a day of apples and pumpkins and the whole works?" I gazed at him, my eyes just over the rim of the mug. He looked me in the eyes and seriously replied.

"I sure am. Can't wait to spend the day with my two gals." He glanced over at Julia and reached out giving her cheek a gentle pinch. Looking back over at me, he gave me a wink that made me blush. I looked down at my plate, knowing that I was the worst person on the planet.

The leaves were various shades of yellows, oranges, and brick red. The sun was shining, but the air was cool and crisp. It was by far the most perfect fall day so far. I felt Julia's soft little hand as her fingers stretched to cover the side of my own hands. Her little grip was tight with excitement and I looked over as her other hand was tightly squeezing one of Kyle's hands as well. I was instantly warm and happy, as I had always pictured our little family to be this way.

My slight smile faded into a sad frown as images of Paul and I in bed together floated around in my head. I could so vividly see his bare skin and smell his cologne at the memory of us being intertwined in his sheets. His touch, his voice. I quickly squeezed my eyes shut as I so clearly remembered running my hand down his back, across the tiny beads of sweat that had started to form. While I kept my eyes shut, I brought my free hand up to my forehead and pushed my fingertips tight against my skin, hoping to force the memories and images out of my mind.

"Headache, Vi?" My eyes instantly popped open and I looked over at Kyle as his face was covered with concern.

"Yeah, I was just getting a headache for a second, but I think it's gone now." The concern left his face believing my excuse.

Turning my gaze ahead, I saw the beginning of the orchard with its large fence that curved upwards into a grand opening. Above the fence was a large wooden carved sign that read: Honey Pine Orchard. The letters were carved out and the inside of the wood was stained with a dark varnish. I remembered the sign from last year, and again like last year, I found myself wondering if they had made it by hand.

I felt Julia's tight grip squeeze my hand even harder with excitement as we walked under the sign. A small shop sat directly to our left. At the right were long rows upon rows of different apple trees. Every fourth row had a short wooden sign posted at the beginning with the name of the apples in that particular row. It was so organized that I was amazed when I considered the fact that I could hardly keep my kitchen organized. Yet, this farm and orchard could organize acres.

Julia let go of both our hands simultaneously and skipped up to the little stand where she grabbed three sacks, one for each of us. I couldn't resist a huge smile that came on my face as Julia beamed and glowed with happiness. My heart fluttered as I felt Kyle's hand slide down the bottom of my arm, his fingers slowly interlocking with mine. It had been so long since we had even held hands like this that it almost felt unreal, but not unwanted. I leaned into him with my shoulder so our arms were pressed against each other. I felt his lips against the side of my head as he gave me a slow and soft kiss on my hair.

The sun shined bright and the trees cast splotches of shade along the path that was sprinkled with multicolored leaves that had blown in from other trees. Julia stood in front of us looking at us while we held hands. She continued to stare for a moment before her mouth curved upward in a smile. As she looked up, the light hit her large loose curls and the sun revealed tiny specks of red in her brown hair. She stretched out her arm and handed us our sacks. She turned and skipped some more as she went up to the first small tree. With great precision, she examined each apple before picking what she thought to be the best one from that tree.

“Can you believe how picky she is?” Kyle said humorously.

She chuckled a little and an image of her as a small baby came to my mind. I could see the memory of her, so little sitting in the highchair as I tried desperately to get her to eat one of the ten different food items I had around her tray.

“I sure can. I'm glad she finally learned to eat more than just applesauce.” Kyle nodded his head in agreement. I watched him for a moment as he gazed over at Julia with a warm, proud father smile on his face. I opened my mouth to say I wish he would spend less time at the office and more time with us when I changed my mind and shut my mouth. I didn't feel the need to ruin what was looking to be one of the nicest weekends we've had a chance to have in a very long time.

I suddenly became aware of the fact that we had already spent more time together so far in one morning than I had spent with him for the whole month put together. Then an uneasy thought came over me. *What if he was only spending this time with me because he was about to go away, or he knew he had a few large cases about to fall on his desk and it would be right back to the way it was*. Like when husbands do something to make their wives angry, so they just buy them some jewelry so they will just forget or forgive. Was that what he was doing? He thought he would just spend as much time with us as possible for one weekend so that would cover him for the next six months. I looked down and a frown slowly formed on my face. These possibilities made me angry.

I slowly let go of his hand and he didn't seem to notice my change in mood as he walked ahead and joined Julia to pick some apples. I observed them together as he bent down and listened as she pointed out the imperfections on the apples she didn't like. I took a deep breath as my frown dissolved. I wanted so badly for this to last, for all future weekends to be like this weekend. I was tired of feeling alone or like a single mom. I took a second deep breath, told myself I could at the very least enjoy this day, not think about the inevitable future, and my ever-disappearing husband.

I walked over to them and helped picked some apples. The air was so fresh, not cold where it grabs your throat. I heard Kyle's voice as I took in all the scents of the fall leaves and sweet apples that lingered in the air.

"What's the plan for when we finish here?" As Kyle spoke, I paused and thought for a moment, genuinely surprised he was going to spend even more time with us than he already had. Since she was distracted with apples, I replied in a low voice so Julia wouldn't hear me in case we changed our plans.

"Well, I had thought of taking Julia to the art store or going to get something to eat." Kyle looked down to the ground as he nodded his head. He brought his hand up to his chin and stroked his long index finger just below his bottom lip, a common habit when he was taking a moment to think.

"How about we go grab a cup of coffee at a coffee shop, and Julia can have a muffin or something," he said. I struggled to swallow and felt as if someone had dropped a heavy stone in my stomach. I knew that logically there were several coffee shops in the area to choose from, but with my luck, he would pick my favorite spot and Paul would be there. This would not be an ideal situation. I quickly thought of something completely different to do, so that I could relieve my stress and anxiety of possibly going to the wrong place at the wrong time. I answered.

"Well, I just remembered that I really need to work on her costume for the fall play, but I guess I could do that at another time." Shoot! What am I doing? Why did I say I could work on it at another time? I looked at Kyle and saw that he was getting more comfortable with the idea to take Julia to a coffee shop, but I just couldn't risk even the slightest possibility of running into Paul. So I raised my voice just a fraction to insure my suggestion would prevail.

"I was also thinking that maybe we could grab a pizza and while I worked on the costume, you two could watch a movie?" Julia could have been a hundred yards away and she would have heard the magic word.

"Pizza!" Her voice blasted like a seasoned cheerleader as she bounced up to us, her sack in hand and a large open smile on her mouth. Kyle turned to her and dropped an apple in his sack

"Pizza sounds good to me. Now, let's get some more perfect apples." He took Julia's hand and walked a couple of steps down the row. I waited for them to get out of ear shot before I let out a huge sigh and leaned against the tree. I was fully aware of the fact that the odds of us being at the coffee shop at the same time as Paul would be low, but I couldn't prevent the paranoia. I knew that I didn't always have the best of luck. Now I didn't have to worry about it.

I held on to my sack and started walking toward them at a fast pace to catch up. I was really glad that I had gotten everything I needed to complete Julia's costume, now that I would be making it a week ahead of schedule.

Apples were piled on the table and the smell of dough and sauce filled the kitchen sweeping its way into the living room. Julia sat with her damp hair and in clean pajamas curled up next to Kyle on the couch.

I watched as she tried to tuck her toes under him to gain some warmth. I set down my needle and thread to get up and get her a blanket when I stopped. I watched as Kyle leaned over, pulling the throw from the arm of the couch across him and wrapping it around Julia. I was surprised that he was even aware of the fact she was chilly, considering Kyle didn't hardly notice anything that was going on in this house.

A strong feeling of guilt and remorse filled me. I had been so selfish and presumptuous, thinking Kyle had totally checked out mentally of everything years ago, and that he viewed the importance of his work above everything else. *Have I been wrong? Was the old Kyle that I fell in love with still in there somewhere? If you are, please come out.* I picked my needle and thread back up, and focused on the job of desperately trying to sew more leaves onto the costume. Julia had been assigned the part of the "mum" in the fall play. I wasn't exactly sure how the whole story was going to unfold since she only had a few lines and was a flower. Unlike some over achieving parents, I understood this was a small play put on by a bunch of elementary students, most of who can't really read. I struggled with the needle to push it through the tough material. I wouldn't go as far as to say I was domestically challenged, but I might be close. I could in reality do more domestic things than most of the upper class housewives. Most of which grew up in high class homes, went to high class schools, and now have high class husbands. So the fact that I could turn out a pretty good meal, wash my own laundry and a tiny bit of gardening, was top notch in my book. Sewing, however, was a different story.

I looked back over at the couch as I let out a heavy sigh of frustration at my slow progress of the costume to see Julia asleep against Kyle. She had a faint pleasant smile on her face and Kyle's eyes looked heavy and slumberous. I was relieved that he looked so tired. I couldn't get these thoughts of Paul out of my head, and it had been so long since Kyle and I were physical that I didn't know what would happen if Paul were to dance around in my mind while we were in bed. At that moment, my heart sank with sadness as I looked at Kyle on the couch with Julia. Could all the old memories and history that we shared outweigh my new thoughts? I had missed Kyle's touch for so long. I knew in my heart and in the deepest part of my soul that I would never stop longing for Kyle to love me and touch me. I decided to take the risk and put away this mistake that I could be making, and try to be connected with my husband again.

Guilt lingered still as it stirred around inside me, but I began to hope that perhaps if we could go back even just a little to what we had before, then maybe I could forget about Paul and this thing that had started. I began to pray that, if Kyle loved and held me, it would break the power of the bewitching intoxication Paul had over me.

I still wanted Kyle. I wanted Kyle to be my prince that comes and kisses the sleeping princess to wake her from the evil spell that had been placed on her. I looked at him as he stared at the TV, eyes heavy and his body motionless.

"She's passed out. It's been a long day for her. Did you have fun today?" He looked over at me and his eyes livened up a little as he heard me speak.

"Yeah, I'm so glad I got to spend the day with you, and her. I miss spending time with you guys. You know, when we were in the orchard today, I was thinking that maybe you and I should go away on a vacation. I was thinking Italy or Paris... something like that. Just a couple of weeks. What do you think?" My mouth slowly dropped open as I sat speechless for a few seconds. I was torn between happy that he was even thinking about vacations... and suspicion. *But why? Why now is he thinking about vacations?* I quickly pushed out all the suspicious thoughts and decided to convince myself to be happy. *What's wrong with you, Vi? This is what you have been waiting for. Stop over thinking everything and just go with the flow. Maybe I do sometimes get what I ask for.* I silenced my swirling mind

"Yeah, that would be so great. And if you don't think you could take two weeks off, maybe we could just take a cruise or something?" He thought about it and nodded his head as a wide smile came to his face.

"Yes, a cruise. Remember when we talked all the time about how we were going to take cruises once I got that job at the firm?"

"Yes," I answered pleasantly. I turned my gaze over to the direction of Julia and said,

"It's been a long time since you've been home and not working, and Julia is also sleeping, but we are both awake." After speaking, I looked away from Julia and looked him deep in the eyes. I intentionally licked the corner of my mouth, which clearly indicated my intentions. Kyle slightly squinted his eyes together peering at me with his best seductive sultry look he could muster, the same look that had gotten me in trouble so many times in the past. He said in a smooth and sexy voice that made my heart flutter,

"I'll be upstairs for whenever you're ready." He had a very mischievous look on his face and my heart began to race even faster. Kyle slowly stood up, turned, and picked up Julia as her arms and legs dangled like a rag doll. He lowered his voice to a husky whisper.

"First, I'm going to lay Julia in her bed, *and then,* I'll be waiting for you." I watched him walk slowly up the stairs, Julia's legs swinging with his steps. When he reached the top, I could hear the soft gentle creaks of the floor as he carried her to her room.

I quickly threw the unfinished costume down on the side table and jumped up to turn off the lights and TV. I shuffled my feet as I hustled to the kitchen, grabbing anything and everything that might need to go in the refrigerator. As I placed my hand on the light switch, I looked down at my not so sexy clothes and remembered that I had a basket of folded laundry sitting on top of the dryer. I raced over to the laundry room and clawed through to the bottom of the basket where I found my pink and black plaid pajama shorts with the coordinating tank top. I knew it was not considered sexy but definitely a lot cuter than what I was currently wearing. I flung my old clothes in the hamper and scampered out of the laundry room.

I saw my purse hanging by the stairs and suddenly realized my breath might not be bedroom quality. I grabbed my purse and spent what again felt like an eternity scavenging for some breath mints. I couldn't help but think that not only would I not be able to protect myself if I was attacked, I also wouldn't be able to get fresh breath at a moment's notice either. With a small squeal of glee, I wrapped my fingers around some breath mints and quickly popped one in my mouth, frantically clinking it around my mouth and rubbing it against my tongue.

As I reached the top of the stairs, my stomach felt heavy and sick. My heart was consumed with regret and shame as clear detailed images of Paul came to me once again. I could remember him kissing my knees. The image instantly made me feel even sicker. I squeezed my eyes shut and tried so desperately to think of something else besides sex or men. Clothes, shoes, house curtains, new china, music, or a new workout? Random topics started shuffling through my head and I grabbed onto one temporarily until I wasn't thinking about Paul in particular.

I opened my eyes, peered down the hallway, and saw a faint stream of soft light coming from the bedroom. Excitement filled me to spend some real quality time with Kyle finally. I walked slow and soft down the hall trying not to wake Julia, even though the odds were slim since she was a heavy sleeper, but my luck was not always the best.

I very gradually pushed open the bedroom door. I saw the light from the master closet as it draped along the bedroom floor and across the bottom corner of the bed. Besides the one beam of light, the rest of the bedroom was dark. With the help of the soft beam of light, I could see Kyle in a white tank shirt, lying in the bed on his side facing away from me. I smiled and continued to walk over to the bed as I reached out and touched his bare shoulder. I felt his warm skin as I gave him a soft push with the tips of my fingers. He remained motionless as I pushed him a second time, slightly harder. I stepped back and heard the rhythmic breathing that was shortly followed by brief, light snoring. I crossed my arms and practically stomped around the bed until I stood directly in front of him. I watched, as he laid so peaceful and sleeping on the bed. I leaned forward within inches of his face and said in heavy whisper,

"Kyle. Kyle." I reached forward and poked him in the chest with my outstretched finger as I spoke again.

"Kyle, are you sleeping?" In a state of sleep, he very quietly mumbled something I couldn't understand. I dropped my arms in frustration and walked around to the other side of the bed, throwing back the covers and crawling underneath them. I didn't bother to get up and turn out the closet light as I lay in bed staring at its strip of light across the wall and up the ceiling.

As I lay in bed, crushed, wondering why he couldn't hold on for a few minutes to be with me, the familiar feeling of disappointment and sadness overwhelmed me. This sadness and humiliation strangled and suffocated me. I knew if he had work he wanted to get done, he would have been up all hours of the night in his library, but making love to his wife was more a chore than his actual job was.

Once again, I felt alone as warm tears fell down my face. Images of Paul hesitantly came to my mind. This time I didn't force them out. I didn't want to think about shoes, clothes, or how to redecorate a room in my house. I closed my eyes and thought of feeling loved and alive. Most importantly, not having to worry that someone found me so boring that he much rather sleep than make love to me. And as the thoughts continued to flow, I drifted into both a resentful and guilty slumber.

SIXTEEN

My love of fall was not altered by the light rain that would present itself on occasion, even though the combination of fall weather and rain was less than desirable. The smell of the rain in the air mixed with the leaves from the earth was peaceful and relaxing, but also deceptive. Rain on a chilly day was like someone pushing you with your clothes on in to a cold shower. Each chilly drop that hit your hand caused a sharp irritation. I would much prefer snow. A snowflake could feel warmer when it hit your skin than a drop of cold rain.

I pulled my hand back in through the car window as the frigid water droplets lay scattered around my hand. As I set mail that was now speckled with droplets on the passenger seat, I took a quick glance at the back seat. Draped across the back seat lay the pile of clothes that needed to go to the dry cleaners. As the heat from the vents blew around my face making the inside toasty and warm, I contemplated not running any errands at all today, just curling up and drinking some tea. My mind was changed for me when I caught a glimpse of Julia's unfinished costume that could no longer wait. My shoulders sank in disappointment and I reluctantly took my SUV out of park to run my many errands for the day.

I sat in the warmth of my SUV listening to the rain as it dwindled to a stop. I had an hour or two to kill while I waited for my things to be finished, so I sat contemplating what I should do next. As I looked out the window, I saw the blonde hair of Beth as she walked with long strides down the sidewalk, heading my way. I decided that I would seize the opportunity to chat with Beth and kill some of my spare minutes. I quickly turned off my SUV and grabbed my purse as I shut the door and shuffled my boots around the car, hopping up on the sidewalk. I tightened my belt around my trench coat and fixed my hair, as I pretended to stroll down the sidewalk casually, glancing in the store windows as I passed. Beth looked up from the ground and saw me as a bright smile flashed on her face. She waved her arms frantically, afraid I might duck into a store before I saw her. I leaned forward and looked at her, pretending I had just seen her for the first time. She quickened her pace until we were face to face. Her hair was even more luxurious than the last time I had seen her. *Mental note: ask for name of stylist.*

"Vi! What are you doing on this side of town?" Beth was wearing her beautiful Burberry's and an even lovelier pair of trousers. I couldn't tell what was going on with her, but every time I saw her, she looked more and more rejuvenated.

"I had to drop off some things at the dry cleaners and take Julia's costume to the tailor." I gave her an embarrassed look about the costume. For some reason, I imagined she was one of those women who knew how to sew very well. I pictured her making all the curtains for her house. She looked at me and nodded in total agreement. Then she said,

"Gosh, I need to find a good tailor. I'm not really good at sewing. I can do everything else except that. How did you find your tailor?" I looked at her amazed that we might actually be a little more alike than I had originally thought. I stretched out my hand pointing toward the shop.

"Well, I found her way back when I needed to get my wedding dress altered, so that was about nine years ago." *Nine years? Had it really been that long?* I couldn't hardly believe it had been that long, but on the other hand, there were times it seemed as if it has been much longer than that. Beth looked up and down the street until she spotted the little tailor shop. I watched as her eyes scanned over the shop sign several times, mentally taking in the name for later. She looked back at me and smiled as she eagerly asked,

"What are you doing for lunch? Do you have plans?" Beth looked immediately disappointed making the assumption I had plans. I quickly answered, afraid she might take back her invitation to lunch and I would be left alone with my guilty thoughts and feelings.

"No, I don't have plans. I would love some lunch. I know a really cute little Italian bistro just a few blocks around the corner. Sound good?" Her face lit up and she shook her head so fast she looked like a child that was asked if she wanted candy for dinner.

"Let's head over there." I pointed behind her in the direction of the little Italian bistro and we took off to the restaurant. As we turned the corner, she looked down and saw my knee-high boots and her mouth formed into a small 'o'.

"Fantastic boots! I wish I could get a pair like that." I was once again taken back. Kyle worked very hard so we could have a nice comfortable life. Beth on the other hand, had a considerable amount more in the finance department than I did. I found her statement interesting and decided that perhaps, with Beth, perception was not always reality.

As we passed through the door into the bistro, my mouth began to water as the whole place smelled like fresh dough and ripe tomatoes. We walked over to a quaint little corner booth and hung our jackets on the hooks next to the booth. The warmth of the air and the doughy smell of the fresh Italian bread and hot pizza crust was overwhelmingly addictive. The lights were dim and peaceful and soft classic Italian music faintly played in the background. I realized this would be a perfect romantic lunch get away for Kyle, but probably would never happen.

Then I started to wonder if it would be safe enough to bring Paul. I instantly knew the answer to that question as I looked at Beth seated across the table.

Beth looked around the restaurant taking in all the scenery with all the atmosphere had to offer. I was beginning to wonder if she would spill her new situation that had brought out a light and life I had not seen in her before. I picked up a piece of fresh warm bread from the basket on the table as the waitress placed it down. The crisp outside crackled as tiny specks of bread flaked onto the table releasing a thin ribbon of steam into the air. I turned the bread over in my hand several times trying to decide how I was going to get her to spill her secret. *What if she's also having an affair? Should I tell her about mine? I don't know.* I decided I would see what she revealed first and what her stance was on that sort of situation.

"Beth, I swear you've found the fountain of youth. Every time I see you, you just keep looking better. More relaxed and happy and just, well, glowing." She blushed and looked down at the table with a small coy smile on her face. *Spill already! This isn't working...I need to try something else*. Then, I continued in my most sincere voice.

"That vacation must have been really good for your husband. I'm guessing he must be making you very happy lately, you know, for you to be glowing this much." Beth glanced at me, and then quickly shifted her eyes away, looking off to the side as her lips curled inward and disappeared. She looked extremely guilty as if I had said an obvious lie. Then slowly, she looked back at me, biting on the corner of her bottom lip trying to decide how much to reveal. I took this moment to assure her of my pure respect for confidentiality, with Abby being the exception as always.

"I'm not here to judge, and if it isn't your husband...well, if you don't want to say anything that's fine. I'm a good listener if you do," I said as casually and cautiously as I could, trying not to seem eager, even though the suspense was killing me. Her face slowly softened and she looked me straight in the eyes as she let out a slow breath and opened her mouth.

"Are you two ready to order?" I sharply snapped my head to the side as the tall slender red haired waitress stood next to the table. I was so intent on waiting for Beth to reply that I hadn't even noticed her walking up to the table. I looked across the table and saw that Beth was ready to order. She quickly placed her order and I followed with mine right after. As the waitress strolled away from the table like a tall giraffe, I looked back at Beth as my mind screamed, '*Please don't change your mind. Spill!'* I stared at her intentionally, so she knew I was open to hear her story. Beth opened her mouth again and I leaned in waiting in expectation.

"I'm sorry, what would you ladies like to drink?" I cocked my head upward as the tall waitress stood next to the table again. *A glass of shut up and go away*! I scrunched my eyebrows in annoyance as I heard Beth reply with her drink order.

"Coke please." The waitress looked down at me with virtually no emotion on her face. She had light skin, dark red eyebrows and red eyelashes, but chose to put thick heavy black mascara on both her top and bottom lashes. I wasn't one to judge other's cosmetic habits and styles, but I just imagined how much better she would look without all the black.

"Iced tea." I glanced to the side as the waitress scribbled in her notepad, her face still remaining emotionless. She peered down at me with her droopy eyelids as she gave me a half attempt at a polite smile. I watched as she once again walked away. I slowly looked over at Beth as she sat lining up her silverware and arranging her napkin. As I spoke, I consistently looked to my side for any signs off the jack-in-the box waitress to appear.

"What were you about to say, Beth?" I stared at her as she continued to arrange her area. I glanced over my shoulder and quickly scanned the restaurant as I heard her take a breath. This time, without looking up and not being interrupted, she said,

"I'm having an affair." *I knew it! I just knew she was having an affair. This means I'm not the only one.* I looked down at the dark stained wood tabletop. I slid my hand across the top of the table pushing the crumbs together in a pile. *Be calm.*

"Really? Has it been going on for long?" Beth stopped arranging her area and squeezed her hands together, interlocking her fingers. She then placed her elbows on the table as she set her chin on top of her knuckles. Her blonde hair fell around her face, but she didn't seem to mind. A sense of relaxation seemed to come over her as if she had gotten a huge burden of her chest. As Beth spoke, there was coolness and I sensed she did not share my feeling of remorse.

"No, not long, only a couple of months, but it has been so fantastic. He is so wonderful. Very sweet and wonderful... Nothing like my husband. Just...Wonderful." A million questions began to run through my mind. I randomly plucked one as they raced around.

"Do you think you would leave your husband for him?" I leaned so far in my ribs were now pressed up against the table as I was completely engulfed with curiosity. Her head teetered back and forth as if she was sarcastically knocking the question about in her mind for the answer.

"In a heartbeat! I'd run away with him and be happy. Just the thought of actually being happy had become so impossible." Beth's smile quickly turned into a frown as she continued.

"But my husband made me sign a lock tight pre-nup before we got married, so I'd have nothing." She looked down at the table still frowning and then glanced back up at me as she spoke some more.

"And not only is there a pre-nup, he's pretty vengeful and I think about what would happen with Ginger. Where would she live? Remember when I told you that I wouldn't even care if he had a mistress?" I nodded my head still intrigued by every word that came out of her mouth. She continued, "Well that would be the best thing for me. Then I could get out of the marriage and not have to worry about being completely penniless or lose Ginger. If he has an affair, then the pre-nup is void." Her face slowly started to light back up as she was obviously thinking of her lover. Beth shot me a quick glance before she made a brief statement that was nowhere near a question.

"I know this is pretty crazy for you to hear. You are so lucky to have Kyle. I'm not trying to be disrespectful. Kyle is handsome, and seems so wonderful and near perfect. You must think I'm a horrible person for what I'm doing." *Is she kidding me? Perfect, yeah, my husband is so perfect that I cry myself to sleep some nights because I'm so lonely. And what good is a handsome husband if he never seduces you. At this point, I'd rather have a homely husband that can't keep his hands off me! Poor Beth, she knows so little.* I had nothing to say to her statement without going into great personal detail on my life. So I kept my mouth shut on her statement and pushed even closer to the table. I asked another of the many questions that I had.

"How did you meet this man? How did it start off?" I had more questions I wanted to ask but tried to limit my questions to a few at a time. She looked at me a little embarrassed as her cheeks flushed pink for a moment. I wondered if perhaps it was one of the younger trainers at the gym, I was sure it had to be.

"I didn't intend for something to happen, but there was just this...spark, right off. I don't really know how to explain it? Almost as if I had found a soul mate. Even if that does sound a little cliché." I looked at her as her eyes sparkled and twinkled. Her face once again lit up like I had never seen before in all the years that I had seen her around. I also had a new feeling of closeness with her. It was like we both shared a huge secret and common situation that most others did not. I also had a feeling that it would be easier to tell her, instead of Abby.

However, as I watched her face, I couldn't help but notice her face and her expressions lacked something that I was constantly dealing with, guilt. I slowly asked her my next question in a tone to indicate I was not passing judgment.

"Do you ever feel...guilty about it?" She looked at me in the eyes for a long pause, thinking about my question. I could tell she wanted to be as truthful as possible.

"At first I did, but being loved, confident and happy, outweighed my feeling of guilt. Well, I can't say that my guilt was for what I was doing to my husband, but how I might look in my daughter's eyes if anyone found out. I don't love my husband so I don't have guilt about what it would do to him." Beth glanced down at the table and I looked over and realized for the first time that our drinks were sitting in front of us. I was so compelled by every word from her mouth that I had not even noticed the waitress when she set them next to us. She looked back up, and to my surprise, she asked me a question,

"Do you think I'm selfish?" Beth looked at me with inquisitive eyes. She had a look on her face that was so desperate for approval and I knew she wanted me to tell her she was not a bad person. I knew now even though she said she didn't have guilt that she was still having her moments of guilt, because I didn't think a woman who really didn't feel guilty would even ask a question like that. I thought for a while on what to say, and then I spoke,

"I don't think I'm the best person to give advice on relationships. I don't really know this other guy and I have only seen your husband a few times. But I don't think it's selfish to want to be happy. I guess it's just the way you try to get that level of happiness you want that complicates life. It complicates everyone's life." I immediately knew I had said this out loud more for myself than I was saying it for her. Beth looked at me and nodded her head as she pondered my words. I really wanted to know more so I tried to lighten the mood so she would enlighten me with more information. With a more positive tone, I asked,

"So tell me a little more about this man?" Her face changed back to a sly smile and she spoke almost like a love struck teenager.

"He's wonderful. Charming, sophisticated, intelligent, handsome, and in good shape...*and* energetic." Her red lips melted across her face as a large smile appeared, her white teeth shone through. She looked up at the ceiling and let out a sigh while still smiling. She now looked as much like a teenager in love as she sounded like one. I was not in the least surprised she said good shape, because her husband, while not fat, was just a little on the pudgy side.

She looked back at me and her smile softened as one of her eyebrows raised just slightly. She leaned in and lowered her voice, as her demeanor was both mischievous and naughty.

"I don't know how much you want to know, but he is so passionate." After a brief pause, she quickly said,

"I'm sorry if that was too much information." She looked at me, her eyes almost pleading for me to ask her to go on and continue. I couldn't resist the temptation to know as much as possible, so without saying a word, I nodded for her to continue.

"We don't have sex. We make love on a completely different level. I experience something with him that I don't think I ever had with my husband. My husband is dry and boring, but this guy is not any of those things. He gets me to do things that I would have never done with my husband. One day, we actually just stayed in bed *all* day long." I didn't think considering how close I was already to the table I could be even more on the edge of my seat, but I was.

"What about Ginger? Where is she at when you two are together?" I pictured Beth holding hands with one of the trainers at the gym, or lying down on a mat while he leaned in and snuck a quick kiss at work, all while Ginger was sitting next to Julia in school coloring a picture.

"Well, one weekend Ginger wanted to go stay with her cousins so my sister watched her for the whole weekend. That was when my husband was on vacation. My sister only lives an hour away so it wasn't a big deal." A little smile came on her face, as she appeared to be reminiscing about the whole weekend. I found even more questions jumping into my mind.

"What does he do for a living?" Her smile faded gently and a slight look of embarrassment came on her face.
Her cheeks flushed pink as she spoke,

"I'd rather not say."

This peaked my curiosity to the highest level. Was this why she was so worried about divorcing her husband and being penniless? It did almost seem cliché for a wealthy housewife to leave her husband for her personal trainer at the gym, but what if I was wrong? Images of Beth holding hands started dancing in my head, images of her with an artist or maybe a musician. *No, I couldn't see her with a musician, maybe a writer, a struggling writer? Taxi driver? No, I couldn't see that either. Maybe the trainer. Or maybe a trashy but sexy bar owner?* Now I was the one smiling. I could picture Beth with a bad boy bar owner who was the complete opposite of her husband. Driving her around town on the back of his motorcycle. Even though I was aware I was most likely completely wrong, I was satisfied with my conclusion that made me smile.

As we looked down upon the food that had seemed magically to appear just as the drinks had, we gave our conversation of affairs a rest. I had decided to keep my own escapades to myself for the time being. We ate the wonderful food and finished our lunch with talk of the girls fall play and Pilates moves. I, at that moment, knew that Beth and I were at the beginning of what could be a strong and perhaps lasting friendship.

SEVENTEEN

The room, which was both warm and cozy, had the safe and familiar scent of coffee sweeping throughout the air. I was lucky enough to snag my favorite leather chair near the fireplace. The usual rustic cabin shop had been lightly decorated with fall colors and artificial autumn leaves. I took a deep breath and tried to relax as I sipped on a newfound favorite, pumpkin chai latte. I inhaled the sweet and spicy smell of the steam from my chai, amazed that they could combine such two flavors to create a masterpiece. I was grateful that Beth had asked if she could take Julia with her and Ginger to the movies to give me some time alone. I had the sense she felt bad for putting her story on my shoulders, which I obviously did not mind.

My jacket draped across the arm of the chair and I unwound my long crimson red silk scarf from around my neck, draping it across my lap. I ran my fingertips along the folds of the scarf and remembered opening the box it had been in. It was a gift from Kyle five Christmases ago. I loved my scarf and I wore it every year as soon as autumn hit. Kyle always had a smile on his face when he saw me wear it.

As I sat there, I could so easily see the portrait of Beth, sitting in front of me at the restaurant a week earlier. I had been continuously thinking about our conversation since we had lunch together. My mind was still amazed at her complete transformation into a woman of pure happiness and contentment with her life now. Beth had made it extremely clear that she would leave her husband in an instant if the situation permitted. *Could I ever leave Kyle?* I had wondered that question on several different occasions before, but somehow seeing Beth and listening to her story made the question more alive and real. Beth and I were not the same, and we did not have the same situation. As I looked back down at my scarf, running my fingertips across it again, I knew I could no longer deny the fact that I was just beginning to feel something for Paul. Was it love... or lust? Paul was starting to consume my thoughts entirely. He was in my mind when I went to bed, through my dreams and he was with me during the day. All my thoughts, daydreams, and images left me with another all too familiar acquaintance; guilt. Guilt and remorse followed me constantly, everywhere I went at every minute of the day. But I still could not stop, which only allowed the cycle to repeat itself.

Short bursts of cool air repeatedly brushed along the back of my neck as the tiny bell on the door jingled with every opening. The rhythmic sound and hissing of the espresso machine along with the soft music playing from the speakers were enough to calm my heavy heart. I leaned over the seat and reached into my bag pulling out my book that I had been attempting to read for several weeks now. My mind and heart were so torn and overworked that I was almost unable to focus on even the simplest of tasks.

I opened my book, slowly flipping through the pages, unfocused on the words that laid on the page. I stared blankly at the page as the words blurred together as one big ink stain and my mind started to drift yet again to both Kyle and Paul. My head slumped down in exhaustion as a couple more short bursts of cool air rushed in, followed by the tiny bell. I let out a long sigh and stared at my silk scarf, turning it over in my hands and sliding it in between my fingers. I could feel the warm tears starting to come to my eyes and I quickly took a sip of my drink while pushing them back.

A warm sensation and slight tingle gradually flowed down my body as I felt the touch of a warm finger on the back of my neck. The finger floated along the back of my neck and behind my earlobe. I sat perfectly still as the finger then glided across my cheek stopping to rest on my lips. I quickly recognized the additively familiar scents of fabric softener and faint cologne. I became astonished that a slight touch could have such a significant reaction from me. My body became instantly flushed with warmth, and guilt was easily replaced with desire.

Paul slid into the leather chair diagonally across from me. The chairs were usually sitting side by side, but a previous person must had moved it for some reason. Paul looked handsome in his caramel colored lightweight wool pea coat. He had a dark brown sweater on underneath and a matching scarf that was draped around his neck, laying gently against the coat. As he sat there, his clothes were neat and pressed with not a wrinkle or crease. I couldn't keep myself from the old habit whenever I saw a man of imagining Kyle in the same thing and thinking he would be able to pull off the look equally as well, or better.

Paul gazed at me and his eyes sparkled with excitement. Even though the odds were slim, I quickly glance around the shop for anyone who might know me, or Kyle, for that matter. After I was instantly reassured, I turned my attention back to Paul. I slowly closed my book and crossed my legs, tilting my head down and giving him a sultry glare and sly smile. The left corner of his mouth curled up in a flirty smile as his eyebrow raised ever so slightly. I blushed as I chuckled quietly and looked down at my closed book, feeling somewhat childish for my display of teenage, hormonal flirtation.

I felt his warm hand as it lightly landed on top of mine and I felt the heat from my cheeks, as they blushed even more. My body transitioned from warm to hot and as I looked up into his eyes. His flirtatious smirk was replaced by a look of genuine affection. Paul looked at me as he spoke.

"Feels like I haven't seen you for a while. I miss you." My smile too became genuine and I briefly contemplated the fact that Kyle hadn't said such a thing to me in years. *Did Kyle ever miss me anymore?* In complete honesty, I replied,

"I've been thinking about you a lot. You are on my mind, always." For a moment, his face flickered with a look of concern, and then he half seriously asked,

"I hope it's good things you're thinking? Are you no longer interested in me?" I looked at him a little stunned, even if his question was only half sincere, I was still taken back that he seemed unaware that I was so drawn to him. Apparently, the flame did not know the power it had over the moth.

"Yeah, I'm thinking good things. Or more like naughty... guilty things." Even though my words seemed flirtatious, my tone was laced with the truth of reality. I had been thinking plenty of naughty things, which in return, caused me a great deal of remorse. I chose not to answer or address his question about dumping him, because even though I could feel myself being pulled deeper into this intoxicating affair, I couldn't utter the words of ending our relationship with my whole heart. The guilt was always with me. Even when it seemed to disappear, it was the reality lurking and hiding just below the surface for the slightest reminder of Kyle to stab itself into my conscience. Again, I pictured Beth and almost, for a moment, envied her new guiltless love. Nevertheless, no matter how small I envied her affair, I never had envy for her marriage. Maybe that was the real truth, you can't be envied for both your marriage and your indiscretions.

I gradually started to gain an understanding about why my guilt lingered. It didn't take someone of great intelligence to notice that many people, mainly women, envied me because I had married Kyle. I had somehow managed to land the type of husband that most women only wished for; loving, hardworking, handsome and faithful, hopefully. So I already knew in my core what I was envied for, and I also began to understand what I would be resented for. Is that the real reason I had decided not to share my story with Beth? Fear of resentment from her because she told me how much respect she had for Kyle?

Another short burst of cool air brushed against the back of my neck and I looked over to see Paul looking at me, waiting for a reply.

Then he spoke,

"Where did you go? You went off into your own world for a moment. Is everything okay?" I nodded my head letting him know I was fine, I pushed back my thoughts and focused on the temptation in front of me. His hand was still on top of mine and the warmth was comforting. I placed my other hand on top of his, and with both hands, I wrapped my fingers around his wrist and gently brought his hand up to my mouth, kissing it. He smiled and his face softened at my gesture of gentle affection.

Without saying a word, he looked over to the door and then back at me signaling his desire to leave and go elsewhere. I gave a short, quick nod, and stood as I threw my coat on, which seemed to increase in weight, and then I wrapped my scarf around my neck.

Paul opened the door and the once short bursts of cool air on my neck, now seemed more like an explosion of crisp fall air as it hit my face. I looked over at Paul as he slid his arm around my waist, causing me to look away as I remembered walking very similar with Kyle a short time ago in the orchard. We stopped right next to the door of my SUV and he leaned in, pressing against me with his body. I seemed to melt against my door. He brought his soft lips close to mine, and he spoke so soft and seductive that it made my legs weak with excitement.

"Vi, could you spare me an hour of your time?" His face was completely overcome with an expression of desire for an afternoon of intimacy and fornication. Before I could answer, he faintly pressed his soft lips to the side of my mouth, kissing me. I could feel the warmth of his cheek near my mouth and my knees became weaker ever more. Kyle was now dancing through my mind as Paul had been doing so much of lately. I closed my eyes and imagined the smell of crisp leaves and sweet apples of the orchard. I hesitantly remembered the excitement and love of that day, but I quickly remembered the disappointment and sadness when I found him passed out later that night.

My thoughts began to repeat themselves over and over again like a broken record. "Just say no, just say no, just say no...end it." I opened my eyes and saw Paul smiling at me as he brought his hand up, moving a piece of hair out of my face. My skin was burning hot and my face flushed. My heart was heavy because it was torn between two men, and I knew in my core what the right thing was to do. But my weak knees were barely able to hold me up along with a pounding heart, and my overwhelming desire to be wanted and loved, took over again as I answered:

"Yes, I have an hour of time you can have." I closed my eyes as a wave of regret swept upon me. He leaned in, kissed me for an instant, and then pulled back as I opened my eyes. I instinctively glanced around to make sure by my luck I wouldn't be seen by a familiar face. The parking lot and quaint little shops were slow and quiet. Slightly more relaxed I leaned into him and kissed him passionately. I jumped as I felt his hand slid under my coat, his warm fingers touching the edge of my button on my pants. I sharply pulled back as I flirtatiously said,

"What are you doing? I didn't know my hour started now." He nodded in agreement with a coy smile.

"Well, technically, it's my hour since the presence of your company is all my pleasure." I swiftly replied,

"Oh, it's my pleasure also." We both stared at each other and then let out breathy laughs at each other. I motioned for him to jump in my SUV, and silently, he walked around and did so. I pulled out and took off down the street, heading to his apartment.

I looked up at the ceiling as I felt a small bead of sweat run down the side of my head. Paul's room was toasty, and the combination of that and passionate body heat made his apartment feel more like a hot summer afternoon in the jungles of Africa than an apartment in a cool autumn afternoon.

I rolled over on my side letting the new silk sheets float off my body revealing my bare skin. I was a little amazed how quickly I overcame my hang-ups about my body, and how I could now show him my bare skin almost effortlessly. I placed my hand on the silk sheets admiring both their rich burnt caramel color and silky seductive feel. Paul had his hands behind his head as he was looking up at the ceiling.

"I'm going to sound like a girl right now, but these are really nice sheets." He smiled almost deviously as he replied still looking at the ceiling,

"I got them for you. I've had them on for days hoping you would be here on them." I felt touched that he went out and got sheets because he was thinking about me. Did he think about me as much as I thought about him? I imagined him sitting in the car, not noticing a green light because he was too busy thinking about me. This brought a smile to my face, as it felt good to know that I was thought about. My smile faded as the next question forced itself onto me. W*hat about Kyle? Does he* *still think of me?* I knew he had to think of me at least a couple of times a day, since I was his wife. I wondered if he randomly thought of me when he wasn't thinking about home things and what not. Would Kyle just go out and get something for me like this? He hadn't in a long time. I started to feel embarrassed and disappointed in myself for even having such thoughts. Here I was worried about what Kyle was thinking, and I was lying next to another man.

I let out a huge sigh and pushed all the thoughts to the back of my mind. I had been eating myself alive in my own head. Paul turned to me and tenderly let his finger glide down my side and over my hip. I looked at him and was strangely unembarrassed and comfortable. I had the thought that I couldn't imagine Paul falling asleep on me and losing an opportunity to make love to me. His facial expression became more serious as he spoke with so much love and emotion in his voice.

"Vi...I'm so in love with you." He looked me dead in the eye. His eyes burned with affection and the hope that I felt the same. Even though I had been caught off balance, I was beyond flattered and the overwhelming emotion of gratitude swept over me. I loved how his words made me not feel alone anymore, and I recognized the intense power of being loved and knowing someone wanted you, really wanted you.

I closed my eyes, my feeling of happiness was over shadowed by rushing waves of guilt, and remorse, as images of my history with Kyle crashed against my mind. I sensed the warmth of my tears as a single drop ran down my face. I wanted to reach out, grab Paul, kiss him, and tell him that I felt something for him too. My throat was dry and I could hardly swallow, let alone speak out loud. His hand was still resting on my hip and the warmth seemed to increase with every passing second. Why had I talked to him the first time in the coffee shop? I knew I was attracted to him and I knew he wanted me. He made it clear from the beginning how he felt and he left the ball in my court. I never thought I would be in this situation, but I was. Now I was lying entirely exposed next to a man that loved me, and I knew I was starting to feel something for him. I thought I would be strong enough to pull out of this affair after I overcame my temptation of him with both parties unharmed. I was in deep, really deep, because there was something growing, more than a fling, more than a spark.

With my eyes still closed as I fought back tears, I felt his hand raise off my hip and then stroke my cheek. I heard his accent through his soft voice,

"Vi, it's okay if you don't feel the same. I just wanted to tell you how I felt. Don't be upset, you don't have to say anything." His touch on my cheek was so gentle that I couldn't hardly hold back my tears and they began to stream down my face as I brought my hands up to my eyes. Quiet, breathy sobs came from my lips, and I felt the need to say something before I looked like I was having a complete breakdown. I uncovered my eyes and looked at his caring, sympathetic face.

"I do feel something for you. I feel so much I can't even hardly put it into words. I just can't get this guilt about what I'm doing to Kyle off my chest so I can be totally happy. Please don't think I'm a nut case." As I spoke, his caring, sympathetic look changed into one of sadness and gloom. His mouth turned downward into a frown and his eyebrows scrunched together, in both frustration and pout. Paul said,

"He doesn't deserve you. He's already had his chance and blew it. I *love* you, Vi. I love you so much that work would never come before you. I can't imagine you not being part of my life. It's just not fair. It's just not fair."

He rolled to his back and looked up at the ceiling with an enormous look of defeat on his face. I wiped the tears from under my eyes and reached down for the sheets to cover my bare skin. I was hesitant to say anything more since the look of his brokenhearted face was almost too much to tolerate. Was he right? Had Kyle already blown his chance? Would it be fair to be with the man that just confessed his love for me? Loud and clear, without hesitation, my conscience told me no. Kyle was far from perfect and was extremely ambitious when it came to his career, but he had always been a good father and he had never intentionally tried to hurt or mistreat me.

I was at the least intelligent enough to recognize that Kyle was just like so many other clueless husbands, not knowing how they affect their wives. But what I didn't fully know yet was whether or not this situation was fair to *me*? I also didn't know if Kyle was really having an affair with Olivia. I had been so torn and wracked with my own guilt that even the thought of Olivia had become miles away.

I pulled the silky smooth sheets tight to my skin and sat up, inching my way to the edge of the bed, letting my feet hit the floor. I felt Paul's warm hand against the back of my arm as he calmly wrapped his fingers around it just above my elbow. I turned my head looking back at him, still too nervous to say anything, yet I let him do the talking.

"I'm sorry, Vi, I just have this feeling for you and I can't help it." As he inched closer to me, I leaned slightly back toward him, letting him kiss me on the side of my mouth. I turned my body facing him. My heart was so happy when I was with him and having someone want me and listen to me, and actually feeling like I existed to someone. It all has made me come alive again. But even with all that, I couldn't say the word love yet. I admired Paul, I adored Paul, and I definitely cared so deeply for him. Whatever this feeling was that was growing inside of me, it just wasn't at the love stage yet. Most importantly, I still didn't have that feeling for Paul that I have had for so many years for Kyle. Yet, here I was with this man that I just couldn't let go of. I just couldn't go back to the everyday depression of being ignored or trying all kinds of tricks to get my husband to acknowledge me. So I gathered some courage and I looked at him, truthfully saying,

"I care for you so deeply, Paul. You mean so much to me and I don't want you to leave me." His face softened again as he seemed pleased with what I had just told him. He nodded and I was instantaneously drawn to him once again as we began to kiss. I let the silk sheets drop and we leaned back into the bed, kissing with increased passion.

As we intertwined ourselves together again, visions of Kyle's sad and betrayed face appeared in my head, as if I had just confessed all. I lost my feeling of comfort as my heart became heavy with remorseful humiliation. Nevertheless, I did not stop, as the endless cosmic black hole had become too powerful and deep for me to fight against my own sheer willpower. I was too deep, gone. Lost in my own transgressions.

EIGHTEEN

As Kyle and I walked down the carpeted red aisle toward the front of the auditorium, I was glad that we made such good time that we could get a seat closer to the front. Kyle looked back toward me, reached out his hand, and with a warm and tender smile grasped my hand, pulling me closer to him as we approached the third row. We shuffled ourselves a few seats in and as we sat down, I quickly set my purse and our coats on the chair next to me. The auditorium was warm and slightly dry which reminded me of the familiar atmosphere you got the first day after turning on the heater. I could smell not only the faint aroma of crayons and craft paper but fresh paint as well, most likely from stage props that had just recently received their finishing touches. I could hear soft whispers and giggles as the curtain appeared possessed with lively little ghosts, floating and moving about. I caught a glimpse of Mrs. Majorette with her long wavy dark brown hair. She was very petite and always wore all black for some reason. She was the Theater and Performing Arts for Elementary Development Director, AKA, a fancy title so that wealthy parents think their children are receiving a far

superior education than average kids. I guess you had to give even the rich some peace of mind as they wrote their checks to the school.
I smiled as I heard the distinct laughter of Julia followed by a squeal that belonged to Ginger. After hearing Ginger, I scanned for Beth and spotted her on the far end of the second row. I looked at Kyle as he flipped through the program, trying to fill time while we waited. I said,

"I think I'm going to go over and say hello to Beth, then run to the restroom." Kyle looked over at me and stared at me for a moment, his eyes searching for some clue as to the identity of Beth. I hadn't felt the need or temptation to reveal even the slightest hint of Beth's affairs to Kyle. I decided to put him out of his misery since he couldn't seem to remember who Beth was.

"Beth's daughter is Ginger. Julia and Ginger are pretty much best friends. Beth is really nice." As he nodded his head, pretending that he remembered who she was, I smiled and rolled my eyes, standing to make my way out of the aisle. I looked over toward Beth as she sat with her legs crossed and her hands folded across her lap. Her back was completely straight and her recent glow seemed significantly dimmed. She had almost a gloomy disposition about her this evening. I made my way to the end of my aisle hoping to cross between the first row and the large gap in front of the stage. As I moved toward the stage, still watching Beth, I could see that just on her left side sat a larger man in a blue sweater. He leaned forward and I immediately understood Beth's current gloomy disposition as the man sitting next to her was her husband. I stopped and pretended to bend down as if I dropped something, trying to decide if I should go over to her to be friendly even if her husband was sitting next to her. I decided not to, as I stood and turned, walking toward the back door to use the restroom instead.

I could so clearly remember the concerned look on Beth's face, as she talked about her husband's prenuptial. I decided that my saying hello to her might trigger a very uncomfortable nervousness that she might not forgive me for. Our friendship was too new for her to know me well enough to trust that I wouldn't let any of her secrets slip out of my mouth in front of her husband.

The hall was cool and breezy from all the parents opening the doors from the outside. After coming out of the restroom, I glanced down the hall toward Julia's classroom, looking for any sign of Paul. I knew he had to be here. Even if he was not the teacher that produced the play, he was the teacher of one of the classes that were performing tonight. I stood against the wall as I heard more parents talking and shuffling into the auditorium. I gazed at his classroom thinking of the caramel silk sheets and the soft feeling of them on my bare skin. I could feel my face get hot, as I vividly remembered Paul as he tossed me on my back. I could almost smell his faint cologne while it mixed with the smell of sweat and minty saliva. It was quiet for a moment as the door eagerly awaited another small burst of parents to pass through it to the auditorium.

I felt a pair of warm, soft lips on the back of my earlobe. My body flushed with heat and my heart began to race. I stood like a mannequin as I felt his warm hand slide under my sweater and along the crease of my back. I smiled as images of him kissing my thighs while tangled in his silk sheets rushed to my mind. My body became even hotter as he started to reach his hand around the front, touching my stomach. I heard the door open, and was startled and hit with a wave of embarrassment and caution as I quickly turned to look Paul in the face, warning him to be careful.

"Kyle?" I looked at Kyle as he stood behind me with a seductive and affectionate smile on his face. I quickly took the look of surprise off my face and promptly replaced it with one of flirtation. He didn't seem to notice my expression of surprise and smiled, looking down at me as he said,

"What? I can't kiss my wife? You know, we could pretend we are in high school and I'm the school nerd and you're a hot cheerleader." He raised his eyebrows up and down looking at me with both a charming look and a little flirtatiousness, and then his face lit up a little as he gave me a soft laugh. I tried to pretend that I disapproved of his childish behavior, but my fake frown couldn't hide my smile. As I looked up at Kyle, I felt his familiar charm that he had possessed years ago, giving me a glimpse into the Kyle that once was. My smile faded as I hastily asked,

"What about our seats?" He gave me a look that eased my nerves.

"Don't worry about it. I put a coat in each chair. I just felt like I was sitting there forever, so I decided to come and get a drink of water. Then I saw you standing here and it just seemed like I was looking at the old Vi. I just wanted to come over and be romantic with my wife... that's all." After he spoke, he leaned down and kissed me on the lips while squeezing my hands tight. I blushed and said,

"Okay. I'm going to get a drink of water and I'll be there in one minute. Please make sure pirates haven't taken our seats." Kyle nodded and turned to head toward the auditorium. With a soft smile still on my face, I spun around and took a few steps to the drinking fountain. I was flushed and my mouth was dry making the water taste like pure heaven. I felt Kyle's hand as it slipped under my sweater and near the rim of my pants just below my bellybutton. I stood back, appreciative of his persistence for romance. Before turning around, my legs became weak as I was hit with the faint smell of cologne and fabric softener. My heart rate increased and my breaths became heavy.

"Vi." I turned almost fearful that Kyle might decide to come back out to the hall. Paul stood with a sad look on his face. Even with the fresh taste of Kyle's lips on my mouth I was still lured in by Paul's intoxicating appeal.

"Paul...hi." I stopped not knowing what else to say. He released his hand and put it in his pocket as another small group of parents entered down the hall, rushing into the auditorium. He gave me a soft smile as he spoke in his ever charming British accent.

"I've been thinking about you constantly." He looked down toward the floor. His look of enjoyment dissipated, and the hurt, sad look reappeared on his face as he continued.

"I take it that man fondling you was your husband." Without lifting his head, he glanced up from the floor. His eyes glistened with more than sadness now, and there was a look of jealousy in them. I swallowed and then as I felt my face getting red, I spoke.

"Yeah, that was Kyle. It's not a secret that I'm married." He looked back down and then slowly nodded his head as he grasped my words, realizing his lack of position even to be jealous by any nature. He spoke low in almost a whisper.

"You're right, Vi. I'm sorry. I can't help it. I love you." It was now my turn to look down at the floor as I felt a compiled mixture of guilt, remorse, shame and probably above all, self-loathing. Why did I get myself into this mess? The minute I asked myself this question I knew the answer. It was the same answer I told myself over and over again to justify everything I was doing with Paul. I was unloved, unappreciated and invisible. I looked back at Paul not really knowing what to say or how to respond. There was no denying my attraction and the allure he had over me. I started to grasp the comprehension that perhaps the main allure was due in part to the element of excitement. That same type of excitement that most housewives remember from their earlier romances with their now boring husbands, romances that have in time dissipated and shrank to dull mundane everyday life. *Was this what his appeal and hold over me really was? Just excitement... something out of the ordinary?*

As I looked into his soft tender eyes, the warm feeling in my heart outweighed my thoughts of shame and remorse. I was also apprehensive of even the thought or fear of going back to life without his attention and affection. Because in truth, I never knew when Kyle would go back to working all hours and falling asleep rather than making love, so I hesitantly spoke.

"You know I can't wait to see you again, but I have to get back to my seat." I fought back the urge to grab him and kiss him, even though it had only been moments earlier that I had kissed my husband. I caught a glimpse of Mr. Kaufman and his protruding belly, and without saying another word, I walked back into the auditorium before Mr. Kaufman and his ever-running mouth spotted me.

As my heels clinked against the floor, I felt a chill down my spine, and I cringed at a thought. *What kind of person am I? Wanting to kiss another man seconds after I kissed my husband. I bet even prostitutes wait longer than forty seconds between men.* I shuddered at the horror that I might in character resemble the women I had judged on those crazy talk shows. The women that sit in an overstuffed chair or a high bar stool and find they need five different paternity tests because they have no clue as to which man their baby belongs.

As I walked through the entrance, I noticed the lights had been dimmed a considerable amount and the room was virtually dark. As I careful made my way toward the front, I spotted a new couple in what had been our seats. I stopped and with a frown, I looked around for any sign of Kyle. I heard him cough just a few feet away and I followed in the direction of the sound. We were now seated several rows back from the front with the parents who had not made it there early enough for the great seats. I shuffled past a few empty seats as Kyle moved my coat and purse from the seat next to him. He looked up at me, and in the faint light from the stage, his face expression was one of sincere apology. I sat and cast my gaze directly at him, and crossing my arms while giving him a stern disapproving look, I asked,

"Ummm, so what happened?" I sat gazing at him with my eyebrows scrunched together, my arms still in their crossed position.

He looked down at the floor his eyes shuffling from left to right as his lips scrunched together, holding back any incriminating speech. He opened them and spoke as he let out a huge sigh, as if confessing some awful truth.

"Sorry, Vi, I guess when I tossed the coats on the chair, yours slid off on the floor and some people didn't realize the seats were taken. I'm sorry that we're stuck back here now." I stared at him for just a few moments longer with my stern look. I had already forgiven him since we usually were late for events like this and sat even further back than we are now. That and I had already forgiven him because I was disgusted with myself for desperately wanting to kiss Paul just moments ago in the hall, while Kyle was just yards away.

I unfolded my arms and softened the look on my face letting him know I forgave him. He placed my hand in his and brought my hand up to his mouth kissing the inside palm of my hand. I sat there staring at Kyle, frozen with apprehension.

The tears gradually began to form in my eyes. I wanted Kyle to be like this forever, but I could not curb my disbelief toward his sudden change of heart. I had been riding on this emotional roller coaster for far too long to truly believe in any existence of permanent change in him. I knew full well, for me to have any real faith would require a big step and continual actions, like cutting his clients in half.

I could not have confidence that Kyle would neglect even part of his career to strengthen our marriage. Unfortunately, with Kyle's priorities, it would not be for lack of love for me, but for the love of ambition for his career. Even after all that, I still found myself wishing it would change and be better, no matter how slim the odds were against it.

"Don't worry about it. We're actually closer than we usually are anyway." He stretched out his arm and curled it around me pulling me into him comfortably. I closed my eyes as he kissed the top of my head, his lips resting on my hair. While my eyes were still closed, I snuggled my head near his collar and wished that I could erase the overwhelming feeling of guilt, as images of Paul flickered in and out of my mind. What I longed for even more was the desire to want to toss out my attraction and addiction to Paul. I was saddened by the truth. I still felt dependent on Paul's attention and excitement.

I opened my eyes as the lights dimmed to their lowest ability and the faint whispers of parents hushing their partners echoed like a quiet domino effect throughout the air. I heard a distinctive cough, followed by a man clearing his throat that came from behind me, directly behind me. I sat up in my seat almost rigid, as I recognized the sounds that belonged to Paul. As the stage lit up and the curtain raised, I focused on relaxing and enjoying Julia's performance. The slight scent of Paul's cologne floated across my face, making it impossible to forget, my mind full of thoughts and pictures of my affair. His smell and presence even behind me caused a warm sensation to sweep through my body.

I felt my face get hot and I began to smile at the irony of the situation. It hadn't seemed that long ago that we were in the other auditorium and Paul was sitting in front of me, instead of behind me like he was now. Once again, my cheeks were flushed and I was finding it hard to focus on the stage as my mind and emotions raced with each other.

Kyle looked over and leaned close to my face asking,

"You look really flushed. Are you okay?" He paused for a moment as he too remembered the ballet recital. He leaned back over and said,

"You must not do well in crowded rooms, because you were flushed at the ballet recital as well." He scratched his head and then held my hand, gently squeezing it as he whispered,

"When this is over you should go get some fresh air. I can go to the back and get Julia." I nodded my head and I cast my gaze back to the stage, fully aware the entire time that Paul was right behind me.

Julia stuck out as a star performer and to my satisfaction, her costume was far better than most of her classmates. Unfortunately, I knew I would not be able to take full credit for it, as a part of the credit would have to go to my seamstress. The play came to an end and the audience burst out with applause and support for their children. I caught a glimpse of Beth in the front clapping for Ginger.

As everyone stood like sprouting plants from the earth, the lights began to brighten. I stood with an increasing amount of dread. I turned and saw the jealous gaze of Paul piercing the back of Kyle's head. Kyle leisurely stood and stretched his arms out in front of him while smiling out of pleasure and pride for Julia's performance. I continued to watch Paul as he started a performance of his own. His face softened and his eyes became gentle and kind, all in time as Kyle turned toward me, catching a quick glimpse of Paul as he was still gazing in his direction. Paul stood and gave me a wide smile, flashing his white teeth as he spoke in his charming British accent.

"Oh, Mrs. Taylor, I didn't know that was you in front of me?" Kyle, still standing, had a look of curiosity on his face, as he appeared to be searching for any memory of this man that stood facing us from the row behind. I swallowed hard, and without showing the increased effort it took, I said,

"Oh, Mr. Conway. It's nice to see you. Let me introduce you to my husband." I quickly turned to Kyle, keeping myself in control of the conversation.

"Kyle, this is Mr. Conway, Julia's teacher." Kyle's face changed, as he seemed relieved he hadn't actually forgotten a person all together. I sharply turned toward Paul, after picking up a hint of amusement in his smile.

"Mr. Conway, this is my husband, Kyle." I was nervous for a moment that Kyle might have noticed my clear over annunciation of the title husband when I spoke, but luckily, he didn't.

Paul pleasantly gave Kyle a faint smile and they both leaned forward reaching their hands out to shake. As I watched their hands lock together, my heart sank and my legs felt weak. I could read past Paul's fake smile while Kyle was genuinely pleasant and respectful. After they released from the handshake, I heard Kyle say politely,

"I've heard good things about you. Julia really likes you." Kyle pressed forward putting himself closer to Paul as he said in a lower voice,

"Julia even said you're nicer than Mrs. Nolan. Didn't she just say that the other night at dinner, Vi?" I couldn't prevent myself from looking down and mumbling, "Yeah, anyone would be better than Mrs. J." Then I quickly spoke up in agreement.

"Uh, yeah, yeah I think she did." Kyle turned toward me with a look on his face that he was ready for us to end this conversation so we could take off. I heard Paul clear his throat and then with great expression say,

"Oh, Mrs. Taylor, I almost forgot something." As he spoke those words, I felt even weaker than before. Without hesitation, I found myself praying he was not jealous enough to destroy my marriage with a single proclamation from his mouth. Paul turned to the side and leaned down, reaching into the seat next to him for something I was unable to see because his body blocked my view.

Kyle glanced at me with a curious look on his face, indicating he was wondering as much as I was as to what it might be. I shrugged my shoulders at Kyle indicating my own bewilderment.

As Paul tilted his body around, I locked my mouth shut as I had the sudden desire to vomit with the sudden wave of nausea. Out of the corner of my eye, I saw Kyle tilt his head while his body language was inquisitive.

Paul's hands held my red scarf. He had it neatly folded, as it lay so gentle across his palms. I could imagine the words, your wife left this at my house after we made love, play out like a bad movie. That was only one of many scenarios that ran through my mind as I stood, staring at the scarf, unable to speak. My heart was pounding so loudly in my ears I barely heard Kyle say with some wonder,

"Is that your scarf, Vi?" Terrified, I took my gaze slowly from the scarf up to Paul's face, searching it for a clue as to what he might say or do. Paul's eyes locked with mine and he smiled a soft smirky smile out of the corner of his mouth as he spoke.

"Yes it is. Mrs. Taylor dropped it a couple of days ago when she came to pick up Julia. I tried to get it to her but it was too late and I couldn't catch her. I brought it on a chance she might be here tonight." I was frozen, still locked in a trance by his gaze, like a cobra about to devour a tiny mouse. Kyle reached forward and graciously took the scarf from Paul's hand before I had a chance to retrieve it. Paul's smile faltered slightly as Kyle smiled turning the scarf over in his hands. Kyle then lovingly placed it around my neck, speaking as he did so.

"Thanks, my good man. This was a gift a couple of years ago. I practically had to travel to the ends of the earth to find her that scarf. Glad you saved the day." He quickly leaned forward and gave Paul a hearty tap on his arm, as if Paul was an old college lacrosse teammate of his. Kyle leaned back with a smile and gave me a quick kiss before he spoke.

"I'm going to get Julia. I'll meet you in the hall in five minutes." I looked Kyle in the eyes and was momentarily relieved that he appeared utterly clueless to the connection between Paul and me.

Kyle reached the end of the aisle and looked over. He gave Paul a wave and a smile as he loudly said,

"Nice to meet you Mr. Conway! Thanks for the scarf rescue." And in a blink of an eye, he had vanished out into the hallway. I sharply turned my gaze to Paul scrunching my face in disapproval.

"What do you think you're doing? Are you trying to end my

marriage?" I spoke both cautiously and quietly so the remaining auditorium stragglers could not over hear our conversation.

Paul quickly looked remorseful after he caught an eyeful of my expression that conveyed horrified disapproval.

"I wasn't trying to put you in a bad spot. I just happened to bring your scarf. I also just happened to get a seat behind you. Don't be angry about it." His eyes and face were pleading with me for forgiveness. While the pounding of my heart slowed, so did my anger. I looked at him and gave him a smirk out of the corner of my mouth. He smiled at me and his eyes regained their sparkle. Paul hastily picked up his coat to leave, trying to prevent the atmosphere between us from becoming awkward. He looked at me while flipping up his coat collar and in a low voice he seductively said,

"I can't wait to see you again. I'm already thinking about you, me, and a nice afternoon." He leaned in close to my face, but far enough it didn't appear intimate before he said in a breathy whisper,

"I would never do anything to hurt or embarrass you, Vi. You've no need to worry, love." I realized Paul was not the one I would need to worry about hurting me or embarrassing me. It was what I *could* and *was* doing all by myself.

Paul gave me a wink and then with great haste, he took off up the aisle, vanishing out into the hall. As my body slowly started to relax, I made my way to the end of the row and looked up to see Beth staring at me with a bright, wide eyed look. Her husband was not by her side.

"Vi, I didn't see you come in. I was down in the front row. If I had seen you, we could have sat together." I didn't have the heart to tell her that I lacked the desire to sit next to her while in a gloomy state, attached to an even gloomier husband.

"I did see you in front, but all the seats were already taken. Where did your husband go?" Beth's face lit up even more and she shrugged her shoulders indicating she could care less about his whereabouts. She brought her fingers up imitating quotations.

"He had to go to the office and get some things done." I reached out and grabbed her arm, interlocking it with mine as we walked toward the exit. She seemed happy that I had embraced her in this act of friendship, which I did with honesty.

"Was that Mr. Conway you were talking to when I came up to you?" My throat became dry, as I was fearful that she might have read my body language and realized I was having an affair. I pulled myself together and answered her question.

"Yes. Kyle had not met Julia's teacher yet, so I was just introducing them. Plus, I dropped a scarf. He picked it up for me." As I spoke, Beth appeared to only be half listening to my statement. She turned and replied lazily,

"Oh, that was nice of him. Well, I'm off to get Ginger. I'm so glad I at least got to see you tonight. I really enjoyed going out to lunch and would love to do it again if you'd like?"

"Sure, that would be nice."

Beth gave me a wave and walked around the hall corner in search of Ginger. I spotted Kyle and Julia talking near the door. Julia squealed and laughed as Kyle held her hand while she twirled in circles.

The vents in the car blew warm air from the heater onto my face causing me to become drowsy. It was just after dusk, but it was deceptively dark, appearing later than it actually was. Julia sat in the back with her head resting against the bottom of the window. Her eyes were heavy and she was using any energy she had left trying unsuccessfully to stay awake.

Kyle sat behind the wheel and I leaned against the side of the door and propped my elbow against the ledge of the window, resting my cheek in my hand. I soaked in the comforts of the warm air and the faint sounds of the radio while I tried to relax from the last two hours. I heard Kyle speak.

"I don't think you like Mr. Conway." I looked out the window hiding the fact that I was completely blown away by his statement. I had no idea how to respond to his statement. I decided to try to see what else he might be thinking.

"You think so? Why do you say that?" I continued to look out the window, cloaking my anxiety with indifference.

"Well, you looked annoyed by the whole scarf thing. I don't think he realized it though, but I picked up on it. Plus, I don't know, something about him is off." I mustered all my energy to give a live or die performance as I turned looking at him.

"I wasn't annoyed at Mr. Conway. Truth be told, I was really annoyed with myself for losing it in the first place. And of course there's something off about him, he's British." I gave Kyle a smile and he looked over at me and nodded his head in agreement before letting out a soft chuckle. I looked back out the window and secretively let out a low sigh. I was put at ease as Kyle leaned over and turned the radio up as he had already forgotten about the brief conversation about Paul.

After a quick dinner, Julia had no hesitation in falling asleep. I pulled out some nightclothes from my dresser while Kyle whistled in the background. I had little doubt he was looking forward to some physical romance considering he was both eager and flirtatious most of the evening. In months past, I would have been enthusiastically thrilled at an opportunity such as this, but tonight, I was too exhausted to get on this roller coaster. Even with his mood this evening, nothing in this house with Kyle was a hundred percent guaranteed. I was rung dry by my thoughts to have too much enthusiasm left for my husband.

I crawled onto the bed and let the exhaustion take me over. I had no energy left to think or feel guilty, remorse, love, anger or even desire. I thought not of Paul or Kyle, not of affairs or fixing my marriage. My mind drifted to shoes, sales, and hairstyles. As I, for the first time in a while, finally became completely relaxed, I felt the soft touch of the fleece throw as it was gently being draped over me. I did not open my eyes, or even care to, as I felt Kyle's soft lips on my forehead. Just as sleep began to carry me away, I heard the switch of the lamp turning off, while Kyle slid in bed next to me. The warmth from his body and the slow relaxed breathing from his mouth as he lay next to me fueled my state of exhaustion even further as I let go and fell into a deep, almost comatose state of sleep.

NINETEEN

A constant, daily state of uneasiness was what my life had become. The very start of this tempting affair started with so much splendor, promise, excitement, and reassurance that I was still desirable to the male species. Now my memories of the past with Kyle and our once strong stable love haunted me daily. Perhaps, if it had been a year or even months ago, Kyle's sudden change would have been welcomed with open arms and overwhelming excitement, but now, it just adds to my conscious level of uncertainty about relationships and men in general.

Both my mind and heart leaned toward Kyle. Paul had become a little more than just a guilty pleasure. I continuously tricked and eased my guilt by telling myself that this guilty pleasure was permissible, as long as no one turned a flashlight towards our dark secret. What people didn't know couldn't hurt them, right? It was like that old question; if a tree is in the woods and falls and no one is around...does it still make a sound? My biggest problem was that I always answered yes.

I was also smart enough to realize that the odds were not in my favor that this affair could go on indefinitely without being exposed. Unfortunately, I wasn't in a place where I could throw Paul back out to sea for another woman to snatch him up, and at this rate, I wasn't sure if I'd ever get there. I just loved being wanted, knowing that a man wanted me so badly that he was jealous of any other man in my life. The plain truth was that it felt good to be desired.

I looked in my rearview mirror at Julia as she sat with her pink little pony in her lap. She looked down at it while she brushed its hair and I could hear her mumbling under her breath, having a conversation with her toy. I smiled, and for an instant, forgot about Kyle and Paul until I pulled around the corner with the school in my sight. I could hardly look at the front doors without flashing back to Kyle's seduction and Paul's jealousy. I began to feel like a tweaking crackhead, as the compulsion to see Paul became overwhelmingly strong and almost uncontrollable.

I pulled into the nearest parking spot and put it in park as Julia looked up, and with an alarming look on her face, she asked meekly,

"You're not going to drop me off at the door, are you? Am I in trouble?" I was surprised that she would ask such a question since she had never really been in trouble before, notwithstanding the incident with Mr. Kaufman's son. I peered at her through the rearview mirror and gave her a reassuring smile.

"No. I just need to ask Pa--, Mr. Conway, a question about field trips and parent teacher conferences." I was very careful with the words I used since Julia was like every small child and had no problem repeating everything verbatim. She gave me a sigh of relief as she clumsily attempted to button up her jacket. The air outside had become frigid practically overnight. I had lived on the East Coast long enough to know we would have a few more days of at least fall like weather, and then a couple of weeks of chilly weather before winter would hit us hard.

I shut the door and cinched my pea coat together, while gently pressing my burgundy scarf inside. I then stretched out my hand toward Julia so we could walk up the steps. Each step I took caused my heart to beat faster. I couldn't wait to see Paul's face, while at the same time forcing images of Kyle to go to the back of my mind with each step.

The warmth of the school comforted us as we walked toward the classroom. I was uncharacteristically on time, more accurately, I was a little early. Julia let go of my hand, quickly taking off her pink coat and hanging it, and with such rhythm, she tossed her matching pink hat as it glided through the air and easily found its home with her coat. She giggled, and with her little pony still in her hand, she bounced across the room and sat next to Ginger.

Only half the class was there already and I could hear some movement in the supply closet at the back of the room. The door was cracked less than two feet and I reached in my pocket, searching with my hands for some lip-gloss. The cold air had dried my lips, which I never remembered that happening when I was in my early twenties. I glanced back toward Julia as I continued to walk toward the closet, checking to make sure she was oblivious to any expressions my face might give away.

As I reached the closet, a long frail hand reached around the door and opened it. I looked in the eyes of a strange new face. A tall, thin, younger woman looked back at me with wide blue eyes. She had light brown hair that was cut just above her shoulder. I stopped and stared for a few seconds too long, causing her to feel uncomfortable.

"Hi, can I help you?" My mind raced with a million questions and fears about Paul. Had he left? Did something happen? Who was this woman in his room? I pulled my self together and calmly responded,

"Yes, I was looking for Mr. Conway?" She looked more relaxed as she stepped out from behind the door with a bin of crayons tucked under her arm like a basketball. I didn't even have to ask if she played basketball in high school or college, as it was obviously apparent with her handling of the plastic bin of crayons. She had a very strong tomboy characteristic about her, yet somehow, she was extremely feminine.

"Oh, I'm a substitute. I'm the new substitute and floater for the school. I was told Mr. Conway was not feeling well today." I nodded my head and gave the illusion of the sympathetic, yet unattached parent, knowing full well that would be the response she would get all day. I smiled at her and pleasantly said,

"Well, welcome to the school. I hope you like it here." She gave me a gracious look and I turned heading back to the door. While my back was to her, my smile quickly faded and a feeling of disappointment came over me, since I didn't get what I had come in the room for, a chance to experience the excitement of Paul. I reached the door and turned, blowing Julia a kiss just as she looked over from Ginger. She smiled and waved and I headed back to the cold, icy air outside.

The heat was blowing on my face full blast, as I sat behind the wheel, staring at the school. I knew Paul had to be sick, because if he had wanted a day off, he would be spending it with me. I leaned over, opened my glove box, and fished around for the paper I had put in there.

Paul had given me his number, which I in return, decided to write on a small piece of paper. I hardly used my smart phone, to Abby's disappointment, which left my phone book on the small side. I also wanted to keep the number out of my phone to rid myself of the temptation to call Paul when the desire hit me. I finally found the small piece of paper after what seemed like an eternity. I pulled out the paper and unfolded it several times before the small numbers looked up at me. I smiled, as I was closer to getting my fix. I paused, thinking if I should take him soup or pick him up a sandwich from a deli. I wouldn't mind being there to take care of him. I reached into the bottom of my purse and pulled out my cell phone. With the heat still blowing on my hands, I punched in the numbers on my phone. It rang several times before I heard Paul's faint voice.

"Hello?" His voice was faint as if he had just woken up, or could hardly speak with a sore throat.

"Hi Paul, it's Vi. I just left the school and was told you are sick. Are you okay?" His voice was soft and he sounded pleased that I would be thinking of him.

"I'm just a tad under the weather today, but I will be recovered by tomorrow I suspect. Don't worry about me, love. I'm just glad you called." My heart became warm and I wanted to be there to hold him and care for him.

"Can I bring you something? Some soup or cold medicine?" I was desperately hoping he would say yes.

"No, I don't want you to catch what I have. I couldn't bear to see you get sick. We'll spend some time together when I'm better. Is that okay?" I couldn't hide the disappointment in my voice, still trying one last time to persuade him.

"Yeah, that's fine. Are you sure you don't want me to come over? I won't get sick. I never seem to get sick when others around me are." That wasn't really the truth, but I didn't even care if I got sick. He replied, with his voice even softer and weaker but his resolution was firm.

"Vi, I love you, but I don't want you to get sick. Please love, let me get some rest and I will be fresh and new in a couple of days and we can have our time then. I love you. Bye." I was startled by the sudden click of the line as he hung up at the end of his sentence.

I slowly put my phone back in my purse, amazed that he had been so firm. He hadn't been that firm before. I was wondering what kind of sickness he could have. Maybe he was a closet germaphobe; after all, his place was incredibly clean and sterile. My mind suddenly switched gears as memories of Kyle came racing to the front of my mind. I remembered on different occasions when Kyle was sick and I took care of him, I would fall under the same virus days later, while he would stand there looking at me, clueless as to what he could do to help. I found it astonishing that men were like helpless babies around sickness. I had thought it was just my husband for most of our marriage, until all the complaining I overheard from other women over the years assured me that it was not.

The large heavy doors barely missed my backside as they closed behind me. I could hear Olivia's flirtatious laugh from around the corner. Just the sound of it made my skin crawl and my blood boil. Olivia walked around the corner in a tight, navy blue V-neck dress that hit just above her knees. Her long lean legs flowed down into another pair of designer heels. As she walked toward me, her happy look faded into slight scowl.

"Oh, Mrs. Taylor, it's so nice to see you. Let me go and see if Kyle is available." As she slowly started to rotate around to head back around the corner, I spoke up, speaking sharply and distinctively.

"No, I'll go check myself, he won't mind." I slid off my coat as I took long determined strides toward the hall. Olivia turned back around with her head cocked slightly to the side and a faint snarl on her lips. I didn't bother engaging her in further conversation, as I already had too many stresses and mental battles going on in my mind. I dropped my pleasant facade so that she could see I had another side. If she was having an affair with Kyle, it would give her a preview of what was possible. I brushed past her and felt choked by her heavy drenching of expensive perfume. I brought my hand to my mouth, coughing on it as I walked past her, letting her know she had committed perfume overkill.

With ease, I gently pushed open the door and saw Kyle sitting at his desk. He glanced up from his computer and a wide happy smile came across his face. Kyle stood immediately and walked around the desk to greet me at the door, still beaming from ear to ear.

"Vi, I was just thinking about you. Do you want to grab an early lunch?" He came close to me and wrapped his hand around the middle of my arm, pulling me into him and giving me a soft gentle kiss on my cheek. I was completely stunned and frozen with surprise. I had not anticipated Kyle asking me to lunch. I had only planned to come and be pushed aside like the countless other occasions that I had become so familiar with. I thought it was worth a long shot, but I never thought I would actually hit anything.

I stood looking at Kyle as he watched my face, studying it for my reply. I thought of Kyle and the missed opportunity I would have had if I hadn't of come to his office.

"Yeah, that would be great." I tried not to sound so skeptical but my voice was unable to hide it. He nodded, understanding my skepticism. He released my arms and still smiling, he walked around the desk, stroking his hand down his tie. He moved some papers around his desk as he spoke.

"I'm just going to put some files up and finish one last thing on my computer. It will take me five minutes tops." He looked at me and winked as I took a few steps before I dropped down into one of the large leather chairs. I was extremely curious as to the actual amount of time this would take, and how far from five minutes that it would be. I watched him as he typed a few more sentences and with a fluent gliding sweep, he managed to save his document and log off the computer.

Kyle grabbed a file and with the moves of a Latin ballroom dancer, swung around in his chair, and slid the file into the cabinet like dipping a lady. He stood up. Still facing me and watching my face, he reached around behind him and scooped up his blazer. All of his movements were done with rhythm and grace like dancing. He looked at me with a sparkle in his eye and said,

"Ready?" I smiled, and for a tiny, split moment of time, I had the same nervous and excited feeling I had so long ago when we first started dating. My heart ached as that feeling was quickly replaced with the visions of Paul on top of me as we rolled around in his bed.

"Mr. Taylor?" In perfect unison, both Kyle and I turned our heads toward the door, as Olivia stood there with a piece of notepaper in her hand. She cleared her throat and tried to pretend she was sorry for interrupting. She was a bad actress however.

"I'm sorry. There's a Mr. Lowry on the phone. He says it's urgent. I told him I wasn't sure if you were still here." I looked down at the floor as I shouted in my head; *I knew it! I knew it!* I knew it! I reached down to grab my purse and didn't even wait for Kyle to reply to Olivia, since I knew the answer already. My guilt regarding Paul didn't come close to evaporating, but somehow, it was lessened by the familiarity of my neglected marriage.

"I'm not here. Tell Lowry I'm not here and you don't know when I'll be back." My head snapped up so fast I almost got whiplash. I didn't have to look at Olivia since I could feel her jealousy as it radiated throughout the room. I heard her sharp heels against the floor as she practically stomped back to the front desk.

"Kyle, are you sure you don't want to take that call?" He looked at me with a playful disapproving look and shook his head as he grabbed my hand, leading me to the front door.

I felt pleased as I brushed past Olivia and her overwhelming effort to hide the resentful look on her face. As we headed out into the crisp cold air, I was still slightly in a state of shock at Kyle's change in priorities.

I climbed into the passenger seat of Kyle's car and without hesitation, turned the heat up full blast to help fight off the chill. It was one of those days that seemed colder and gloomier than what reality was, due to a lack of sunlight. I looked out the window as everything seemed cold and gray, the beginning stages of hibernation and death was now showing itself.

Kyle stretched over to me and kissed my lips softly. He lingered with his mouth just inches from mine and then leaned in again, kissing me more passionately than before. My nervousness made it virtually impossible for me to enjoy his affection. I began to wonder what the real reason was for his increased passion and greater effort toward our marriage. Was it out of guilt because he was doing something behind my back? Was he suspicious that I was doing something? Did he know something? I gave him a faint smile back as he took off down the road. The heat was full blast and hot, but I found myself wishing it was cold again, since all the anxiety and nervousness was making my skin burn. For a second, I thought maybe he had won a huge settlement for a client and we would be cashing in a large check soon. It was not uncommon for Kyle to take on cases on the agreement to be paid after final trial, which was rare for a lawyer. I decided to let myself believe this last theory so that I could enjoy my lunch. Kyle's voice was smooth and pleasant as he spoke.

"I was thinking of going to the deli, but would you rather go somewhere else?" I immediately knew what deli he was talking about, even if I could never remember its name. I started to have a craving for that fantastic Italian restaurant that I ate at with Beth when she spilled all her secrets to me. I knew it was further out from Kyle's office and would put him at a long lunch, which was something he hardly ever did. I swallowed my assumptions and decided to suggest something different.

"Well, actually there is this really great Italian place, but it's a practically across town. So whatever you want to eat is fine."

"Did you say really great?" I nodded my head nonchalantly, pretending indifferent to the whole situation. He made a sharp turn down a street that promptly led him to the freeway. He began to talk, still in a chipper mood.

"I'm so glad you suggested something else. I was starting to get tired of eating at that deli. Olivia decided she loves it, so she has been convincing everyone in the office to eat there all the time." I didn't even pretend to contain my snarl, letting my lip curl up to the bottom of my nose. He looked over at my face and paused for a long moment while a look of confusion crossed his face. He continued,

"So either you hate the deli, or you are not a fan of Olivia?" I let out a loud breathy huff that I couldn't contain. Was Kyle really that oblivious? Could he really not feel the tension in the room when she walked in and I was there? I completely left all reserve behind as I spoke.

"Really, Kyle? You haven't sensed the tension from that slut? She's a classless act in five inch heels! Oh... and I love the deli."

Kyle looked astonished and baffled as the words came out of my mouth. I could see him thinking about my statement while his look softened and he seemed to understand at least part of what I said. Kyle spoke, in part, I think to soften my hate.

"I think the last time we were at the deli, we were all celebrating the fact that she just got engaged, but she is flirtatious, that's true. She flirts with everyone at the office, except her uncle, who got her the job in the first place. And to be honest with you, Vi, she is the worst receptionist we have ever had."

After I got over my initial surprise that she was getting married yet again, I felt a little better knowing that she was such a bad employee. However, I didn't feel that much better knowing that she flirted with everyone. That just made her even more scandalous. Even though this brought a small fraction of comfort, I started to wonder if there was a connection between Olivia getting married and Kyle's sudden positive outlook on our marriage. I quickly stuffed those thoughts out of my mind before they had time to start spinning into images and wild theories. Besides, there was hardly anything that I could think in regards to Kyle that might alleviate my guilt enough to let me return to my previous remorse-free life.

"It's not surprising she is getting married. She has to have some way to afford all those shoes." I smiled and chuckled under my breath. I made the comment more for my own amusement than for Kyle. I couldn't wait to see Abby and tell her about Olivia. I knew she would have so many funny things to say. Kyle, in a more serious tone said,

"There was something I wanted to talk to you about." He then brought his finger to his mouth while he thought for a second. "You know, I think I'll wait 'til it's a little more ironed out before I say anything. Never mind." This made my stomach flip. My guilt overloaded mind began to spin frantically with possibilities. I was now nauseous and weak, as I could feel the color drain from my face. Did he know? Is he being so nice because he's going to serve me with papers?

"Is it something... bad?" He looked over at me and laughed out loud as he shook his head.

"No, Vi, you always think the worst. It's something that I think will be good for us. Don't worry, I'll tell you when things look more solid. Just think of it as a surprise." I sure was thinking of it as a surprise. *Surprise, we're getting a divorce.* That was now going to be rolling around in my head with all the other thoughts I've been having. Then I thought, maybe he's going to open his own practice, but I didn't know how that was going to be good for us. That would just mean more hours and less time from home.

I relaxed my shoulders and focused on the fact that for a rare moment in time, I was going to have lunch with my husband. I closed my eyes and let all doubt and wild thoughts fall off into a land of nothingness. I opened my eyes just as Kyle asked,

"Okay, so where is this place at?" I smiled, reached down, and took his warm hand while his left hand stayed firmly gripped to the wheel.

"It's on the same street as the old bookshop and seamstress. I'll tell you when we get close to it." He looked over at my neck and smiled as if he just realized something for the first time.

"I love when you wear that scarf."

"Thanks. I love this scarf."

"Vi?"

"Yes?"

"I love you."

TWENTY

The weather was starting to have its yearly warmer days before winter showed herself. Usually, I looked forward to this time of year on the East Coast. In the years past, it had lifted my spirits, but not today. Today I was beyond scared; I was terrified. It was almost funny how neglectful I had been with the term karma, and now karma itself was more real than I could have ever imagined.

I reached up and put my hands to my face, letting the tears fall. I could hardly believe that just yesterday, the problems that I thought were enormous now seemed like nothing more than high school drama. *Is this what I deserved? Had I done Kyle so wrong that this is what my karma would be?*

I sniffed and wiped tears from my cheeks as I stepped out of the SUV. My legs were as heavy as lead as I painfully walked up several steps to Abby's front door, longing for the comfort of my best friend.

Abby swung open her door with a frantic look on her face. Abby motioned for me to come in and shut the door behind me as she spun around.

“What is going on, Vi? You are totally freaking me out!” Her eyes were wild with worry as her chest heaved up and down.

I turned, struggling to lift my heavy legs. I made my way to the nearest chair and sat down. Abby scurried across the floor and sat down in the chair next to mine as she mumbled to herself.

“Good thinking, let's sit down.” Abby looked so sick that I took a deep breath and let out all my fear in a single sentence.

“This morning in the shower, I found a small lump on my breast.” I was unable to control the tears as they swelled up in my eyes. Abby's face drained of color and her repetitive swallowing told me her mouth became instantly dry. I continued talking through teary eyes to release some of the tension that had quickly built up inside of me.

“I already made an appointment for this week, but I am so scared, Abby. What if I didn't find it soon enough? What if it's cancer and is already spreading to the rest of my body? What will happen if Julia has no mom? I'm so upset right now.” I put my head in my hands and for the fifth time, began to sob like a war widow.

I felt the light touch of Abby's hand as she placed it on my back, rhythmically gliding it up and down to soothe me. I immediately felt comforted by her mother-like instincts and actions. Even though I could hear the slight sound of fear in her voice, Abby took great effort to speak in a calm and reassuring tone.

“Everything will be okay. I'm sure you found it early, and it might not even be cancer. I'll be here for you. Please don't cry. I'm sure everything is going to be okay.” I raised my head, sniffed back some tears, and wiped my cheeks.

"You're right. I know you're right. I'm probably over reacting. I just get a little crazy sometimes when I even hear the word cancer. I know you understand." She placed her arm around my shoulders and squeezed me toward her in a hug. I knew Abby was the one person that would understand my reaction. She knew that I had lost two aunts to breast cancer, my mom's only two sisters when I first married Kyle. They passed away only three years apart.

I could sense that she was terrified for me, but still held herself together to be strong in front of my face. Both my body and soul were heavy and exhausted, not only by the new alarming events of this morning, but also by the affair I was having. I looked at Abby and paused for a moment. I desperately wanted to lift the weight of the affair off my chest by telling her everything. However, knowing Abby, she would neither agree with the affair, nor be able to handle two pieces of information of this magnitude in one sitting. At this moment, I would continue to keep the affair to myself. The overwhelming feeling I had was that I would have to end it the minute that I let the secret out, and I was still not ready to give up Paul. I knew that I was being selfish, but I didn't seem to be able to stop myself.

My attention was snapped back to the thought of this new lump. I couldn't shake the idea that this lump was karma for my adulterous betrayal. I had betrayed Kyle and even though I knew in my core that it was wrong, I couldn't control myself enough to do the right thing. I wanted to do the right thing, but I was too selfish to make myself. These thoughts made my eyes swell with tears again and Abby began to smooth my hair as I brought my hands up to my face. I heard her voice as it was soft and quiet.

"Shh, don't cry, Vi. Let's go to the back room and have a drink. Would that be a good idea?" I looked over at her and gave her a sad nod and weak smile, as we walked to the back part of the house.

The back room was more like a lounge room. There were no traces of beer signs, pool tables or tacky pictures of playboy bunnies. Instead, the bar area was extremely sleek and sophisticated with the long glossy marble top counter that sat above smooth, dark finished wood. The perfect amount of dim, dropped, retro lighting bounced beautifully off every piece of silver and chrome that lay around the room. The back wall featured a wide wooden wine rack that housed some of the best wines from around the globe. Placed not more than a couple of yards on the wall to the left lay a vast modern fireplace to liven up the room with soft retro chairs that faced it.

The two of us had spent a decent amount of time in this room. While it might be the smallest room in her place, I had a strong feeling that for most people, it would be bigger than any one room they owned.

Abby stood, facing her wine shelf with her back to me. She took her fingers and swayed back and forth trying to pick one. With forced optimism she said,

"I know this is not a celebration, but let's have a really good expensive bottle. You know, to cheer things up and show good faith for the fact that everything is going to be fine." She turned around with a rich green bottle that appeared to turn brown with the mixture of its deep burgundy content. I smiled wide at the cream colored vintage looking label sporting the red letters that could easily be read Petrus.

She smiled back at me and lightly shook the bottle as she spoke in a teasing tone.

"Oops. Looks like I have someone's favorite." I felt my spirits lift with her attempt to use humor to cheer me up. Abby held a favorite of both of us in her hand. She reached out and slid off two beautiful sparkling clear wine glasses from the hanging glass rack.

Everything in this room was in perfect condition. She sat down and poured me a large glass. I brought the glass up to my nose and was immediately hit with the sweet aroma of berries. Abby took a small drink from her glass as we began to talk.

"Have you told Kyle?" Abby paused and then took a larger drink from her glass.

"No, I think I'm going to wait 'til after my appointment. I don't know. Do you think I should?" She looked down at her glass and curled the left side of her mouth inwards as she thought for a moment.

"I really don't know? I guess if your appointment is in a couple of days, maybe you should just wait. He will freak out the minute you tell him. Kyle might not seem like he is there all the time, but that man loves you." Abby had been there as my best friend since the very beginning of our relationship, and she had a knack for seeing the deeper level of peoples relationships than what they show most in public. I always suspected she was good at that, mainly in part because of her own mishap.

"I know you're right. I'm thinking that probably I'm just going to wait." I did believe Abby was right about Kyle becoming upset about the news, but a part of me still had doubts that he still cared for me as he once did.

Abby looked down at her glass that was now half gone and smiled as she spoke.

"Do you remember the first time we saw Kyle? I still remember you leaning over and telling me that he was so gorgeous. Do you remember what I said to you?" She looked over with an amusing look on her face, waiting for me to reply as I laughed.

"Yeah, you said, well, go get that man!" Abby laughed and shook her head as she recalled our conversation on the bench at the lacrosse game. Then as Abby pondered a question, she said it out loud.

"Can you imagine if we didn't go to that game? We almost didn't. What if we had gone to that stupid party instead?" She looked over at me and I pictured what could have been. I chuckled a little and replied in a storyteller's voice,

"We would have met two average brothers that delivered pizzas for a living. We both would have had five kids, gained forty five pounds, and then lived happily ever after." I looked at her and with every effort, tried to keep my serious face. Abby looked at me as if considering the possibility in her mind, and then we both burst out with laughter.

Abby reached over and pulled out a tissue to dab the wet tears away from under her eyes. I caught my breath and took another drink. I pictured Abby with five bratty kids running around as she screamed and chased after them. Under my breath, I laughed a little more. Then I heard Abby.

"I still remember you thought Kyle was too good looking for

you. But you've always had something that men just love." Abby spoke with a very serious, factual tone that I found her statement most flattering. I looked over at Abby and said in a sarcastic tone,

"Wait a minute. Did you open a bottle before I got here?" In response, Abby rolled her eyes. A tiny smirk curled up on the side of her mouth as she replied,

"Fine, fine. I was just giving you a compliment. It's true though. Even if you don't believe it." My heart was grateful for Abby's positive compliments and I knew I was really lucky to have a true friend like her.

I looked up at the ceiling and stared at the tiny specks of light while they sparkled like fairies. I could feel the relaxation of the wine kicking in, so I closed my eyes and felt a small fraction of my stress drain. I heard the click of the remote starter as it was placed back on the table. I opened my eyes to see the fireplace lit with crackling flames. I instantly became mesmerized by the flickering color of the vibrant streams of fire.

"I thought it might be nice to take the chill off. Besides, nothing goes with fine wine better than a fire." I nodded my head since I agreed with that. Then a slow rationalization crept up on me as I wondered out loud,

"Did you *ever* think you'd be sitting in your own lounge, with a remote controlled fireplace, drinking wine that's more than a grand a bottle?" I was still staring at the flames as I really began to think about our lives and where we had started. Abby responded in all truthfulness.

"No, I think about all those times growing up when my mom

was living paycheck to paycheck." The room became quiet for a moment and I glanced over just as Abby looked down, the hint of a frown creeping up on her face. She appeared to be remembering tough times in her childhood. Then she smiled and looked over at me and said,

"Do you remember that piece of junk car I had our freshman year?" Abby knew I would never forget that car, since it was incredibly hideous and awful.

"Yes, I still have nightmares about that car." We both laughed and Abby let out a long sigh and then said,

"Yeah, but don't you just miss riding around town in my red Pinto. Come on, you know you loved the one gray door and the smell of exhaust in the air." She lifted her hand and waved it around her nose as if imitating the smell of something wonderful. In the spirit of the conversation, I added,

"Oh, yes, and don't forget the great pick up and go. Zero to sixty in about two hours." I saw her face change as an eyebrow slowly lifted and a smile spread across her face. I knew the next flashback she was going to bring up.

"Just you, me, and my Pinto. Oh, and that perm of yours too." I crossed my arms in a fake pout as Abby began to laugh uncontrollably. Looking back now, my hair had to be incredibly hilarious. I was quick to remind her.

"I don't know why you're laughing. You permed my hair in the first place. Besides, at least I had hair to perm." Abby abruptly quit laughing and looked over at me while I struggled to keep a stern look on my face. I cracked a smile and we both started to laugh loud. Trying to catch her breath, she struggled to speak as tears streamed down her face.

"Oh Lord, I tried so hard to forget that boy bob cut. That was the worst ten dollar hair cut I ever got. I looked like I was going to audition for Peter Pan, and the streaks of brown and red? You know, looking back, I can't believe guys even talked to us at all." My sides were hurting from laughing so hard. It was even more humorous as the years went by. In all reality, Abby was probably right about it. Back then, we both wanted to be hip and fashionable, but neither of us had the financial ability to accomplish it.

"At least your perm was pretty much out when you saw Kyle for the first time. I have a feeling, if he had seen you with that perm, he would still tease you about it now." I found it hard to smile at that statement since it was true of the old Kyle, but the Kyle that I was now married to was much too self-focused ever to take trips down memory lane with me. Kyle seldom brought up the old days or had the time to reminisce about our past, which was sad to me.

I leaned back in the chair and let out a long sigh as I turned my head over to Abby. Tears from laughter streamed down her face as she tried to catch her breath. I said,

"Thank you so much, Abby. I'm really blessed to have a friend like you in my life. I'm much more relaxed now." Abby turned to me and replied,

"Of course. I am always here for you, Vi. You are my one and only sister. Maybe not by blood, but that's how the world should be. Everything's going to be fine, I just know it." Hearing Abby's words brought a wave of comfort and confidence that for the moment, made me believe I could fight and survive anything.

TWENTY-ONE

A smile crossed my lips, as the leaves were extra crisp, crunching under my shoes. My nerves had been on edge and my mind had been all over the place since I found the lump a few days ago. Tomorrow was my appointment and I was on the edge of being terrified, and hopeful that I would get reassuring news, giving me the chance to put the whole thing behind me.

I found it rather intriguing that Paul had been flooding my mind lately. Even when I had conversations about Kyle, Paul was always there, lurking like a jealous lover inside my thoughts.

I snapped my fingers back instinctively from the entry doorknob, as it was as cold as ice. I glanced back as Julia carried the smallest bag of groceries. Her purple hat was so low and snug on her face that it covered her eyebrows, letting her brown eyes peep out from underneath. Her brown curls poked out from the bottom and clung to the sides of her cheeks. I nearly dropped my own bag of groceries as the front door swung open. I was greeted by the cheerful, peppy voice of Amber.

"Hello, Mrs. Taylor! Can I help you with those?" I managed to nod my head but could not speak since I was stunned. Amber had been our occasional babysitter up until she got too busy with all her activities. I paused and thought hard if I had called her to come babysit. It had been about a year since I last called her, so I was sure it must be a misunderstanding, but how did she get into the house? I stopped thinking for a moment when I realized Amber had already passed me twice as I stood on the porch frozen with curiosity.

Amber always had an excessive amount of energy and raced back and forth from getting groceries with little effort. I walked through the kitchen, set the final bag of groceries on the island counter, and turned to Amber. Already, Julia was catching her up on her day to day activities and all the things she had done since the last time they saw each other.

"I'm sorry, Amber, I don't remember when I called you?" Amber looked up at me with a puzzled look for a moment and then gave me a goofy smile.

"Oh no, Mrs. Taylor, *you* didn't call me, Mr. Taylor did." Now I was even more baffled. Why would Kyle call her? He had never called any babysitter before. Really, why would he call her? I had these thoughts as I went into auto-mom robot mode, putting away the groceries. I turned to Amber and asked,

"Is Kyle here?" Her eyes got wide and she pressed her lips together before she began to speak in her highly energetic cheerleading voice.

"Oh, good gosh, Mrs. Taylor! I'm sorry. I like totally forgot that Mr. Taylor is upstairs. He got home only a few minutes before you and headed upstairs to change. He said if you got home before he came down to let you know he was home. Then he said I could have anything in the fridge. Is that okay?" With Amber's eyes still wide and her varsity coat on her small petite frame, I found it so easy to like her youthful spirit. It was a reminder that I too was that young once with a youthful spirit and a glow around me. I responded,

"Thanks. I'll run upstairs in a second. And as always, you can have anything in the fridge or the pantry. I'm not sure what Kyle has planned, but I will leave out a cake mix if you want to make cupcakes." I desperately tried to lower my voice when I said the word cupcakes, but my effort was futile. Julia raised her eyebrows so high they could have touched the ceiling. Then Julia's face lit up and was followed by the longest humming noise I had ever heard. Amber responded with an equally happy look on her face as well. Who could have known cupcakes was the magic word to make all girls happy.

"Yeah, that would be so cool. I'm totally hungry for some chocolate." I turned as the two of them started conversing about all the different kinds of cupcakes there were and which ones they liked best. I set the mix on the counter and placed both a bowl and the hand mixer next to the box.

I headed upstairs leaving the two of them in the kitchen now discussing all the possible cupcakes that they might like to invent.

The light from the master closet poured out unto the dimly lit bedroom. The evidence of a shower hit me as the moist air smelled of soap and expensive aftershave, as the leftover steam floated out of the master bathroom like eerie fog. I heard some rustling in the closet as I raised my voice so he could hear me.

"Kyle, is everything okay? Why is Amber here?" Kyle stepped out of the closet with a freshly pressed pair of dark trousers on. Kyle's chiseled abs and broad shoulders glistened in the light from the closet. I looked at him with his dark wet hair, which looked freshly cut. I wasn't sure how he had managed it, but he looked strikingly handsome and even better looking as he aged. He spoke with a soft pleasant smile that his eyes glistened with joy.

"Well, I thought I would take my best gal out to dinner." I looked at him and said with a very sly tone,

"That's nice. How'd she like it?" He chuckled a little at my joke and nodded in the direction of the master bed just as he pulled his undershirt over his head. I turned to see a small black box with a red ribbon neatly around it laying on the top of the bed. I took a few steps over and picked up the box as I gave Kyle a quick, curious glance. He already had on his shirt as he began to button it. Glancing back up at me, he smiled wide, his white teeth sparkled in the light and Kyle couldn't keep his excitement from his voice.

"Well, don't you want to open it?"

I carefully untied the ribbon with my fingers, treating the thin pieces of silk as if the present was meant more for royalty than me. I set the ribbon down on the table next to the bed and slowly opened the lid to the box. Inside was a brilliant diamond and ruby bracelet. The diamonds sparkled around the edge of the white gold bracelet as the deep red gems lined up the middle. I had a very similar version of it once when I was much younger, except mine was the cheap plastic kind with cubic zirconium and fake rubies. However, this one was the expensive and genuine version. My heart was touched that he even remembered I had a similar bracelet, considering I only wore it a handful of times when we first met, right before it broke.

I turned to Kyle, his face frozen in a smile. I was so taken aback that I struggled to get the words out.

"Thank you, it's so beautiful. How did you know I would like it?" A look of pride came over his face

"Believe it or not, I saw it in the jewelry store and I had a faint memory that you had something close to it. So I just had to get it for you."

"Well, it's amazing." I was completely overwhelmed by his generosity, knowing full well I was undeserving of it. I reached into the box and hesitantly slid the bracelet out of the box to put it on my wrist. It felt strange and wrong for some reason even to take the bracelet out of its box, as if the minute I put it on my wrist I was betraying Kyle on some deeper level. It was hard for me to grasp why I had this feeling, but it was just there.

Kyle took a few steps over to me and slid the bracelet out of my hands to clasp it around my wrist. I smiled and turned toward the bed as I looked at it on my wrist. It was beautiful and exactly what I would have picked out for myself. My heart dropped for a moment as I wondered if I would forget this at Paul's apartment one day in the future.

The rubies stared back at me, like tiny scarlet symbols of my affair. A gift like this would have made any wife ecstatic, but I was left with a feeling of self-loathing. Each diamond and ruby I admired made me hate myself a tiny bit more than the last one. I couldn't shake the feeling of self-loathing that lingered because I was so undeserving. It felt like I was wearing thirty pieces of silver on my wrist. I turned to Kyle.

“I hardly know what to say, Kyle. It's so beautiful and thoughtful. Why did you do this?” Kyle softly placed his hands on my shoulder and looked down into my eyes, and then he said wholeheartily,

“Vi, I'm so sorry that I have been distant and disconnected for such a long time. I think I finally understand that these past couple of years have been hard on you, with all my obsessive time at work. So, I just wanted to get you something as a very small token of my sincerity.” My legs were heavy like bricks, stuck to the floor, as I was momentarily motionless from the shock.

Fear seized me. I was afraid that I had become so infatuated with my newfound flame, completely won over by lust that even this huge amount of kindness would not turn my complete affection back to Kyle. It was hard for me to admit this fear, even to my own self, but I desperately didn't want this strong possibility to come true. What I really wanted was to go back to the way things were, or as close as my conscience would allow them to be.

I closed my eyes just as a memory of Paul kissing the lower crease of my back pushed through my head. I threw my hands up to my face as the remorse and guilt smashed against me like a ton of bricks. I cried as huge sobs came out that were muffled by my trembling hands. I felt Kyle's arms wrap around me as he pulled me into his chest. He gently rested his chin on top of my head. Kyle spoke with so much guilt of his own.

"I'm so sorry, Vi. I'm so very sorry. I've been such a workaholic jerk. Do you think you can forgive me? Please?" My sobs came out even harder, as my conscience was wreaked even further by the reality that he was not the only one in the room who needed forgiveness. I felt my wall weaken and for a brief moment, I wanted to confess all my transgressions and ease this unbearable weight. I pulled my hands from my face as Kyle leaned back with a sad remorseful appearance on his face. I opened my mouth to confess when I hesitated for an instant. Peering into Kyle's eyes, I softly said through my tears that had calmed down to a simmer.

"Of course I'll forgive you. It's my fault too. I kept all my feelings to myself and never told you how lonely and sad I was. I really want things to be as they were in the beginning. Do you want that?"

"More than anything." Kyle's sad look slowly softened and a small excited smile graced his face as he changed the mood in the room, making it more pleasant.

"Shall we finish getting dressed so we can make our reservations in time? But don't feel rushed." I reached over and plucked a tissue off the night table, gently patting away the tears off my wet cheeks. I wasn't entirely sure what was more shocking, the nice gift or the fact that he actually called a babysitter *and* made reservations. I was beginning to think my husband had been a victim of an alien body snatching. But if that was a possibility, I would take it because they were miracle working aliens.

I walked over to the bathroom and took a long look at my face in the mirror. Mascara and eyeliner were smeared all around my eyes and I felt like a complete wreck. I popped my head out of the bathroom as Kyle sat on the edge of the bed putting on some socks.

"Do I have time to take a shower?" He glanced at his watch and with great ease replied,

"Sure. I'm almost ready, so maybe I'll just go to the study for a moment and..." He shook his head at himself as he cut his sentence short. He realized that change was easier said than done. I was severely impressed that he even caught his possible slide back into his work addiction. Kyle continued talking as he finished putting on his sock.

"Go ahead. I'll just wait for you here. No work tonight for me."

I unclasped my bracelet, set it on the counter, jumped in the shower, and for the first time in a very long while, I had a feeling that I almost didn't recognize from my husband. I felt that my husband actually wanted me. This renewed feeling was comforting but it was wrapped in a cloth of unfamiliarity. It was welcomed, but so very foreign at the same time. I would have been more comfortable at that moment in a completely different country than in my own shower with a husband who had appeared to have a total transformation.

The warm water pushed against me. Each drop that touched my bare body was a reminder of Paul's fingertips, and that had become familiar with my naked skin. I couldn't get Paul's face and touch out of my head even though Kyle's aftershave was still fresh and alive in the bathroom. The water, past warm and almost hot, made memories of Paul real and vivid. My stomach turned and ached, as I could almost feel the presence of his breath on my neck.

I could hear the fluctuation of Kyle whistling as he walked around the bedroom. An increasing wave of uneasiness swept over me and my body became tense and painful, as knots started to form in between my shoulders and back. My stomach ached and stress pushed against my mind, body, and soul. I was overwhelmed and tense. Everything piled up, stacking one thing on top of another.

I had a lump in my breast that I was terrified was cancer. I had a husband who had been distant and self-absorbed for so long that I fell into the arms of another man, but now the old Kyle had started to reappear as he once was. However, the worst was I had a lover who I didn't think I was able to give up just yet, because of my own selfishness. I was beginning to loathe the very person I had become.

I closed my eyes and let the drops beat against my face while I let out a long sigh, spitting out water as I did so. I greatly wanted to blame Kyle for my infidelity to relieve even a fraction of this tension and guilt, but down to my core, I knew I couldn't. I had never asked. I never asked Kyle to stay home, I never asked him to refuse a call and I never asked him to look at me and listen to me. I just was. I was just quiet and supportive and never asked or demanded *anything* for myself. So now, instead of having a husband that knew his wife needed him, I took a lover instead of demanding I be given the priority I deserved. I didn't fight, I sat back, and I just... was.

The smell of fine wine and French cuisine embodied the elegant and beautiful atmosphere. The candles set off a warm, romantic glow throughout the restaurant under the dim lighting. It was both beautifully done and relaxing at the same time. Our table was draped in satin bisque colored tablecloth and the restaurant resembled an old royal castle to the best of any imagination.

Kyle looked up at me and smiled. With a menu in hand, he looked as handsome as ever. While I looked at Kyle, my mind replaced the vision of him with Paul. I imagined for a brief moment that Paul was sitting in the seat and peering at me on the other side of the candle. For that temporary pause in time, my heart fluttered, and I was then snapped back into reality by my own shame. I looked at Kyle as the long thin flame of the candle made shadows dance upon his face. Kyle was just about everything any woman could want. He was intelligent, strikingly handsome, and had a successful career that provided more than a comfortable living, but here I was fantasizing about Paul. I did not know why I couldn't get Paul out of my mind, why I couldn't turn all my focus on Kyle, all my efforts seemed useless.

Yet, I loved Kyle. I lusted after the excitement of Paul, but Kyle, I truly loved. I didn't understand how I could still be torn. Perhaps I had been adrift for so long out in the vast ocean of the forgotten, drowning in Kyle's shadows. Paul had become my life raft. He brought me back into the light and out of the shadows. He romanced me, caressed me, and touched me in ways that I had almost forgotten even existed.

“Everything alright, Vi?” I looked over at him as I realized I had drifted off into my own thoughts. I smiled and nodded as I looked down at the menu before I spoke.

"This place is really nice. I can't remember the last time we went out to dinner like this." I was looking through my menu as I spoke. I prepared myself that at any moment, his phone would ring and we would cut our meal abruptly short, so he could get some things done. My thoughts lingered on this since my memory reminded me of the last time we had a babysitter and went out to dinner.

"I'm so glad you like this place, and you're right, it has been a long time. This reminds me... there's something I want to talk to you about." My stomach dropped, I continued to keep my eyes on the script writing throughout the menu. It always seemed so rare that Kyle ever gave me really good news. I mustered the energy to keep myself from acting alarmed as I casually replied,

"Oh really? What did you want to tell me?" I glanced up and his eyes were like beams into my soul. He locked my gaze and started to speak with such sincerity and conviction.

"First, I wanted to tell you that I made partner." My mouth curled upward in a wide genuine smile. I was happy for Kyle since I knew this was something he had wanted. As I sat there excited for him, I slowly became aware of the fact that this would mean even more time at work and away from home. This current realization shined a possible light on his lavish gifts and fancy dinners. Maybe Kyle was attempting to butter me up before he threw me back out into that vast sea of loneliness. My heart sank and then thoughts of Paul crept back in. As I was slightly taken aback by the mood of Kyle, he spoke in a way that placed his heart on his sleeve.

"I also wanted to tell you about a new divorce client I had." His mood became somber and sad, like what you might expect from an addict when they finally admit they have a problem.

"She was a real nice lady. When she came for her consultation, she couldn't keep from crying. I almost didn't have the heart to represent her. I thought she wasn't even ready for a divorce. She told me her whole story about how much she loved him and everything she did for him, and that he was very successful in his career. Why she took care of stuff behind the scenes, then she said, every year her husband spent more time away from home." Kyle took his eyes off me and looked down at the table as he continued to tell me his story.

"It nearly killed me when she said, 'I just wanted him to appreciate everything I did for him, and I just wanted to know that I meant something to him. But I haven't even heard I love you for the last five years.' And, Vi... the whole time she was talking all I could do was think of you." His eyes glanced back up toward mine and I did not move a muscle on my face as a tear slid down my cheek. I didn't know what to say in response to his story. There were so many things I could have said, but I sat there and stared at his face. Kyle saw my pain and reached across the table, placing his hand on top of mine.

"This client really opened my eyes, which is why I have also decided that I am going to get an assistant. I am going to be spending less time at work and more time at home. A career is nothing but a title you give a job, but you, Vi, you are my everything. The last thing I want is you sitting across from some lawyer ten years from now telling the same story I heard." I was frozen. I couldn't move as the tears slowly fell down my face. I had a feeling of relief, like waiting years for my husband to return home from war and now here he was. But to my self-created misfortune, I hadn't waited in an act of fidelity.

I picked up the linen napkin off the table and gently wiped my wet cheeks. The feeling of pressure on my chest regarding my upcoming doctor's appointment pushed against me, as I looked over at Kyle, desperately wanting to tell him about the lump I had found. I had a sudden urgent desire to share as many things as possible with him, including what I had done with Paul. Unfortunately, my habit of keeping things to myself overruled and I quickly threw the idea of telling him out of my head. I looked Kyle in the eyes and spoke with honesty, still reserving the most intimate secrets for another time.

"Do you really mean what you say? Or am I going to go back to being a single mom two months from now?" I had not intended to sound as harsh as I did, but I had already opened my mouth and put my thoughts out on the table, so there was no point in taking it back. Kyle looked at me neither surprised nor insulted by my tone and questions. He appeared to be humbled by my reaction to his statements.

"Yes, I mean every word of it. I have interviews this week to hire an assistant. I've already made a month vacation each year part of the deal to be partner. Julia is growing so fast, and I don't even see you guys but maybe ten minutes a day. I want *us* to have a life."

I stared down at my hand that was resting on my lap and studied the wedding ring on my finger. I was exhausted by everything, mainly everything I had done to myself, but I also felt hopeful for the possibility of things. I wasn't sure what else to say to Kyle as he sat across from me in nervous silence. I glanced back up from my ring and caught his gaze into my eyes. All the hope and wishing in the world couldn't completely erase my skepticism, but I was willing to push it to the back corner of my mind for the time being. Like I did all my other emotions and thoughts.

"That's all I ever wanted, Kyle, for me and Julia. I love you, Kyle. I always have." As I said these words, his eyes glistened as the bottom part of his lid showed signs of tears forming. He replied,

"I love you so much, Mrs. Taylor."

TWENTY-TWO

The room seemed cold and eerie as I sat on the edge of the examination table. Even with their best attempts to make the room calm and relaxing, it just wasn't. I looked at the chairs sitting against the wall and considered making a run for it as I waited for the doctor to return. My thoughts were cut short as I heard two gentle taps on the door as it slowly opened.

Doctor Benson walked in the room and gently closed the door behind him, taking a few steps, and standing directly in front of me. His eyes peered into mine with such intensity that my stomach felt as if it had fallen to the floor. While he softened his face and gave me a gentle smile of grandfather quality, I could feel the color drain from my cheeks. He had the look that most parents get, right before they tell their children the family pet passed away. He was fairly handsome for an older man with the majority of his thick hair now gray. He also had a strong presence and stance, and he smelled slightly like hospital soap and classic aftershave. He was the kind of doctor you could imagine put half dozen kids through college and now reads books to his grandchildren by an open fire. He opened his mouth and I abruptly cut him off in a panic, as I spoke in a high-pitched voice.

"What is it?" My heart was racing and my nerves were on edge. He placed his hand lightly on my shoulder as he spoke calmly and with authority.

"Mrs. Taylor, we have the results back and I'm sorry to say it is not great news." He paused for a moment and the room tilted as if I was about to faint. He pressed his lips together as he collected the next couple of sentences before he spoke.

"It is cancer, but there is good news in the fact that we did catch it extremely early and there are a couple of approaches we can take in this situation." As the words came out of his mouth, every syllable spoken appeared to come slower and slower until the whole room seemed to stop, along with my heart. I couldn't comprehend anything after the word cancer passed from his mouth into the air. The word alone was like poison gas floating in the air. The whole room slowed and spun. It tilted like a ship rocking at sea, but it was all in a dream like state. I felt almost numb in both body and mind. I had a weak thought that perhaps this really was a bad dream in which I would awake from any moment. I could hear the doctor as he continued to talk but his voice was millions of miles away, as if he was also speaking a foreign language. I couldn't grasp a single word he said.

I stared at the wall while still encased in my state of shock. There was still the far off voice of the doctor as I glanced up at the ceiling. All I could seem to be able to clearly hear and focus on was the faint humming from the overhead halogen light, which gradually got louder with every second, as it drowned out the doctor's voice. My focus shifted on the dreary room, with its gray blue walls and cement colored ceiling. The eerie light that poured down from above with that annoying hum was straight out of a horror movie. I forced myself to come back to reality.

I looked at the doctor who was still standing in front of me. He had stopped talking and had both his arms around his clipboard. He stood as if waiting for me to come out of my trance. In all honesty, he could have left the room and I would have never known. I looked down at the floor as I heard his calm voice again. This time it wasn't millions of miles away.

"Are you alright, Mrs. Taylor?" My natural reaction to this sort of situation was to make a joke. I had no energy or wit even to calm myself in that manner. I had a strong overwhelming feeling of anger, but I didn't know where to direct it. Whose fault was it that I had cancer? Was it mine, was it the whole karma thing coming to bite me in the ---

"Mrs. Taylor, are you alright?" I looked at the doctor through an almost hazy dreamlike state. I instinctively and quietly mumbled,

"Yeah, I'm just shocked." I began to feel dizzy once again as the sound of people walking outside in the hall reminded me that I was not in a dream.

Dr. Benson reached up and placed his aged hands for a second time on my shoulder. It seemed like an unnatural movement for him so I imagined he mentally told himself to do a physical act in order to comfort me. He continued to talk in his calm voice.

"I understand that hearing this news can be a shock at first, but I don't want you to become upset, Mrs. Taylor, because I feel extremely confident that we caught this so early that your odds are fantastic. Now I understand this is a lot to take in at the moment, so why don't you take a few days and we'll sit down and go over the treatment options for you. It will be helpful and a great support to let your family and close friends know what is going on. Support is always helpful even if it is in the early stage." I stared down at the floor in between my feet as he spoke, struggling to catch every word he said. It was all still dreamlike.

It was strange that at that moment, I thought I would have pictured Kyle or Paul, but I didn't. All I could see was the face of Julia. My thoughts and mind slowly started to think about all the negative and horrible possibilities that could happen, even if it was unlikely. I began to wonder what would happen if they couldn't cure it or get rid of it, and I died. What would happen to Julia? Would Kyle remarry? I started envisioning Julia, coming home from grade school as she bounced up to the front door while some strange woman opened the door. But I couldn't imagine a face. I knew that the odds were great that Kyle would most likely remarry, but I just didn't know what *kind* of woman he would remarry. Would she be the same age as Kyle and me? Would she be much younger, or even much older? I got a sharp pain in my stomach as I pictured my only baby calling some other woman mom. Would Kyle let Julia call another woman mom? Of course, that would happen. Kyle's never home enough to know what's going on in his own house.

My stomach turned and the sharp pain worsened with the

thought. What if he married Olivia? She was a snake and was always looking for the next mouse to divorce. I could easily see her dropping everything and going after a vulnerable widower. I couldn't stomach the thought of Olivia being there and taking care of Julia, teaching her how to wear slutty clothes and use men like cup holders.

I jumped off the table as my stomach did the last and final flip. In one instantaneous move, I fell to my knees in front of the wastebasket and clung to it with both hands for dear life, as I vomited so intensely that I thought I might die right there before cancer could get the best of me.

I felt a slight breeze as I realized the door was now cracked open. I pulled back, still slumped slightly forward, released my grip on the wastebasket, and let my hands fall on top of my knees. I could hear the shuffle of feet down the hall as a nurse came into the room. She was short and plump, but had a very pleasant mother like quality about her. Her brown eyes showed signs of aging as they sat behind small rimmed glasses and her short dark brown hair fit just behind her ears. I caught a brief glimpse of her badge as it clinked against one of the pins she had attached to her light blue scrubs. The badge read, Rose. As Rose spoke, her voice was filled with so much sympathy and compassion that it was a pleasant surprise in this day and age.

"Oh, Honey, here, come sit in this chair. Let me get you a wet cloth for your face." She patted the vinyl covered chair against the room wall, making it seem so inviting. Without hesitation, I reverted to a childlike demeanor and nodded my head in obedience, and as I pulled myself off the floor, I said weakly,

"I'm sorry about the wastebasket." She turned from the sink with a damp cloth and patted my head as I sat there with a frown plastered on my face. She spoke again in her loving and motherly voice.

"Don't worry about that wastebasket, Dear. Believe me, you are not the first one to get sick in here. Besides, if you can't toss your cookies in the hospital, where can you get sick?" Rose gave me a little crooked smile showing her dimples in her chubby cheeks. Without moving my head from under the cloth that she had gently against my forehead, I glanced up with my eyes and smiled back. Rose removed the cloth and took a few steps back before she asked in a sympathetic voice,

"Can I get you something to drink?" Still recovering from a state of shock, I nodded like a small child that just wanted my mom to take care of me and tuck me in bed. Rose gave me a quick nod in return and scurried out of the room like a woman with a mission as she closed the door behind her on the way out.

I leaned back in the chair and rested the back of my head against the wall as I looked up at the ceiling, staring at the overhead lights again. I started to think about all that I would leave behind if I didn't pull my act together and get this taken care of. At that moment, I started to have regrets for going into a state of shock and not hearing all the doctor had told me. I knew I had only caught the first sentence. I then started to think about both Kyle and Paul. Who would really care if I were gone? The past couple of days I have had with Kyle were beyond wonderful. Kyle was finally doing and saying exactly what I had dreamed of for so long, but I couldn't completely shake the fear that things would go right back to the way they were before.

I envisioned lying in bed sick and having the depressing feeling of being all alone. If I had to come for appointments and maybe even some type of treatment, would Kyle really miss that much work? Would he even really care when I told him I had cancer? My mind then started to shift over to Paul. I wasn't so naive to think that Paul would always be as attentive and loving as he was now, but would he care more if I told him about the cancer? Would he be willing to take me to my appointments and do whatever I needed if I asked him? I envisioned myself lying sick in Paul's bed and pictured him sitting next to me reading poetry out of his leather bound book. This thought made me smile, but then it faded. Even all the wonderful thoughts and visions of future possibilities with Paul couldn't erase or cover my memory of the first time I saw Kyle.

“Here you go, Honey. Here's a little soda pop to help your stomach.” I turned my head as Rose slid back into the room caring a Styrofoam cup with a straw. I sat up and put my thoughts of Kyle and Paul away as I took a little sip from the straw, finally deleting the awful acidic taste from my mouth. I let out a little sigh as I said to Rose,

“Thank you so much.” She smiled while her eyes squinted, reminding me of Christmas cards with pictures of Mrs. Claus on them.

“You’re welcome. All your paperwork is at the front desk and they'll schedule your next meeting with Dr. Benson. If you need to take a few more minutes to relax, please take them. I'll see you upfront whenever you’re ready.” Her voice was relaxing and comforting. She gave me one last pleasant smile as she slowly walked out of the room, leaving the door cracked slightly.

I picked up my purse from the floor and headed for the front, while I thought about whom I would tell this awful piece of news to first. It didn't take me long before Abby jumped into my mind.

As I walked down the long narrow hall with numb legs, everything was hazy, as my mind circled with nothingness, while I pretended cancer lacked existence.

Against my own intelligence, I crossed my fingers and prayed that I had only been in a very realistic dream this whole time, one I would awake from at any moment. I knew it was all real, too real. I also knew that perhaps this is what I deserved. What goes around comes around, isn't that what everyone says? *Maybe I really did deserve this*, I thought to myself. Because, even in the face of cancer, I still was intoxicated by thoughts and desires for Paul. My affair was not only toxic to my marriage, but to my soul and body as well. I had turned into an addict, an addict for the excitement and attention that I had been deprived of for so long. I knew like most addicts that I wouldn't be able to cut myself off cold turkey, no matter how much I desperately wished that I could.

TWENTY-THREE

The whole room smelled old and musty, and the air was so humid and hot it was suffocating. The thick heavy drapes were swirled with ugly orange and brown flowers. I rolled over on my back, exposing my bare body while the blankets and comforter lay crumpled in a pile next to the bed. I glanced over by the air conditioning unit half expecting to see a cockroach around the wall. Thankfully, my expectation was not indulged. Everything felt dirty and immoral, and my main desire at the moment was to take a scalding hot shower to cleanse myself of all impropriety.

I could hear the hustle of cars and trucks as they drove along the highway overpass that was less than a block from the motel parking lot. The one unbroken bathroom light cast a small beam of light into the room. The remainder of light came from the sunlight that pressed down from the small gaps at the bottom of the heavy drapes. I heard the clinking of metal against the door just as the key took its final twist and it cracked open. I rolled over to my side and lay my arm along my hip, while resting my head in my other hand that was propped up by my elbow.

Paul walked through the door, tightly holding two sodas and a small cheap plastic bucket filled with ice. He closed the door and locked it, turning on the light switch that seemed to do nothing. I heard him mumble something as he made his way to the side of the bed, setting the bucket and cans on the cheap bedside table. I glanced up at him as he turned on the light, revealing a sly and mischievous smile as he returned my glance. Paul scanned me over and gazed at my exposure of skin. It was delightful how the musty smell of the room seemed to evaporate in the seductive presence of Paul's cologne and fabric softener. He casually crossed his arms, grabbing the bottom of his t-shirt and pulling it off over his head to expose his smooth, bare chest. He picked up a can of soda and twirled it around in an imaginary circle as he spoke,

"Are you thirsty? The vending machine put up a good fight, but I won in the end." I laughed under my breath as I pictured Paul yelling in his British accent, 'Bloody Hell' at the vending machine.

"Not now, but maybe later," I lied. I was feeling a little thirsty but I was afraid to drink anything from this motel, even if it came out of a can.

Paul sat down on the edge of the bed with his back to me and I reached out and gracefully dragged my finger straight down his spine. My mouth became instantly dry as a memory of Kyle rushed to my mind of me doing the same exact thing when we were both in college. A strange depressing sadness sat on me, dwelling in the knowledge of my betrayal. I snatched my finger back and while clenching my hand in a fist, I rolled over on my back again.

I stared up at the ceiling as I heard Paul take long drinks from the can. With my fingertips, I pressed them into my breast to locate my small lump, which was less than the size of a pea. Every time I touched the lump, all I could think about at that moment was karma. The two were always inseparable in my mind. Was it even possible that my immoral pleasure could cause such a toxic situation? I knew scientifically and anatomically this was not possible, but I was still unable to shake the looming thought of the 'what ifs' from my questions, but yet, I still couldn't stop myself with Paul. My thoughts were interrupted by Paul's voice.

"You look so lovely when you lie on your back. What are you doing with your fingers?" I glanced over to see his face expression change from flirtatious to baffled in one instantaneous second. I paused to think whether I should tell Paul about my diagnosis, especially considering I had not yet told Kyle. There was the strong desire to tell Paul, since all of my experience with him up to this point let me know that if one person would see me and listen to me, it would be him. So considering at that moment I desperately wanted to be heard, I said,

"Well, I have a lump in my breast. I went to the doctor and he said it was cancer. But it's very early and I shouldn't be too scared about it." The words just flew out of my mouth with such emotionless speed. I watched him as confusion stretched across his face. He looked down at the bed for a moment and scratched his head, obviously in deep contemplation. He looked back up at me with an inquisitive expression, almost void of any type of true emotion.

"When did you find this out?" I assumed I had misjudged his expression and he was upset that I had not come to him for comfort and support. Turning back to my side, I answered him.

"Earlier this week. I haven't really told anyone, not even Kyle knows yet. Only my best friend Abby knows." He shook his head and appeared satisfied by my answer. He stood and took a few steps to the small plastic trashcan as he tossed his can inside. He turned, and in a gentle voice, he asked me a few more questions.

"So they caught it early? The doctor said that it is treatable, correct?" Paul spoke in a tone that bordered on professional rather than personal or sympathetic. I was slightly taken aback by his whole tone and mood. I was not entirely sure what I had expected by telling him, I just knew I had not expected what I got. I didn't linger on my thoughts too long. I told myself perhaps this was his personal way of dealing with uncomfortable news.

"Yes, the final outcome looks very promising." Even with all the positive information and favorable outcomes, the fear did not completely leave me. The tone of my voice did not hide my fear and concern, as I knew I came across scared. Paul reached out and put his hand on top of mine while he spoke, this time slightly more sympathetic.

"Don't worry, love, everything will be just fine. You'll look back on this and it'll be like nothing." He patted my hand a couple times and then leaned in and kissed me on my cheek. Could that be true? Could having cancer, even in the early stage be like nothing a few months or years from now? Would I run into a long lost friend and say,

'Yeah, I had cancer, but it was nothing.'

Paul reached over and picked up the other can as he asked me again,

"Sure you don't want it?" I shook my head, and without purposely intending to, I crinkled my nose at the can that looked just as dirty as the room. Paul said apologetically,

"I'm really sorry about the room. I wish the apartment complex had cleaned my carpets early in the morning so the floor could be dry by now, but we won't have to come here again. This is just a one-time thing." I sarcastically let out a huge sigh of relief and wiped my hand across my forehead, like a criminal who's no longer going to be executed. Paul laughed a little and then threw back his head as he drank from the can vigorously. He set down the can and tried to catch his breath as he panted from drinking so fast.

"Wow, you're really thirsty."

"Yeah, it seems really hot in here. I had no idea this hotel was going to be like this when I picked it. I only suggested this one because I drove past it one time and thought the location looked good. I'm sorry and I hope you will forgive me." He looked deep into my eyes as he climbed in next to me with his nose was only inches from mine. I smiled as my heart started to race. I was still intoxicated by his presence and alluring nature. I answered,

"You know I will, as long as we never have to come here again." Humorously, I glared at him without blinking like a mother scolding a child.

"Deal."

Paul leaned in and kissed me on the cheek. I closed my eyes and without warning, I envisioned the bracelet that Kyle had gotten for me, which I couldn't bear to wear when I was with Paul. I could feel the warm touch of Paul's lips on my neck but my mind couldn't erase the picture of Kyle's face when I opened the gift that I didn't deserve.

It even haunted me that after dinner, Kyle and I had made love. Deep, passionate, soul connecting love. I had feared he would know I had been with another man, but in truth, it had been so long that even Kyle seemed like another man. Even so, what was I doing? Why was I here in this musty smelly motel with Paul? Why was I so drawn to Paul and was unable to control myself with him, being easily seduced.

My eyes started to swell with tears that burned as they fell from my eyes. Paul looked up and saw my tears. His face saddened as he quickly kissed me from cheek to cheek and the corners of my mouth, speaking softly in between kisses.

"Don't cry, Love. Please don't cry. Everything will be fine." I calmed myself down and said nothing, misleading him to think my crying was a result of the cancer. I rubbed underneath my eyes with my fingers as I spoke calmly.

"I'm okay now. I don't want to ruin this time we have together." My statement was a half lie. I did hope this time we had would be ruined, because I lacked the willpower to do so myself.

"I think I need to get going. I actually have a teacher review with the school board in a couple of hours and I should get moving along." I sat up so quickly that I became dizzy from the blood rushing to my head. Did my crying scare him off? I said timidly,

"Are you leaving because of me?" He sat up as well, slid closer to me, and wrapped his arms around me, pulling me into him. I could feel the heat of his skin against mine and the side of his cheek pressed against mine as he spoke softly in my ear.

"Love, you could never do or say anything to make me leave. I really need to go get ready for this review I have." As he finished his sentence, he wrapped his arms tighter around me, placing his exceedingly warm hands against the spine of my back. His embrace mixed with his words of tender affirmations made my blood rush and my skin tingle with excitement. Now I was clear why I was so addicted. It was not necessarily him, but the feeling of being loved and existing again that I so treasured.

Paul gradually released me from his firm embrace and warm hands as he slid off the bed. Standing, he put the t-shirt back on that he had just taken off minutes earlier. He glanced down at his watch and then with increased speed, finished dressing as I sat on the bed watching him.

I got out of bed and started to dress as well, not desiring to stay any longer in this musty motel. As I finished dressing, I turned to see Paul standing near the door. I was stunned that he would try to leave so quickly, considering the plan to get together today had been in the works for a week. He looked over at me and then with great speed and purpose, walked straight to me. Throwing his coat on the bed, he grabbed me and kissed me so intently and passionately that my legs wobbled. Paul released me with the same haste that he had used to kiss me, causing me to lose balance momentarily, almost falling. Paul smiled and picked up his coat as he said,

"I love you." He then walked to the door and as it was closing behind him, all I could mumble was,

"Bye."

The crisp air hit me with such delight. I took in a long deep breath of the clean air, delighted to be free of that musty smelling rat hole. The hustle of the cars and trucks on the freeway overpass was incredibly louder in the parking lot than in our room, which I guess was one small thing to have been thankful for. I didn't waste any time jumping in my SUV and pulled out of the half broken cement and gravel parking lot.

I reached down to turn on my radio as I heard the car behind me honking. Startled, I glanced up into my review mirror, and was surprised to see Abby directly behind me. Abby then put on her right signal, obviously implying she wanted me to pull over. Times like this made me wish I were not in the habit of turning off my cell phone.

My heart raced as I wondered if Abby had seen me pull out of the motel. I knew her better than I knew anyone else and I was terrified knowing the level of disappointment she would have if she found out my secret. She always watched my back and wanted the best for my life and me, and it was too much to think that I had let her down.

I drove a few more blocks before I found a spot to pull over. I took a deep breath. Rolling down the windows on the passenger side, I said a quick prayer that she hadn't seen me at the motel as I heard her approaching footsteps on the gravel.

"Goodness, Vi, don't you ever turn on your cell phone? Or did you lose it again?" Abby was dressed beautifully and she looked like she just had her hair professionally styled as well. I could tell that her question was a rhetorical one, as she didn't wait for an answer before opening the door and sliding in the passenger side of my SUV.

"I didn't lose it. My cell is just turned on silent." Appearing not to hear me, Abby rubbed her hands together frantically trying to warm them. She turned toward me with a serious stare as if I was sitting in an interrogation room.

"What were you doing at that piece of crap motel?" Her glare into my eyes was so intense that I could no longer make eye contact with her. I tried to buy a little time by messing with buttons on the door, rolling her window back up. I looked down at the floor. Noticing her new shoes, I decided to use them as a diversion, hoping she would not notice my forced attempt.

"Wow. Great shoes. You look really nice today. Did you have a meeting of some kind?" I strained to remove the guilt out of my voice as I forced a tone of cheerfulness. Abby glanced down and twisted her ankle as she spoke factually.

"Yeah, everything I'm wearing is new. I had a lunch date. I mean a date, at lunch time." She looked back over at me and I could sense that she was not going to forget so easily, so I continued in a positive voice.

"A date? With who?" She raised her shoulders up and down as she let out a sigh, as if she had a lottery ticket in her hand that was not a winner.

"This guy that I met through my finance guy. He was supposed to be a really nice guy. But it's the same old story." I looked at her, egging the conversation on.

"What story is that?"

"You know. The rich guys are jerks who only want super models with huge breasts. And the average guys want to make you their sugar mama as soon as they find out you have money." She rolled her eyes, sighing once more, she crossed her arms displaying that she had for all intense purpose given up on true love. I felt bad for her and was no longer thinking of my situation as I kept the conversation going.

"Maybe you should enter a dating service and lie about the money. So after a guy falls completely in love with you, bam! You pull out the fact you got money and everyone's happy." I clapped my hands together making a loud pop. A faint smile curled up on Abby's face. I heard her laugh a little under her breath. I smiled too, as I looked down at her shoes once again, getting ready to ask if I could borrow them when she spoke abruptly.

"Okay, don't change the subject this time. What was going on in that motel?" Still unable to look her directly in the face I glanced past her and out the passenger window behind her. I did notice that her arms were crossed and I could hear the tapping of her shoe on the floor. I hesitated and then said in a low breathy voice that was just above a whisper, unable to carry the burden of this secret from Abby on my shoulders any longer.

"I met Paul there." I didn't have to indulge her in any more information at the moment for her to understand what had just taken place. Abby's mouth fell open in surprise right before it curled down into a frown. Abby then spoke, her voice carrying so much scrutiny, but I could tell she was trying not to judge me.

"Oh, Vi, what are you doing? Who is this Paul anyway? And please tell me this was a mistake and one-time thing?" She studied my face for emotion to help her understand any answers I was about to give.

"Paul is Julia's teacher, also known as Mr. Conway. Remember, I talked about him once or twice? And no, this isn't the first time." My head dropped down and I stared at my hands before I said the words out loud with hesitation.

"I've been having an affair with Paul." I couldn't hardly believe the enormous amount of shame and humiliation I felt at that moment. Perhaps it was saying the words out loud, or maybe it was telling my dirty secret to my closest and dearest friend, whom I respected. A look of disappointment mixed with slight anger washed over her face as she crossed her arms and spoke through a frown,

"I can't believe you didn't tell me? When did we stop telling each other everything? I'm shocked. I'm your best friend." With her arms still crossed, she softened her voice slightly as she continued.

"Vi, I'm not judging you. Everything I say is because I love you more than a sister. But you know me, I don't sugarcoat a lot of things." I shook my head knowing that she was preparing me for the hard truth. My eyes swelled with tears as I began slowly to feel weight and pressure being lifted off my shoulders. It was release from a secret that had been eating me inside, but the weight lifted from telling the truth was quickly replaced with the unbearable reality of tremendous guilt.

Seconds passed before I glanced up, realizing that the air was too quiet for comfort. Silently, Abby sat looking at me with a sad disapproving look on her face. In a kind inquiring tone, she asked,

"What are you doing, Vi?" I knew she was hurt that I had not told her about the affair earlier. More importantly, she was upset because she was the kind of woman who only wanted the best things for the important people in her life. I took a deep breath and reminded myself I was in the company of a long time trusted friend, not a judge who would hang me. I spoke with slightly more ease as I started to confess.

"I don't really know what I'm doing, Abby. I guess I was just tired of being lonely all the time. Then this charming, attractive man practically falls in my lap and I felt something I hadn't felt in a long time. Loved. I know, I honestly know what I'm doing is not right, it's wrong, but I can't stop. I just can't. I don't know how to end it. I don't even know if I *want* to end it. I just don't know, Abby. I just don't know."

Abby's head slowly bobbed up and down with every word I said, intently listening.

"What about Kyle? Are you going to leave Kyle for this guy?" She was trying to figure out exactly my level of feelings for Paul.

"No, I love Kyle. I've always loved Kyle. I can't say I love Paul, but I love how he makes me feel. I love how he treats me. I love being around him. I don't know, maybe that's what real love is." Abby looked at me and then rolled her eyes letting out a short hiss from her lips.

"Real love? Oh, Vi, I know that I have never been married, but I have been in plenty of relationships with different types of men to know that just because a man tells you what you want to hear, and is really nice to you, doesn't mean that's real love." Abby's voice was filled with wisdom. I felt like I was sitting next to an old soul with much to share. In a factual tone, Abby continued.

"Real love is when you want good things for the other person, even when you're angry at them. It's when you are at your worst, but don't have to pretend to be something you're not, because you know that he'll love you even at that worst. Love is not perfect, it's far from it."

Abby paused and I noticed for the first time her foot had finally stopped tapping. The cars on the busy street seemed far off and the whole inside of the SUV was still. The warm air blew through the vents like a million tiny whispers. I had to get more off my chest.

"Sometimes, everything with Paul seems like an illusion. Everything with Kyle is the opposite. It's reality. But I'm so tired of *my* reality. My life is dull, boring, all the time. Kyle's never home. I just felt like I needed to escape, even if it was escaping to an illusion. Now that I'm here, I can't imagine going back to that. I don't want to leave or lose Kyle because I still love him, but I can't be so miserable again. I just can't!" With that, I threw up my hands to my face and let out a low agonizing groan, and then while my hands were still on my face, I cried out loud in my defense saying,

"I didn't look to have an affair! It just happened." I heard Abby let out a small sigh of frustration. Abby always believed everyone should step up and take responsibility for their own actions. I picked my head up from my hands and looked over as she started in on me.

"Love isn't the illusion of perfection. It is the reality of forgiveness, compromise, and having the comfort to know that no matter what, no matter how hard, it will endure because it has in the past." She looked me dead in the eye and with forceful, yet compassionate words, tried to push some sense into my head.

"So what do you think is going to happen, Vi? Are you going to keep seeing Paul on the side for years and just cross your fingers that Kyle never finds out? And what happens if you start to fall in love with Paul? Do you really think the longer you keep this up, the easier it's going to end? The longer this goes on, the greater chance everyone is going to be hurt. As of now, if Kyle found out about this he would be devastated, absolutely devastated." I wasn't sure why, but I started to get angry. Probably because I didn't want to hear about my mistakes anymore and who I was hurting. What about me? Didn't I deserve to be happy? Besides, weren't affairs and infidelity expected and tolerated in other cultures around the world. Many people cheated all the time and that didn't make them bad.

"Don't I deserve happiness? Paul makes me feel happy, and it's exciting. So what's wrong with that?" I glared at her almost challenging her to question my firm statement. Abby glared back at me and then squinted her eyes together ready for confrontation. I should have known Abby would not have backed down. She never has before in her life.

"Oh, no you didn't! Listen Vi, you are my best friend, you are more than a sister, so I say this with all the love in my heart. You have to get yourself together and knock this off! I'll always have your back, but if you want me to say what you want to hear and tell you that it's okay for someone to get something on the side, I'm not going to say it. I won't agree with something that I don't think is right. Kyle loves you. He is crazy in love with you." I was still angry with her because I wanted to be right, and I wanted to be told that it was okay to have Paul since Kyle had been so neglectful. But there was a tiny feeling of appreciation towards Abby for being the one and only person who would set things straight for me. So with sincere humility I asked,

"What if I can't let go of Paul?"

"The word can't shouldn't exist in that sentence. You can't have your cake and eat it too, now that's something you just *can't* have. Listen Vi, I love you. You're my best friend in this whole world, I'm not trying to be hard on you. This is gonna end badly and I'm sure you know that you know what you got to do."

"I know, I know, I know." Even as I spoke the words, I was terrified that I was past the point of doing what I knew I had to do, and stuck in the world of doing what I knew I shouldn't do.

TWENTY-FOUR

"I really wish I had my own indoor pool right about now." Abby was once again referring to the temperature outside. After our long heart to heart about my affair, I had managed to talk her into swimming with me a few days later at the gym. I had been on such an emotional roller coaster since the start of the affair and my diagnosis that, I felt like I was going stark raving mad. I could also tell even though Abby was trying to show a positive attitude about the whole cancer situation, it was in reality scaring her inside. She didn't hesitate to come to the gym with me and I knew what I really needed was a good swim to help clear my head. Something about water always seemed to do the trick for me. Besides, I knew if I gave Abby a few days to let the information sink in, I might be able to open up a little more about the affair and finally have someone to give details to. I figured it would be nice for a change to let things out verbally instead of having everything tossing around in my mind.

The air had become more frigid over the last few days, showing signs that winter was much closer than I was prepared for. I could still hear Abby mumbling as she walked toward me from her car, carrying a small gym bag in her hand. Without looking back, Abby clenched her key remote tightly as she pointed it behind her, pressing the lock button. A shiny new black Mercedes lit up and beeped letting us know it was locked.

"Is that a new car?" I asked, glancing at the prestigious looking Mercedes.

"Yep, that's what you do when you have money but can't find a good man. You buy a great car." She was beaming from cheek to cheek, letting me know she was in love with her new purchase. I looked at the car with a ping of jealousy as I thought to myself, maybe I'll trade two men for a really nice car? My mouth curled up and I giggled just a little.

"Are you laughing at me because I'm cold?" Abby looked down right mad. The seriousness in her voice almost made me want to start laughing at her.

"No, I was laughing because I was thinking about trading two guys for a car." She looked at me puzzled for a moment, clearly not understanding either what the joke was, or how it was humorous.

"Never mind. Just forget it."

The constant echoing shower room was just off the indoor pool, and was hot and humid as we attempted to rinse off our feet before we went into the pool, a habit we picked up in college, as it was a requirement of us.

Abby had on a lovely sapphire blue one piece suit that looked like it cost a fortune, and it probably did. I concentrated on rinsing off my feet as well, while Abby strolled over to a full length mirror that was facing away from the showers.

“Does this suit look bad on me?” She poked the side of her belly and whispered. The echo was loud enough to carry her voice over to me. I rolled my eyes and ignored her question. Abby had been an extremely chubby child and teenager so she always carried a fear deep down that the weight would slowly creep back up on her, especially considering how much she loved to eat. She tried again, this time a fraction louder.

“Vi, does this suit make me look pudgy?” I didn't even try to lower my voice.

“Nooooo, Abby! For Pete's sake, you’re not even close to fat. Your body is practically perfect, so stop asking me.” Abby turned back to look in the mirror, then turned again and squinted her eyes as she examined her rear end. I stood outside the shower and just waited as she finally shrugged her shoulders and grabbed her towel off the hook.

“So do you want to talk about anything in particular?” Abby asked me. My heart dropped a few feet as I became terrified that someone would overhear even the slightest mention of my affair.

“Maybe after we get in the pool and swim a little, and there's not such an echo,” I whispered. She nodded her head in agreement, since she had not considered the noise level. Abby stopped as we went over to one of the many wooden benches along the long wall and curiously asked as she set her towel down,

“Where is Julia today? I know there's no school on Saturday.” I did a quick survey of the pool and was glad there were fewer than four people in it.

"Oh, she's spending the day with Kyle. I think he is taking her to a movie and then out for lunch and ice cream, or something like that." Abby was impressed as she raised one eyebrow and crossed her arms.

"Oh really? That is a really great dad right there. Those types of men are hard to find." She gave me a little look with her eyebrow still raised. I should have known since she didn't have the opportunity to talk about Paul being evil. She would instead talk about how great Kyle was looking these days.

"Yeah, it is great that he's doing that, but before you give him the father of the year award, let me ask, how many dinners has he missed? How many hours has he spent at the office and not with Julia? How many bedtime stories has he read her? Don't get me wrong, I'm happy that he is spending time with her today, but one day doesn't make up for the last couple of years." Abby looked like she was taking it all in with great consideration. Then she said,

"That's true, but you have to give him some credit that he's working on changing, Vi. He really seems like he is trying now. Don't hold the past too tight against him, okay?" I knew she was right. At the same time, my relationship with Kyle had turned into such an emotional roller coaster that it would take a great deal more to convince me that this would be permanent. Especially now considering that I felt there might even be the slightest possibility that I could have permanent happiness with someone else.

"I know, Abby, but I'm totally afraid to accept the change as real, because what if next month everything goes back to the way it was and he is hardly ever home again? I don't think I could take another round of that." We stepped down into the water and were both pleasantly surprised that it was more lukewarm than cold.

"I'm not saying just to jump in and pretend he has been the perfect husband and father all along. All I'm saying is give him a fair chance." I could agree with that. I felt guilty because I knew part of the reason I was being harder on him than I should probably be was because of Paul. If Paul hadn't entered the picture at all, Abby and I would be having a completely different conversation at this moment. I'd be talking about how happy I am that Kyle is trying and how with some work and compromise, things would be better. The truth is that the feeling is there. I love Kyle, but I love the thought of lasting happiness and being brought alive even more, however selfish that might sound.

We waded a little deeper in the pool as an elderly couple got out. The elderly woman had her thin gray hair stuffed inside a flowered swimming cap. The man had a grumpy look on his face as he followed behind her. She was round in the waist and had a chipper smile on her face as I heard her speak in a loud but shaky old voice.

"Come on, Lewis, the doctor said you have to do it. And no salt today either." She seemed not to miss a step as she spoke, her husband right on her heels.

"Blast it! I can't eat without salt. He doesn't know what he's talking about anyway! He probably was getting drunk like all those kids do in college! Maybe he missed the class on salt!" His voice was deep and gruff. He had a small protruding belly under his swimming trunks that were pulled up high past his bellybutton. His legs were long, thin and ghostly white and dark brown hair slid down his chest. They both picked up their expensive towels as she continued walking. Not looking back, I heard her say just as she walked off to the women's locker room.

"Maybe, but he is our son, Lewis. We didn't put him through medical school for nothing."

Abby and I turned and looked at each other and waited until the older man vanished around the opposite corner before we burst out in laughter.

"That could be you and Kyle someday." Abby said with a humorous grin on her face.

"I don't think so. If that were Kyle and me, then we probably wouldn't say two words to each other and I would just remove all the salt from his diet, which he wouldn't even notice." We laughed a little more and I started to imagine what it would be like if it was Paul in the future instead of Kyle. How different would it be? Would I be happier with him than with Kyle? Would I be old and wrinkly in the pool as Paul looked me in the eyes and told me how beautiful I still was to him? Would he say how happy he had been the last forty years since we had been together?

A little smirk of a smile crept on the corners of my mouth as I envisioned all the futuristic ideas in my mind. Abby noticed my little smirk and she started to smile as well.

"What are you thinking about, Vi?" The response flooded to me so quickly that for the first time, I didn't have a chance to think anything, as I opened my mouth and let the words out before I could stop them.

"I think I'm falling in love with Paul." Abby's little smile faded and sadness crept over her expression. For an instant, I was filled with regret for letting this information out, even though I had not planned it. Abby looked down at the water and focused her gaze at her hands as she moved them back and forth under the water. Then she spoke in a soft, but sad tone.

"Well, what are you going to do?" I had no immediate answer for this question. I honestly wasn't sure what I was going to do, but the thought of leaving Kyle was very slowly starting to creep into my mind. All these thoughts bounced around in my head as Abby asked another question.

"Do you still love Kyle?"

"Yes." My response was so immediate that she looked as if she was caught off guard with my reply. Abby was loyal in everything she did. She was a loyal best friend. When she was engaged, she was a loyal fiancée. She was so loyal to people and businesses she truly loved, it didn't matter if something newer came along. I knew having feelings for two men was a foreign concept to her. In truth, I've always had great admiration for this quality in her. Abby asked me another question and sounded curious, almost intrigued.

"Do you love them…equally?"

"Umm, no, I don't know how to explain it. I've always loved Kyle and we have a history. I fell in love with Kyle the minute I saw him. But it's different with Paul." I took a long pause for a moment, thinking about how to let it all out. Considering I just had the realization moments earlier about my feelings for Paul and where they were headed, I wasn't sure how to translate it.

"I think I'm falling in love with Paul because of how he makes me feel, and for the fact that he brought me back to life. Truthfully, it hasn't helped Kyle that I have resentment toward him for not stepping up and being the one to see me and bring me to life. He should have done that a long time ago." Abby looked at me and nodded her head. Then she looked down at the water again as she tilted her head, thinking.

"Did *you* ever tell Kyle how you felt? Did *you* ever tell Kyle that he needed to step up and what he could have done to make the marriage better?" I was not entirely sure why, but I felt a little resentful toward her question.

"Well, no, but why should I have to? I gave and gave and never asked him for anything, and all I got in return was a career obsessed husband and night after night of loneliness." To my surprise, I couldn't fight back tears as they rushed to my eyes. I tried my best to choke a few back as I grabbed a handful of water and splashed my face to wash them away. Abby moved herself closer to me, putting her with in a half a foot to my face as she spoke sympathetically.

"I know, Vi. Did you ever think that maybe that was a part of the problem? You didn't ask. You didn't tell him anything. He's practically been set up to fail from the beginning."

I didn't want to talk about this anymore. I wanted to be in a relaxing quiet place. I glanced around and was relieved to see a large group of young college students come in to get in some laps. I looked at Abby and signaled with my eyes toward the group before I spoke.

"I feel like getting out. Let's just call it a day." Abby looked genuinely relieved as well, since she didn't really want to be in the pool in the first place.

Abby and I stood in the main lobby and I was amazed we managed to change out of our wet suits faster than it took us to put them on. Our whole conversation in the locker room had revolved around cancer, but no matter how hard I tried to focus, I didn't hear any of the words of encouragement Abby had given me. My mind was consumed with Paul the entire time. It was if I had been given a revelation. I was falling in love with Paul. Every time I said that to myself my heart skipped a beat and I felt giddy and happy like a little school girl with her first crush. I was almost overcome with excitement and couldn't wait to tell him. I knew for a fact that I wouldn't be able to wait for the next couple of days until we got a chance to meet again. I would have no other choice but to get out my cell phone and just call him. I had to be one of the very few that didn't live or die by the power of the cell phone. I truly could care less, but in this case, I would make the exception. I had to tell him what was on my heart and how I felt.

"Do you want to come over for a glass of wine this evening?" Abby's voice snapped me out of my thoughts of love and excitement. I looked over as she zipped up her black leather jacket. She took out a pair of sleek black leather gloves and promptly put them on.

"If Kyle isn't too exhausted and is willing to watch Julia tonight,

I'd love to come over for an hour or so." I immediately started to work out the opportunity to arrange a quick rendezvous with Paul. My mind was so in depth with the thought of holding and kissing Paul that I nearly missed Abby's intense gaze as her mouth fell open. She spoke slowly as she raised an eyebrow and unzipped her jacket, taking off her gloves and stuffing them in her pocket.

"Well. Hello." She licked her lips like a starving cat that had just scooped up a small tasty canary to her face. I turned to see what her big fuss was about. My mouth dropped open as well.

Through one of the large, glass, doors to a private class stood the most stunningly attractive man I had ever seen. He was tall and had a near perfect manly physique. He was neither too bulky nor too lean for that matter. He had a thin goatee and dark thick wavy hair that was pulled back into a ponytail. His skin was almost a golden olive color and the light cast shadows on his muscle tone making him look even sexier. He looked like an exotic model. I could easily picture him in a cologne add, riding a horse along the beach.

His stance was powerful and he moved around the class like a strong lion watching his pride. There were only about five women in the class and my gaze was taken off the instructor for a second as I glanced through the glass doors at the women in the room. One in particular caught my eye. It was Beth. All five women were now in the downward dog pose as he moved around the room talking and placing his hands on the spine of a few of the girls. The only reason I knew the name of the pose was thanks to a very brief moment where I had tried to take up yoga. Unfortunately, it didn't work out for me. My huge effort to hide my lack of grace and poise was useless in yoga. So after a week of looking like an utter fool, I quit, but not before learning some of the names to the poses. Besides, how can you forget a name like downward dog?

"With him, I'd do that pose *any* day." Abby was still transfixed on the instructor, as the corners of her mouth appeared to be salivating. She was talking to no one in particular as she concentrated on his every move. Abby continued to mumble some more into thin air.

"I really need to get me one of those." I could barely hear what she was saying since my mind was now filled with questions about Beth. *Was this the guy Beth has been seeing*? *Maybe this is the guy that has turned on a light inside Beth and made her extremely happy*?

I watched while the instructor walked over to Beth and gently, but professionally, placed the palm of his hand between her shoulder blades. I was taken out of my trance by Abby's voice.

"What is this class? How do I get in? How many days a week is it?" I wanted to laugh as she had not only taken off her gloves and coat, but also now packed them in her bag, looking as if she was ready to start the class at that moment.

"I'm not sure, but I think I saw the pamphlet for this class about two months ago. If it is the same class, I guess this guy is supposed to be the best of the best. And it's kinda expensive." Abby glanced over at me with a sly smile on her face. I threw the expensive comment in there just for my own amusement.

"Isn't he gorgeous, Vi?" I shrugged my shoulders as if I hadn't even noticed. I looked back toward the class as they finished. The four women were talking to one another and Beth was talking with the instructor with a bright smile on her face. *This has to be the man she is seeing.* Slowly, one by one, the women trickled out of the room.

"I think I'm going to go talk…" I turned to look at Abby and noticed she had vanished. I spotted her at the main information desk. She was busy chatting up the receptionist, asking questions about the pamphlet she held in her hand.

"Hi Beth." I had made my way over to the door at the same time Beth reached the doorframe. Her face lit up and she stopped directly in front of the instructor making it impossible for him to step around her.

"Hi Vi! Did you just have a swim?"

"Yes we did." Before I could answer, I heard Abby's voice chime in. She must have run from the information desk when she saw me at the door. I looked over as Abby softly ran her fingers through her hair, smiling and batting her eyelashes. I was almost awestruck by her behavior considering the entire length of our friendship I couldn't remember a time she acted so infatuated. Being infatuated was so contrary to Abby's personality. Abby was more of the love em and leave em kind of girl. Always protecting her heart and too intelligent to play all the foolish games that came along with first dates and new relationships. One look at this man had morphed her into a new creature. I could feel everyone waiting on me to bring the conversation together since I was the one common denominator between everyone.

"Do you remember my friend, Abby?" I looked up at Beth as the instructor stood just behind her, patiently waiting and not the least bit in a hurry. This made me believe he had to be foreign. And he must not have been here in America long if he could stand behind someone and not look at his watch at least three times.

"Oh, yes, I believe I've seen you at a couple different activities of Julia's. Is that right?" Abby glanced away from the instructor for a moment and gave Beth a warm smile as she spoke, not wasting anytime.

"That's right. So, I've been looking for a really good yoga class. Is this one any good? How's the instructor?" Abby tried hard to put on her best puzzled performance, as she pretended not to know that the man standing behind Beth was the instructor.

"Yes! I love this class. Actually, this is the instructor." Beth took a step to the side and twisted her body as she pointed to the tall olive skinned man. He took a step forward and a hint of citrus fruit seemed to follow him. He reached out and respectfully shook our hands one at a time. The minute he took Abby's hand, I could hear her breathing increase through her nose as if she was about to have an asthma attack. I had to stick my hand in my pocket and poke myself so I wouldn't laugh. When he spoke, his accent was very thick and sultry. It almost blew Paul's run of the mill British accent out of the water.

"If you are interested in the class, I could go over with you the basics of the course if you would like?" I couldn't believe how much power one man could draw from all the females around him. I could even feel the eyes of other women around the gym as they passed by the door. I had wondered in the past if there was a type of man that could seduce and hold power over large numbers of women. Now I knew that answer was yes, and I was looking at him.

"Actually, my friend isn't really into yoga, but I have been *dying* to find a really good class, and I would love to join. I'm sorry, I didn't catch your name?" I was relieved that Abby remembered my humiliating encounter with yoga and didn't try to drag me into the class with her. The instructor gently placed his hand against his chest as he graciously replied to Abby's question.

"My apologies, ladies. I am Marcelo Fernando Santos, but most people call me Marc." Every word that came out of his mouth sounded even sexier than the last one. If he decided to have a conversation about garbage and maggots, it would probably be the sexiest sounding garbage I had ever heard about. It was also nice that he didn't have that womanizing aspect that Hollywood portrays foreign men with thick accents to have. Maybe that was a huge part of his appeal to every female in the gym. Even though he was strong, he had that, I'm not about to chase after a hundred women all day, attitude about him. Whatever his real thoughts were on women, it was definitely working a number on Abby. That's probably what she really needed was to feel like she had to chase after a man instead of men chasing after her and her money.

"It is so nice to meet you, Marc. I'd love to stay and chat, but I really need to go. I'll call you later about tonight, Abby." I turned and tried to catch Abby's eyes, but she refused to break her gaze with Marcelo, and just gave me a little nod to acknowledge my statement.

"I'll walk with you to the door so Abby can ask more questions about the class." Beth stepped out and reached for my arm and I felt really sorry for Abby at that moment. She was going to be crushed when she found out Beth and Marcelo were an item, which I was becoming more certain of as the minutes went by.

"That seems like a really good class?" We were walking to the front and I was using this as an opportunity to get the information out of Beth about her relationship with Marcelo.

"Oh, yes it is. He is a really good instructor and I am way more flexible than I was a month ago." She spoke factually. *I bet he has made her more flexible.*

"He is very, umm...attractive." I wanted just to come right out and ask her if Marcelo was her secret lover, but I didn't think this was really the place to do that. So I kept at my other approach to get something more readable out of her.

"Yeah, he is. Last week, I even saw a lesbian ogling at him." She did a half eye roll and a little chuckle. Like one might expect if I had asked if women found Brad Pitt attractive. She turned to me as we reached the front door. Her eyes were bright and excited with happiness. She did a quick glance around us and then lowered her voice so quietly I just barely caught her words.

"I probably shouldn't say this right here, but you are the only one that knows about my...lover. I'm going to go out to lunch with him in a few minutes, and I'm thinking I really am going to leave my husband for him. Just him, me, and Ginger." Beth clasped her hands together and smiled wide and lovingly. I tried to picture what Marcelo would be like as a stepfather. I knew for certain by the time Ginger got to Middle School, all the other pre-teens would be clawing each other to be her friend so they could come over and stare at her handsome stepfather.

I felt awkward with this situation. I wasn't really sure how to act or what to say. Do I congratulate her? Do I hug her? Do I try to talk her out of it on a moral ground, even though I know I have no personal right to do that? I stood there for a few more moments and then finally came up with something, but really nothing.

"Oh, you seem really in love." It was neither an approval nor disapproval, more of a statement. I figured I would be safer with a statement than an opinion.

"Yes, I am. Well, I'm so glad I saw you. I better run to the locker room to change really quickly." She glanced down at her tiny watch and then gave me a smile and wave before she rushed off toward the locker rooms.

There is nothing that makes you feel more sure of a newfound love than seeing someone else in love. Now I could hardly wait to tell Paul how I felt about him. I had already decided I was going to call him now and if he couldn't meet with me, I was going to tell him my feelings over the phone.

As I sat in my SUV and having taken a virtual decade to fish through my bag, I finally grasped my cell phone and pulled it out. And for the millionth time, I told myself I really needed to start making it easier to get too. I opened it and started going through my contacts. I only had about thirty or so contacts on my phone, most of which were businesses and a few parents from the school, whom I had never called but took their numbers out of courtesy. I scrolled down 'til I got to the 'P' section. And right before pizza – Justino's, was Pam-school mom. I had put Paul under the name Pam just in case Kyle randomly decided to go through my phone, not that he ever had before, or was prone to such behavior, but it was better to be safe.

I had my finger on the button and paused. I stared down at the phone in my hand while it sparkled as the sun reflected light around the metal edges. Even though I had already been having an affair, and the betrayal already happened, this was something new. Telling Paul that I was *in* love with him might start a snowball effect that I couldn't control. An image of Kyle's face was right there in my mind, crystal clear with every detail. I thought about what his face would look like if he found out about Paul and how it would rip him apart. That image was haunting, stifling my physical ability to dial the number.

Staring at the phone, I contemplated using the delete button and erasing Paul from my phone. I wanted to do the right thing, but I was so torn that I felt physically ill. Paul might be a new love, but I still loved Kyle. Most importantly, Kyle was my husband. I pushed Kyle out of my mind. I didn't want to think about him at that moment. I didn't want to feel stifled either.

I paused with my finger on the button and a warm smile on my face while my heart fluttered. I felt like a teenager once again, getting ready to ask a boy to come over for my birthday party.

I let out a sigh and glanced up for a moment as Beth walked out of the front gym doors. Her feet seemed light as air as she practically bounced with each step. Her skin was glowing as she illuminated with pure joy and happiness. I watched as her beautiful blonde hair bounced up and down with each step and her ultra-white teeth sparkled. Beth looked happy, really, really happy. I was extremely envious and had to capture some of that happiness Beth had for myself too. That feeling I saw in Beth was in my grasp, and I could not let it go!

I mustered up the courage to stop feeling so girlish, just call Paul, and tell him. Beth threw all caution to the wind and now she is higher than ever on life. Watching Beth in the height of her enthusiastic state and my finger still resting on the button, I took my final breath before I prepared to confess my heart to Paul.

I can't breathe... I can't breathe! The sharp pain in my stomach was so intense I could almost see a tiny man with a tiny knife stabbing me in the stomach. My heart stopped. The amount of pressure on my chest was enormous. *I can't breathe*. I tried to take a deep breath. I felt like I might be having a panic attack, but I knew I wasn't. I caught my breath and my skin began to boil. My skin became hotter and hotter with every beat of my heart. I could feel the heat from my face as it steamed off my cheeks.

Sitting in my SUV and watching, I saw Beth as she had her arms wrapped tightly around him. He leaned down and gave her a long, passionate kiss while letting his hand drift down her back, resting it on the curve of her rear. The air was cold and crisp and I could see a faint cloud of moisture as he grabbed her and motioned for her to come with him to his car.

My stomach heaved and I coughed, keeping back vomit. When Beth had told me months ago that she loved a man with an accent, I never suspected she was referring to Paul's accent. Unaware of my presence, Beth and Paul were just yards in front of my SUV and looking very much in love. My heart started beating at an alarming speed, and I went from not being able to breathe to breathing so intensely that I could hear the air blow from my nostrils. The sound of my heart pounding in my ears was so loud I could hear every beat my heart made. I received a brief moment of comfort from my vision of running up on him and grabbing him by the back of the head while smashing it against the hood of his car, but that comfort was short felt. My anger was quickly replaced by something that was much harder to bear. I was completely, utterly, entirely, and enormously humiliated. I was consumed with feeling unbelievably stupid. What a stupid, stupid, stupid girl I had been.

I found it hard to grasp that I went from not knowing how a woman could be in love with two different men to this. Now I couldn't hardly decide what was worse, feeling all alone and like a ghost to my husband, or being used and betrayed by my lover. Abby was right when she said I couldn't have my cake and eat it too, because apparently, I wasn't the only one eating that piece of cake.

TWENTY-FIVE

Humiliation. I was consumed by it, far worse than I could ever imagine. No matter how hard I tried, I couldn't erase images of Paul. I couldn't seem to get the smell of his cologne and fabric softener out of my nose. Fabric softener. I was willing to bet he was probably doing a great deal of laundry so he could wash off the different kinds of perfume he was surrounded by. Humiliated and crushed. Humiliated and angry. Humiliated and devastated. Humiliated was always attached to any other emotion I had. So many things were starting to make more sense than before. That awful cheap motel when he was having his carpets cleaned, his carpets that probably never were cleaned to begin with. Was Beth stopping by without warning and he was afraid she'd catch us in bed? Beth. Strangely, I wasn't angry toward her, perhaps a little jealous maybe, but not angry. If there was anything I felt for Beth, it was sadness. Sadness that her lover is nothing more than a womanizing player who is using her and is most likely after her money.

I laid on the edge of my bed with my head sunk deeply into the pillow. The house was a little on the chilly side, but I had no energy to get up and go turn the heat up. I also had no energy this morning to take a shower or get dressed. I didn't even have the energy to be surprised and delighted when I told Kyle I had an awful headache and he promptly offered to take Julia to school.

For most of the day, I lay in bed, like a sad depressing lump of a person. I found it nearly impossible to get any real sleep. Every time I closed my eyes, the images of Paul and me in bed would flood my mind. Paul kissing me, touching me. His shoulders. His back. The smell of his sweat. Me lying on his silk sheets totally bare and exposed. Naked. Humiliation swept over me again. I couldn't believe I trusted him enough to lay there naked. Even though we were two grown adults, it's hard to erase that adolescent humiliating fear that he's going to laugh behind my back, telling his buddies that he scored with that chick, and saw her naked!

Deep down, I knew I should suck it up, get out of bed, and move on. It was only a fling. No real harm came out of it, right? That question got me every time I asked it. Sure, I didn't get pregnant, or get caught by my husband and get a divorce … yet. I was haunted with the idea that Kyle could still find out, and that my marriage still might end in disaster.

Even if, and I'm really crossing my fingers on that if...Kyle never finds out, *I* will always know what my secret title is and what I had done, and the memories will never leave me.

I let out a loud grunt and rolled over to my other side. Taking the other pillow, I placed it lightly on my face and cried softly.

"Mommy?" I took the pillow slowly off my face and wiped the tears from under my eyes. Julia sat on the bed with her book bag next to her. I hadn't even felt her climb up on the bed. Her brown hair was pulled up into a high ponytail and her purple shirt didn't match her dark blue jeans with bright pink flowers embroidered on them. But I knew Kyle had done his best and I had nothing to complain about since I was wallowing in my own adulterous grief.

"Hi, honey, how was school today?" She smiled for a moment, and then looked really sad as she spoke in her tiny little voice.

"Are you sad, Mommy? Daddy said your head hurts." She tilted her head and looked puzzled while she tried to figure out if my head hurt so badly it was making me cry.

"Yes, Mommy has a headache. Mommy's not crying. Her eyes are just watering because she is very sleepy." Julia nodded as I spoke, believing every word that came out of my mouth. So now, not only was I a cheater, but I'm also the mother that lies to her daughter. But then again, what was I going to say? Mommy's crying because her lover was sleeping with Ginger's Mommy and now Mommy is humiliated, because she was a slut that cheated on Daddy. That hardly seemed like the right conversation to have with her.

Just like classic child behavior, Julia's short attention span quickly put us on another subject.

"I like when Daddy takes me to school. I like when Daddy doesn't leave to go to work so much." As I looked at her while she spoke wholeheartedly, I realized that she had comprehended a great deal about Kyle's work schedule and its effect on her, more than I had realized she did.

"I know you do, honey. You should tell Daddy to take you more often. I think he will if you ask him." Her face lit up and she smiled wide, her eyes twinkling. Still smiling, she leaned over, opened her bag, and reached inside. She pulled out a rock and held it out in front of my face, beaming proudly as if it was a gift from Tiffany's.

"This is for you, Mommy. It's a special surprise. I showed Daddy and he said it was perfect." Julia had always had a fascination with nature. She loved randomly collecting rocks, leaves, flowers, and had even collected little twigs at one time 'til a boy at school stated that twigs are boy plants. After that, she decided they were too boyish for her collection. But this rock she held in her hand was different and special. It resembled the rock that was in the top drawer of my dresser.

It was a reminder of the very first time I spoke to Kyle after his lacrosse game. Abby and I were walking back to her old beat up Pinto, as Kyle appeared to be in a rush for some reason. He didn't even notice that all the girls were smiling and watching him, me included. His gorgeous dark hair and long eyelashes distracted me, when the top of my shoe tripped over a rock, I lost my balance, and of all cars in the lot, I was flung against his car. It was the stuff of Hollywood movies. What I later would hear referred to as a meet cute. Nevertheless, on that day, as he rushed over to me half-concerned, half intrigued by the whole ordeal, our worlds collided like a cosmic bang. Out of all the girls there, some of whom jealously made false accusations that my stunt was on purpose to snatch the hottest guy, Kyle only noticed me.

"Thanks, honey, it is perfect. Where is Daddy?" I pulled, sat up, and slid back, now sitting against the headboard.

"He's downstairs in the kitchen making some snacks." I heard a light tap on the frame of the door and rubbed the remaining of my tears before I looked over.

"Auntie Abby!" Julia slid off the bed and plopped down on her feet, skipping the few short leaps to meet Abby as she strolled across the room. Abby smiled and touched Julia's hair as she pulled a small lollipop from her pocket. Content and ready to go find the next source of entertainment, she raced over to the bed and grabbed her book bag as she hurried to the bedroom door, her voice bursting out in declaration.

"Thanks, Abby! I'm going to go downstairs and color, Mommy!"

Abby took a few more steps until she was on my side of the bed. She slid into a plush cream high back chair, crossing her legs. Her voice was full of concern.

"What's wrong, Vi? Are you upset about the cancer? Is there anything I can do for you?" I pressed my lips together and shook my head as my tears started to form again. The whole time I was feeling sorry over this revelation about Paul and his con-artist ways, I never thought about the real, honest dilemma in my life, like cancer. Was I this shallow? To mourn the loss of a lover over dealing with and getting rid of cancer? The memory about when I confided in Paul about my cancer in the hotel room, his casual, almost unsympathetic response. Another wave of humiliation came over me again. How foolish I was not to see his true side then.

Guilt followed humiliation once I thought about the fact that I had yet to tell Kyle. I had told my two faced, lying, backstabbing, and betraying player of a lover, before my own husband! Is that worse than the actual physical part of the affair? Either way, I was screwed by all the choices I had made.

Abby got up and sat on the edge of the bed next to me. She slowly stroked my arm trying to comfort me. She really was the sister I never had.

"Tell me what's bothering you, Vi." I nodded my head. I was going to figure out a way to tell her some without confessing everything about the last few times with Paul, since I had promised her that I would break it off. Leading with Beth was the best solution I could figure at the moment.

"I found out that Beth is having an affair, and who with." For a split second, Abby's eyes got wide with excitement. Her mood quickly changed when she realized this kind of news should not make me on the verge of tears. Her eyes flickered to the side as she quickly searched her memory for a clue. A sudden look of panic crossed her face.

"Please, please, don't say Marcelo." She closed her eyes and braced, or said a little prayer (I wasn't quite sure), before I blurted out my answer.

"No, it's Paul." Her eyes popped open and she leaned forward in bewilderment.

"Really? As in Julia's teacher Paul? Your Paul? I can hardly believe it!" I shook my head again to confirm it as she took a deep breath and let out a half laugh, half sigh. I could see her mind racing with a million questions as she kept shaking it back and forth. Her eyes were still wide with disbelief. Then she calmed and her tongue started to make the clicking sound, others would say tsk tsk, but Abby had the whole dramatic sound effect going. She then let out a long sigh and looked down at the floor as her shoulders dropped. I knew at that moment that Abby had believed me when I promised her I would end it with Paul. Abby then had a slight look of relief on her face. She looked over at me and read my face. Her expression changed and became saddened as she asked the next question, in almost an accusative tone.

"Were you still seeing Paul?" I opened my mouth but then bit my lip, and that was all the answer Abby needed.

"Oh Vi! I thought you ended that. Did you fall *in love* with Paul?" I honestly didn't know how to answer that question since who I fell in love with apparently didn't even exist. In my lack of an answer, I bit my lip again and Abby sighed in frustration as she stood up off the bed, crossing her arms.

"Vi, what were you doing? Don't you realize how much you have? What you would have thrown away?" I tried to contemplate what she was saying but wasn't grasping her words. I knew it didn't matter anymore because it was over, but she was on a roll so she continued.

"Look at all you have. What's wrong with this life? Your husband is handsome, has a great career and makes good money. He loves you..." She opened her fingers and began counting on them as if she was listing off a hundred things, and then she continued. "You live in a big expensive house with expensive furniture. You have a perfect daughter who is healthy, smart, and beautiful. And let's not forget the greatest friend anyone could ask for." She smiled and batted her eyelashes while touching her chest, mocking vanity. I looked down at the floor unsure how to respond. Abby was right. I knew she was right. I knew she was right when she told me to drop Paul the first time, but I didn't listen. I couldn't listen. I was too busy being sucked into his black hole of seduction. I was desperate, so desperate in fact that I allowed myself to believe he was the real deal. I wanted what he was offering so badly I made excuses for everything in relation to my affair.

"The grass really isn't greener on the other side, Vi." I looked up at her as she made the statement so matter of fact.

"What do you mean?"

"Sure, the grass might look greener, but once you jump that fence, you find out the grass is brown and dying. If you're not happy with what's going on in your own yard, you fix it. You don't jump the fence." I looked at her with a blank stare on my face before I spoke.

"Seriously? You're going to do the whole 'the grass isn't greener on the other side of the fence' metaphor?" A look of annoyance was on Abby's face and in her voice as she continued.

"Uh, yep. Look, all I'm saying is, if you're not happy with your yard, you fix it. You don't just bail on the situation, and that's kinda what you did. I mean, Kyle isn't perfect, but he can't give you what you want if you allow him to be oblivious to you and the marriage. What you don't do is sneak around and sleep with your daughter's elementary teacher." I was now a little annoyed as well with the assumption that I wanted Kyle to ignore me.

"Allow Kyle?"

"Yes, I know you tell me how you feel when you're pissed off, but every time I ask you if you told Kyle, you just blew it off. As I said before, Vi, you have to give him a fighting chance, a fair shot. Of course, Paul looked like the stupid shining knight in armor. He smelled your desperation, and he knew he could get you in the sack. He was more like a vulture than a knight."

"I know you're right, but do you have to be so mean? I know I'm like the world's worst wife, and mother too for that fact. But I feel like a humiliated slut at the moment!" Abby calmed down a little, and then reached down and touched my arm as she spoke gently.

"I'm sorry, Vi, I just hate seeing you this way. I hate seeing how that jerk made you feel, and most of all, I hate thinking that it could all have been avoided." Then she changed the subject, and I was actually relieved to talk about anything other than Paul, even if it was cancer.

"Did you tell Kyle yet?" I didn't have to ask what she was referring to. It was obvious she wasn't referring to Paul. I took a long easy breath of comfort, happy to be released from our intense conversation about Paul and my affair. I looked up at Abby ready to reply when I stopped breathing.

Abby was as stiff as a block of stone and I couldn't even tell if she was breathing. Her eyes were staring at the door, which made my heart drop to my stomach. I bit my lip and followed her gaze to the bedroom door, terrified as I did so. Kyle stood in the doorway with a tray in his hands with small sandwiches on white plates. My hands and arms started to shake as I looked at his face. He stood there for a moment, emotionless. I was terrified, not knowing how long he had been standing there or even how much he had heard, but hoping he had heard nothing. I could tell by Abby's statue like pose that she was thinking the same thing. We both looked at Kyle and waited for some cue or sign.

"Hi, ladies, I made some sandwiches." Kyle took a step into the room and had a wide proud smile on his face. I literally felt the muscles in Abby's body relax at the same moment mine did.

Kyle set the tray next to the bed and handed me a small glass of orange juice. Abby shook her head in reply to a sandwich and juice and glanced down at her watch. I could tell she was comfortable with leaving me in the hands of Kyle, and she was probably hoping I would take care of my yard.

"Thanks, Kyle, I better take off. I have an appointment in about an hour." Most of the time when Abby said appointment, it was code for date. She leaned down and gave me a quick squeeze of a hug before she waved and headed to the front door.

"Do you want me to walk you out?" Kyle started to walk the door when Abby shook her head and said,

"Oh, no, it's not a big deal. I can let myself out."

A short second later, Kyle sat down on the other side of the bed and handed me a plate with a small sandwich before taking a bite out of his. He chewed quickly and then while looking at his sandwich, asked,

"What are you supposed to tell me?" I nearly choked on the small bite when he asked me. His tone was completely curious and there was no hint of accusation or anger, but I still felt paranoid. So I answered his question with a question.

"What do you mean?" He did a half eye roll and a faint sly smile came on the corner of his mouth.

"When I got to the bedroom door, I heard Abby ask you if you had told me yet. Then before you answered, Abby saw me and looked like she had let a huge secret out." He still had the sly smile on his face that made me extremely curious. So I asked,

"Why are you smiling?" He smiled a little wider, squinted his eyes, and nodded his head in confidence before he said,

"I think I know. Are you pregnant?" I rolled my eyes and thought how complicated *that* would have made everything. I then frowned and shook my head no. His smile disappeared and he looked puzzled as he thought for a moment before taking another bite of his sandwich. I reached over, put my hand on his leg, and then told him all about the cancer. I told him everything about the doctor's appointment, the upcoming surgery, and about how scared I was at first. I also told him all that the doctor had informed me about and the positive outlook. After I finished telling him all this, I looked deep in his eyes and saw something I had not seen when I told Paul. Genuine love. Genuine concern.

"Oh, Vi, why didn't you tell me this earlier? Why didn't you let me be there for you at the appointment? Are you that angry with me for working so much that you left me out of this?" The corner of his eyes glistened and became bloodshot as small tears started to form.

"I'm sorry, Kyle. I just didn't want you to worry, that's all. It's not that big of a deal, really." He looked terribly hurt as he spoke.

"Not a big deal? Vi, you're my wife, so everything concerning you and your health is a big deal. I want to be here for you. Please, let me help you with whatever you need. I love you so much, Vi. I couldn't live without you." Tears were now swelling in my eyes as my heart felt ripped apart. Paul seemed so trivial at this moment, as I said in all sincere honesty,

"I don't deserve you."

TWENTY-SIX

I sat in my SUV basking in the warmth of the heater as the steady stream blew on my neck. I glanced in the rearview mirror to see Julia bundled up in her purple coat. She smiled as I pulled forward in the line of cars to drop her off. It had been two weeks since my surgery and even longer since I lay curled up in my bed, humiliated by the whole situation with Paul. I had been fortunate enough that Kyle was more than willing, even happy to drop Julia off at school and pick her up in the afternoons. I didn't have to worry about the possibility of seeing Paul's face until today. I pulled up to the stairs to the entryway and Julia fumbled with her seat belt, as I quickly glanced up to the doorway, desperately hoping I wouldn't see Paul. I was surprised to see the same tall lanky substitute standing near the edge of the classroom as the time before. I asked Julia just before she jumped out of the door,

"Did you have a substitute teacher yesterday?" She glanced over at the door and then back at me quickly, answering in a fast chatter.

"Yeah. Mr. Conway has been gone for days. I hope he's not sick. If he is, I think I will make him a card. Bye Mommy!" Before I could ask another question, she slammed the door shut and skipped up the stairs, her long brown waves bouncing against the back of her purple coat.

I pulled slowly around the well-landscaped loop in front of the building when I heard my cell phone ring. I pulled over to the curb and slid it out of the front pocket of my Louis Vuitton. The caller ID read private and I frantically pushed the button to send it straight to voice mail. I had been getting calls all week from a private number around the times I would have picked up Julia or dropped her off. Since only a handful of people had my cell number, I was more than certain it was Paul. I set it on my lap and was startled when it rang again. The phone almost jumped off my leg. I held it in my hand while it rang, deciding what to do. Should I answer? I was confident his allure would not wield any control over me in the slightest, but I also felt done with the whole thing. Then I thought what if he keeps calling and calling and one of those times Kyle is next to me, or picks up my phone. I'm sure to forget to turn it off since I have never been good at monitoring my phone, considering I get so few calls.

I pushed the button and lightly cleared my throat so the person on the other end knew I was there. I closed my eyes and crossed my fingers that this was just an annoying telemarketer that got my number by mistake. I had no such luck.

"Vi?" Paul spoke in a hushed voice, seeming uncertain if it was me on the other end. I cleared my throat and even though I don't know why, I answered him back in the same hushed voice.

"Yeah." There was a long silence from him following my

unfriendly, borderline hostile tone. After what seemed like a decade, he continued. His voice was still hushed but also cautious.

"Vi, I haven't heard from you in a while. Is everything okay? How are you feeling? I miss you so much and I can't stand being apart from you for so long." I felt queasy that I even believed his smooth voice and caring lines of crap in the past. I mustered up courage from deep within and said something to Paul that I couldn't have imagined myself saying to him a month ago.

"I don't want you to call my phone or talk to me anymore." I thought I heard a faint gasp on the other end, but wasn't sure. Another decade seemed to go by before he said,

"Did I do something to make you mad? Tell me what it is so we can work on it. Is it your husband, because I love you, Vi, and he doesn't!" I let out a breathy laugh as I blurted out,

"I doubt that!" For the first time since I've listened to everything Paul had said to me, I heard something in his voice as he started to speak. It was desperation of his own.

"But I love y---"

"I'm done, Paul. I...am...done." I ended the call and tossed the phone over on the passenger seat, as if the phone itself was toxic. My hands started to shake and I closed my eyes as I was bombarded with a flood of emotions. I was proud and felt a weight leave me, but at the same time, I was sad that my illusion of him had now completely vanished. I thought how much easier it would have been if I had said that sentence back in the coffee shop before this all started. I wondered what I would have felt then after I said it. Would I have been proud of myself then, or regretful that I didn't try to make myself happy? For weeks, my mind played the first day at Paul's apartment when I had forgotten my keys. If only I had not forgotten my keys, what if I had controlled myself! How I could have avoided all this guilt, shame, and humiliation. No matter how hard I thought about it, I couldn't go back and change the past and live on the what ifs that were always on my mind.

My phone rang again and I grunted out loud in frustration as I snatched it up answering it right away.

"I said, I'm done." I was angry and went to turn it off when I heard the voice of Beth on the other end.

"Vi? Hi. It's Beth. Is this a bad time?" I was relieved and smiled.

"No, sorry, I was just dealing with something. What can I do for you, Beth?"

"I saw you parked over to the side and I was going to come and see if you were alright but it looked like you were on the phone. Julia said you went to the hospital. Are you okay? I just wanted to check on you." I was touched by her sweet generosity. I was put in a spot because I knew that she would be beyond devastated if things continued to go on with her and Paul. But I also didn't want my secret to be known, especially by Beth in particular. I decided I would make up a story about seeing Mr. Conway with a woman and then cross my fingers that Beth might have better luck of putting the pieces together than I did.

"I did have some minor surgery. Are you busy this morning?

Would you like to come with me to grab a cup of coffee?"

"Sure, that would be wonderful."

Fifteen short minutes later, we met at my favorite shop and I walked inside to see Beth sitting at a small wood table by the window. I decided in that moment that I would need to pick a new place to have my coffee as the whole room no longer had the same feel to it. I glanced over at the leather chairs for a brief second remembering when Paul and I sat there. A small chill ran up my spine and I blinked the memory away as I smiled over at Beth and pointed up to the Barista, signaling that I was going to grab a drink.

With my hot latte in front of me, I draped my coat over the back of the wood chair and looked up at Beth as she gave me a faint, weak smile. Her recent glow had seemed to disappear and I noticed her eyes were red and bloodshot. She had the appearance of fighting a terrible flu. She pointed over to the fireplace.

"I love that little fireplace. It really makes this place feel, oh, I don't know the word."

"Cozy." She looked over at me and smiled as she nodded her head in agreement.

"Yes, that's it, cozy." I hoped Beth started coming here so that someone would be able to enjoy this place to its full potential, since I no longer would be able too, at least not for a while.

Beth took a sip of her drink before she looked at me with tired eyes, asking with a concerned voice.

"Ginger told me you were in the hospital? You mentioned

having surgery. Is everything okay?" Beth kept her gaze on my face as she slowly brought the mug to her lips and took another sip of her drink. She looked so sad and tired I had a strong feeling something had happened with Paul but I couldn't put my finger on it yet. I didn't think she knew anything about my involvement with him. However, her demeanor would have been different if she had known something.

"I'm fine now. I had surgery because I found a tiny lump in my breast and it turned out to be cancerous, so I had it removed. The incision is still a little sore because they removed a small amount of tissue around the lump just to make sure, but it was caught so early that the doctors seem very confident with the outcome of the surgery." Beth's bloodshot eyes became as wide as her exhausted face allowed them. Her eyebrows rose higher and she said in a surprised tone.

"I'm so sorry, Vi. Is there anything I can do?" What I really wanted her to do is just spill everything about Paul. Then again, on second thought, I didn't know if I had the stomach to envision all the details of their relationship and another reminder of humiliation.

"Thanks, but I have a follow up next week and then they are going to run another test in about a month. Then I'm going to get tests done every six months from here on out, just to be on the safe side. Thank you though." I smiled at her and took a sip of my own hot drink as Beth pondered my response and then nodded her head in respect for turning down her offer to help. I decided to change the subject, so I casually asked,

"How about you? Are you doing okay? You look a little upset." She frowned a little and looked down at her mug for a long time. I started to panic because I was afraid she was going to burst out in tears at the table and I wouldn't really know how to comfort her. So I quickly said,

“You don't have to tell me. I'm sorry I asked.” Without raising her head, her eyes flickered up at me and then looked out the window. She took a long quiet breath and then let it out in a long depressing sigh before her faint sad voice spoke.

“You know that guy I was seeing? Well, it's over.” I feigned a look of surprise and asked,

“What happened? Did your husband find out?” She shook her head no and said in an even more depressing tone.

“No, worse.” Now my mind was racing. I had once thought about telling Beth about Paul but now that it was over, I didn't want anyone else to know about Paul besides Abby. The less people, the safer I felt, whether that was a fact or not, made no difference. I just felt safer with few knowing.

“What can be worse than you husband finding out?” I literally, for some unknown reason, put my hand under the table and crossed my fingers.

“He had someone else.” I looked at her, my eyes urging her to go on. I locked my fingers even tighter, hoping she didn't know enough to look my direction. Did she know about us together? Did he tell her? Nevertheless, even though I was scared for myself, I felt both sad and happy for her that she wasn't going to get dragged farther along by him.

“A wife.” The statement caused me to snap straight up in my chair as I exclaimed,

"What?" I couldn't believe it. Did he actually have a wife or did she put together tiny clues and flags and just *thought* he had a wife. She stared at me. Her lips pressed tight together as she rhythmically bobbed her head up and down and then shrugged her shoulders as if to say. "Yep, took me by surprise too." I had to have more information so I asked,

"How did you know he had a wife? Did you meet her?" She let out another sigh.

"No, but I heard her voice on the phone, and it gets even worse."

"What? Even *worse*?" I was beginning to notice that it took Beth an incredibly long time to tell a story. I had become too familiar with how Abby told stories in which she blurted almost everything out at once, and I didn't need hardly to ask questions. She just told you straight up.

"Well, he isn't even British." This statement sincerely confused me. What did that mean? And had she even told me she was dating someone who was British? Had she forgotten that she didn't tell me that? I looked at her with wide eyes and asked,

"Beth, tell me what happened."

"Okay, so I was at his place about a week ago. We had just finished having sex on his expensive satin sheets that I bought him." She sighed and looked embarrassed that she had even spent any money on him. I also felt embarrassed because I too had slept with him on those sheets. Beth continued.

"So I get up to go take a shower in the bathroom and I turn the shower on and was just messing around in the bathroom in front of the mirror. I didn't have a towel in the bathroom so I opened the door a crack to grab one out of the hall closet when I saw the bedroom door closed. I stepped out of the bathroom to get the towel when I heard him talking in the bedroom." I leaned to the edge of my chair, trying hard not to visualize Beth sneaking around naked, but I couldn't get the image out of my head. At least it was better than visualizing them both naked having sex.

"But that was the thing. He didn't really sound like himself. I couldn't hear too well because he wasn't talking very loud, but it just didn't sound like him. He obviously thought I was in the shower. I have never done anything like this before, but I tiptoed over to this vintage looking phone he had, you know, one that looks like it's from the twenties. Anyway, I knew he wouldn't be able to hear me if I picked it up off the holder and listened in to the conversation. I've never done anything like that before, eavesdropping." She took a long pause, and she was clearly collecting herself before she finished the rest of her story. Beth took a long, slow sip out of her mug before speaking. Her eyes looked at me and my legs began to shake under the table with anticipation.

"Well, I picked up the phone and couldn't hardly believe my ears. The guy I was seeing had this lush, sexy British accent, but on the phone, there was no accent. None. Well, at least not a British accent. He had this, almost, Boston accent. There wasn't even a hint of a British accent in his voice. I thought I was listening to someone else talking. And he was talking to a woman who did actually have a British accent. It was just so insane." I didn't want her to take a long pause so I blurted out,

"What did they say to each other?"

"That's how I knew she was his wife. They talked a little about her family back home, something about the business and how she couldn't wait for him to come back. Then he told her his grandfather was still doing very poorly and it might be another month or so. Then she said, 'I feel like we've been apart longer than we've been married.' Married! She sounded so sweet and loving. He was feeding her all kinds of crap about how much he loved her and missed her and she would always be the only one. Blah, blah, blah. Only one, my butt!" Her voice trembled and her bottom lip started to quiver as her eyes moistened with new tears. I wanted to reach out and tell her she wasn't the only one that fell for his smooth lines and charming game. Instead, I reached my hand across the table, patted her arm, and said,

"I'm so sorry, Beth. I'm sorry that he turned out to be such a liar." These words were sincere and from my heart, because I had felt what she was feeling. Even though she clearly was more devastated than I had been to lose *her* idea of what Paul was, I still felt bad for her just the same.

"I only listened for a couple of minutes but it was enough for me. I didn't even turn the shower off. I walked in the bedroom, threw my clothes on, and left his place. He just stared at me. He didn't even say a word! Vi, I have never been so crushed in my life. I'm a wreck to be honest. And I haven't even told you this, but he works at the school!" I couldn't imagine what kind of shape she would be in if she found out that she wasn't even the only one he was cheating on his wife with. At this point, I wasn't even sure Beth and I were the only two. What if there were more? I could just imagine Paul, if that was even his real name, having women stashed in England and America, feeding them lines and stories and different accents.

"So what are you going to do?" She looked at me and a sly genuine smile barely touched her lips.

"The only thing I could do. I had him fired." This revelation made me happy. Even though I didn't do it myself, I still shared in some of the proud joy of revenge that was taken. Beth suddenly looked alarmed after she told me that and quickly looked down. I realized that she figured I would put the pieces together since Paul had been out of the classroom for a week. I had no choice but to act surprised and to ask a question. If I did not, she might suspect something between Paul and me, and all I wanted to do at this point was try to sweep away as much as I could of Paul and our affair.

"Was it Pa—Mr. Conway?" Her face looked extremely guilty and she her eyebrows scrunched together as she replied,

"Yes, I know that is so horrible." I wished I could tell her that I too was sucked into his allure, and that my guilt was equally as bad as hers was for sleeping with my daughter's elementary teacher as well. Instead, I just shut my mouth and gave her a look letting her know she was not being judged.

I desperately wanted to call Abby and tell her everything. I was certain I would not be able to keep this information to myself alone. It just had to be shared. I had to ask one final question.

"How *did* you get him fired?" She casually shrugged her

shoulders and said,

“Large donations, followed by strong suggestions turned into results, I guess.”

“Wow.” That was all I could say. That was all I was thinking at that moment. Just. Wow.

A short drive later, I was sitting in my driveway, my mind spinning while it tried to absorb all the heavy information Beth laid on me. The feeling of humiliation started to creep up on me again. I felt used and if it was even possible, sluttier than before.

My hand was wrapped around my cell phone as I started to dial Abby's number. I changed my mind, and decided to run inside, change my clothes and then drive out to her house. This was a story I had to tell her to her face. I quickly unlocked the front door and took a few steps to hang my purse on the banister. I heard some rustling upstairs and yelled up; surprised that Kyle would be home from work at this time in the morning. It wasn't even noon yet.

“Kyle? Is that you upstairs?” I heard him faintly yell down a reply, sounding distracted by whatever he was doing. I glanced over and noticed our luggage packed and sitting a few feet from the front door, stacked against the wall. I stopped breathing as panic rose inside me. Did he somehow find out about the affair? Were those bags filled with my clothes? Was Kyle kicking me out? Were they filled with Kyle’s clothes and he was leaving me forever.

My legs started to shake and I stood there unsure of what to do. How do you fix something like this? I was certain Kyle knew about

Paul and these bags were proof of it. I was going to lose everything because of the affair. I was going to lose the only man that truly loved me.

I heard Kyle walk down the stairs. I couldn't prevent the tears that started to form in my eyes. The room became blurry as I looked out through a layer of tears. Kyle stepped down on the landing holding a small overnight bag. He looked at me with a grave concern look on his face. I blinked and a tear rolled down my cheek. I wanted to leap forward, grab his shirt, and beg him to forgive me. I wanted to beg him to love me, beg him not to hate me.

He reached over and gently touched my arm before saying,

"What is it, Vi? Why are you crying? You're freaking me out." He reached up and wiped my tear away then moved my hair away from my face. My legs almost gave out in relief.

"Nothing, I just heard something on the radio and then got all emotional. No, actually, I'm crying because I realize how much I love you." I wiped my face as he gave me a little smile and a kiss on the side of my cheek. I pointed to bags and asked while praying his smile was a good sign.

"What's this?" His smile grew wider as he answered.

"Well, I've already taken care of all the arrangements. Abby has agreed to watch Julia for us, and we are taking a little weekend getaway. We always talked about taking weekend getaways, and I think it's time we start making good on those promises." I smiled at him as he beamed back, proud and happy.

Because of guilt, I couldn't let myself feel entirely excited since I hadn't made good on my promise of marriage vows.

TWENTY-SEVEN

The first attribute that anyone would note was his physical appearance. He was not handsome in a subtle way, but deeply and undeniably attractive by most standards. He was the man that young women whispered about when he walked down the hallway at the office, but was unmistakably oblivious to any advance, no matter how flirtatious.

However, Kyle Taylor did not consider himself handsome, his well-groomed and up-kept appearance was out of necessity, not vanity. He grew up the second youngest out of five children, lanky and slightly awkward compared to his three older brothers, who competitively teased and harassed him on most given occasions. Kyle was merely thankful that, by the time he went off to college, he finally grew into his ears and could take his braces off, which had been great cause for part of his childhood teasing. Regardless of his brother's teasing and competitive nature towards him as well as each other, he strived to be athletic like them and gain their approval. It was his admiration and quick ability to pick up athletics, particularly lacrosse that helped to earn him a scholarship to college, which was a great relief to the finances of the family. After spending the summer before his senior year running errands for a small law practice, he had made his decision to practice law. It didn't take long for his heart to belong to this area. In a small way, he felt that he was helping and contributing to something greater than his own self. It was easy for him to slide into this field. He owned more books than tennis shoes, was fond of reading, and had no problems with his studies. He was intelligent and clever, easy to converse with and filled with great compassion.

Kyle never grew up believing in love at first sight. He didn't care to chase women or go through the hassle of long awkward advances which he always assumed wouldn't be returned. He never met a girl in any of his classes that sparked his interest or made him want to step outside his comfort zone on faith. However, that changed for Kyle during the last away game of the season. He was beyond physical exertion and sweat was trickling down his face as he reached up to wipe his brow. The sun caught in his eye for a second and that was when he saw her.

He felt his heart drop and his adrenaline took a new charge. Kyle hadn't even cared that they won the game that day or that he was the team captain and was expected to round everyone up for a celebration. All he could think about was the girl in the stand. There wasn't anything particularly attractive about her with her straight brown hair and peg-rolled pants, but there was something about the air around her. It was if the heavens opened when she cast a smile in his direction during the game. So on that first day, Kyle ran to the locker room and grabbed his duffle bag as quickly as possible to try to find that girl before she left. He knew he might never have the opportunity again, and it was the one opportunity he knew he would regret if it got away.

Kyle ran to the parking lot with such speed and focus on finding the girl that he hadn't paid attention to where he was going, and an old rusty bumper that was bent out sliced him just above his right knee. Even though the cut was fairly deep, he couldn't feel the pain as he searched for the girl. That cut would later turn into a scar that Kyle would often think of as a loving reminder of her every time he looked at it.

It was by chance that as he turned around the corner of the gravel parking lot, he caught a glimpse of her. As they locked eyes, she stumbled and was thrown into the car next to her, which happened to be his. That day was what Kyle would often think of when he heard about love at first sight.

ꕤꕤꕤ

The crackling of the fire and soft glow of orange light bounced around the room, casting dancing shadows along the wall and floor. I took a sip of my wine and then leaned over and set it on the antique style side table next to our large comfortable couch.

Kyle had secured us plane tickets and after a fairly short flight and fifteen minute taxi ride, we landed on the steps to the grand entrance to the Biltmore. The beautiful autumn trees as a large pack were even more stunning than a few scattered trees here and there, as I was used to seeing. On the massive grounds, surrounded by the yellow, orange and deep red marigolds, they came alive, almost sparkled even. After a relaxing stroll through the gardens, we came back and curled up on the couch to enjoy some wine and the fireplace.

Kyle set his wine glass down on the side table next to him then inched over and wrapped his arm around me, pulling me into his chest. I leaned into him and rested my head on his chest while he stroked my hair. My eyes fixated on the flames as they glowed, small specks of fire crackling to the side.

"You know what, Vi? I think this suite is bigger than our first apartment." Thinking about his words, I glanced around the large living room with its walls lined with elegant artwork and handcrafted antique furniture. I then peered down the hallway to the large bathroom, and the thought crossed my mind that it seemed so far from where we were sitting.

"Yes, I think you're right. Our first apartment was on the small side, but we weren't in there for very long." I flashed back to our first one bedroom apartment, with its tiny kitchen that was more like a hallway and one small bathroom. The only thing that the apartment had to boast about was the large walk in closet in the average size bedroom. I would joke on a couple of occasions when we first moved in that if I ever got mad at him I was going to move our bed in there, making it the dog house. I looked up at him, his eyes looking at the fire while he continued rhythmically to stroke my hair. I spoke up and asked, wondering if he too remembered as much as I did.

"Do you remember our first apartment? Do you remember how the kitchen was so small that all we seemed to eat was take-out?" A smile formed on his lips and he nodded and glanced down at me, his eyes full of love.

"I still think about that time right after we moved in and I got up in the middle of the night to find you eating leftover Chinese take-out on the rug, naked. I still picture that sometimes." His smile widened and he gave me a mischievous look indicating he was picturing it again at that moment. I rolled my eyes and pretended to be annoyed with his remark, but I couldn't hide the sly smile on my face. I too remembered that night he was talking about. For some odd reason, maybe it was the temporary insanity of my early twenties, I had decided that it would be stylish to buy a faux polar bear rug, complete with a head and paws. After a night of vigorous lovemaking, I snuck out to the small living room and lay on that tacky rug to eat my Chinese.

"Do you ever miss our ever so classy bear rug?" I asked him. Once again, I couldn't hide my smile as memories of vigorous love making *on* the rug came to me.

"When did we get rid of the rug?" His playful and sarcastic tone made me chuckle as I glanced back to the fire and snuggled even harder into his chest. I didn't want the moment to end. I wanted to pause time and freeze it forever.

"Vi?" I closed my eyes and took in all of his essence. I took in the feel of his soft cashmere sweater. The smell of his fresh clean aftershave and the smell of his cologne that I bought him as a gift for his last birthday. I answered practically in a whisper.

"Yeah?" There was a sadness in his voice as he started to speak in such a way it made my heart ache.

"Do you resent me?" I didn't know how to answer his question or why he was asking it in the first place.

"What do you mean? Why would I resent you?"

"You remember the older lady client that I had? One of the things she told me was that her husband worked so much that she started to resent him. She said it started as frustration and just kept growing until it was resentment, then finally hate. And you said to me at dinner during that conversation that you didn't want to go back to being like a single mom." He took a long pause and then went on.

"So I just wanted to know if you resent me. I hope I'm not too late that it's turned into hate." I took a deep breath and thought for a moment on the level of honesty I should answer with. The truth once was that I was becoming resentful towards Kyle, but after cheating on him and having a tremendous amount of remorse, I now had resentment for my own self. However, this was something I could not tell him.

"I missed how we use to sit and talk for hours. I resented that what we had just disappeared. But I never hated you." The significant truth of my last sentence brought tears to my eyes. Weren't the only wives that cheated on their husbands the ones that hated their husbands? However, I never hated Kyle. Yet, I still did the unthinkable to him. I sniffed and then threw my hands up to my face as warm tears flooded my eyes.

Kyle leaned down and kissed the top of my head several times that only made me cry harder.

“Please don't cry, Vi. I truly am sorry for ignoring you. Can I tell you something?” I took the inside of the sleeve around my wrist of my black cotton turtleneck and patted under my eyes as I sniffed a few more times.

“Sure,” I said as Kyle leaned down and kissed me again on my forehead and even though I glanced at the fire, I could feel him looking down at me.

“I was so focused on work and so career driven because I wanted you to be proud of me. I wanted you to be proud to call me your husband. The very first time I saw you at my lacrosse game, I knew that there was something different about you. I wanted to make you happy and I wanted to be able to afford the nice house and stuff for you. That’s why I worked so hard, for so many years. I guess I just got caught up in the routine of it so that I didn't pay attention to you.” He paused and I wrapped my arms around him tightly. Then he quietly said,

“I'm sorry.” The soft sweater touched my lips as I kissed his chest in a gesture of forgiveness.

“I have always been proud to call you my husband. I'm glad you're successful, but that's not the most important thing to me.” I stopped talking just long enough to keep myself from crying again, as images of Paul kissing me and memories of me grabbing his back while sweat dripped down to my fingertips, flashed in my mind like a lightning rod. I battled with the images in my head while each second that passed caused me to feel guiltier and more regretful than the previous second. I was thankful when I heard Kyle's voice. I was hopeful that focusing on whatever he would say might push the visions of Paul out of my mind.

"You know, I did think you were different the first time I saw you." Kyle scooted toward the other end of the couch during his sentence, making room for me to pull my legs up on the couch and rest my head in his lap.

"You mean in the parking lot? Where I tripped like a clumsy idiot?" I let out an over dramatized sigh and a breathy laugh. I could hear the smile on Kyle's face as he continued.

"No, not in the parking lot. When you were sitting in the bleachers with Abby. I looked over at you a couple of times when you weren't paying attention. You were just different from the other girls in the stand. They all looked snotty and full of themselves. But you... you just had something about you." Oh, God, what have I done? A million women in the world would probably feel lucky to be in the arms of such a gorgeous man who truly loves them, but I'm the one idiot that went out and had an affair.

I looked at the fire and thought that if I could stick my arm in the flames and it would erase what I had done, I would gladly bear the pain. But it will never be that easy, and the past will never be erased.

Kyle took the back of his finger and stroked my cheek. I wanted to say so many things to Kyle in response to his confession, but I couldn't. I didn't deserve to say anything.

"It was in the parking lot that I hoped that you would be my wife someday." I was amazed at this revelation, because this was the first time in all the years we had been together, he had ever told me this.

"Really? You knew during our first conversation in the parking lot that you wanted me to be your wife?" He leaned down and gave me another slow lingering kiss on my head before he said,

"Yeah, they say when you know, you just know. And well, I just knew." I didn't think it was possible to be both happy and miserable at the same time, but I was. The more that he told me, and the harder he tried, the worse it made me feel. I sat up, burning from all my internal agony and roaring fire.

"I'm going to go to the bedroom and change out of this warm shirt." Kyle gave me a quick smile and crossed his arms, pulling his sweater over his head revealing his dark gray tank top. The way the orange glow of the fire bounced off his chiseled shoulders and his strong jaw line made him irresistible at that moment. I just sat there mesmerized by his glossy thick hair as he carelessly ran his fingers through it. For me, he was nearly perfect, and I couldn't think of a movie star or model in a magazine ad that could compare. At that moment, looking at Kyle, I fully grasped that Paul was nowhere near an equal to my husband.

Kyle leaned back into the couch after draping his sweater over the arm and I stood up to head to the bedroom. Just as I started to pass my purse, I heard my phone ring.

"Is that your phone? I don't think I ever heard your phone ring. You better get that." My body started to fall into a state of panic as my hands started to tremble ever so slightly. I was grateful that it was dark enough that it wasn't noticeable. I tried desperately to play mellow, when in reality all I could picture was Paul's voice on the phone while Kyle sat on the couch looking at me wondering who it is.

"Oh, yeah, it's probably just Abby or Beth. Or a wrong number." I slid my purse over to the edge of the table. My phone stopped ringing and I took a sigh of relief internally. Kyle shrugged his shoulders in agreement and then asked casually,

"Are you hungry? I can order us some room service if you want?"

"Sure." I fished my phone out of my purse and held it in my hand to take it with me to the bedroom just as it lit up again and began to ring. The caller ID read private and my heart sank.

"Seriously, you better get that. What if it's an emergency?" I swallowed hard and my heart began to beat so fast I could hear the pounding in my ears. Sweat formed around the edge of my hairline and I glanced at Kyle as he smiled and gave me a pretend scolding look.

"Are you going to answer that, Vi, or have you forgotten how to use your phone already?" He chuckled and took a sip of his wine, and I gave a laugh in response that came off more nervous than I had wanted. I answered my phone and brought it to my ear as I turned to walk to the bedroom, pretending I was going to multitask and change while I took a casual phone call.

"Hey Vi!" I exhaled and my shoulders slumped down just as I heard Abby's voice. I turned toward Kyle, covered the phone briefly with my hand, and whispered to him.

"It's Abby. I'm going to change and see what's going on." He nodded his head, leaned back into the couch as I escaped into the bedroom, closing the door behind me.

"Hey, Abby, your number came up private?"

"Yeah, I switched my service so my number is always private now. So, how do you like the place? It's beautiful isn't it?" I smiled and sat on the edge of the bed, relieved and refreshed now that I had taken off my turtleneck and was letting the cool air touch my skin while I sat on the bed in my bra.

"Yes, it is so amazing here, and Kyle has been just wonderful. How is Julia?"

"Perfect Angel. We went to the park and then I took her for ice cream and I think tomorrow I'm going to take her to the zoo if that's alright?" I leaned back into the bed and just imagined Abby and Julia having their fun filled long weekend.

"She would love that." I wanted to tell Abby about my lunch with Beth because I didn't have the opportunity to do it before we left for the Biltmore. I wanted to get it off my chest so badly. I got up and cracked open the door to see Kyle on the phone with room service. I closed the door and went to the far end of the room from the door before I started to speak in a low voice.

"Okay, I have to tell you about my lunch with Beth." I heard some excitement in Abby's voice. She could always tell when I had something interesting to tell her.

"Please do." I gave her the brief synopsis of Beth's story, but included the full detail of his phone call conversation with his wife, accent fraud and everything. I could hear her gasp and then she spoke, each word drawn out in a long dramatized fashion.

"What? That is some crazy mess." She laughed for a moment and then said,

"You got a serial-marrying secretary, a wife that screws clowns, and a British playboy who isn't even British! There's never a dull moment when you have a little money. I think the rich *must* be crazy." I knew it was pointless to point out to Abby for the millionth time that she was richer than anyone else that we knew, but she loved to talk like she wasn't really in that category of craziness.

We made a few more jokes and I got off the phone and slipped into a soft oversized t-shirt that Kyle had packed for me. I took my pants off and found a pair of cotton shorts in the bag that he had also put in there.

I walked down the hall and saw the cart of food sitting in the living room as Kyle opened the silver lids to peek under them. He smiled as I walked out in my oversized t-shirt.

"I love when you wear that t-shirt." For some odd reason, his statement made me blush. He seemed different here, now. He was relaxed, rejuvenated and I could sense a strong sexual attraction toward me that I hadn't felt in a long time. I sat on the edge the couch, wheeled the tray over to me, and sat next to him. Even though I was only wearing an old baggy t-shirt and shorts, and he was wearing a tank top and his pants, the chemistry was stronger than ever. I could tell he felt the energy as well. He reached over and softly touched my arm that sent chills up and down my body from excitement, just like the very first time we were together. In what only took a flash of a moment, but seemed to play in slow motion, Kyle's lips were on my neck. I closed my eyes and a single tear ran down my cheek, as the pain was almost unbearable while Paul's conceited face smiled and laughed at me in my thoughts. My heart ached as I thought that all the love that Kyle had for me would disappear if he ever knew. Above all, I knew my pain was nothing compared to the torture and agony he would feel if he found out.

Kyle's lips found his way to mine and he paused and leaned a few inches from my face, as he looked me dead in the eyes.

"I love you so much, Violet. I am so lucky to have you." I bit my lip and replied with every ounce of my heart.

"No. I'm the one who's lucky." Before he could say anything or argue with my statement, I kissed him so passionately, and was so consumed with his entirety that for the first time in weeks, Paul had become less than a memory.

TWENTY-EIGHT

Eighteen Months Later...

"Julia, have you seen my other shoe?" I shouted as I lifted up the edge of the bed skirt. I was on my knees as I leaned forward, putting all my weight on my elbows. I sat up in frustration and blew a long piece of curled hair out of my face. I heard Julia's voice as it came from her bedroom down the hall.

"I think I saw it in the blue room Mommy, but I don't know."

I grunted and pulled myself up with the side of the comforter hanging off the bed and limped over to the blue room across the hall. It was named for the fact that the previous owners had painted it in several shades of blue.

I tripped over a moving box that had not been unpacked yet. We had been in our new house for over three months and still had a few boxes scattered around, as well as plenty of walls that still needed to be painted. The new house was slightly smaller than the one we had before, but it was still larger than what we honestly need, but it was located in a nice, less pretentious neighborhood. In addition, it was closer to Abby's house.

I saw my other dress sandal sitting on top of a moving box right under the windowsill. I could tell that Julia had been trying it on. I rolled my eyes, as I reached down and snatched up the shoe. I took a quick glance through the narrow opening in the top of the box and my eye caught a glimpse of some photos. I opened the light brown box and snatched up the first couple of photos off the top of the pile. I smiled while gazing at the photo from a trip to the zoo late last summer with Beth and our girls. Everyone in the photo looked authentically happy. Beth filed for divorce roughly two months after the revelation she had in Paul's apartment. That day inside Paul's apartment made something inside her snap. Beth hired a top-notch private investigator, and in less than two weeks, she had plenty of photos of her husband with more than his fair share of mistresses. I wasn't sure what a fair share was (or if anyone really deserved any kind of share) but whatever it was, he had tripled that, according to Beth. I never shared our common secret with Beth and didn't regret my choice to keep that from her.

In the end, she did not need photos to ask for a divorce; Beth knew they would help her case. She immediately wanted to hire Kyle as her attorney. I had been a little uneasy at first when she asked Kyle to represent her, but considering the amount of money her husband had to hire the best representation, Kyle was a smart and competitive choice. Thanks to her trusty private investigator and some indisputable photos, Beth was fairly compensated, and retained full custody of her child. Beth had found a perpetual state of peace.

I put the photos back in the box with a smile and picked up the shoe, strapping it to my foot. I turned and called out to Julia so we could head out the front door.

I could smell all the different flowers as they mixed in the air. I could smell the lilacs in particular, as several bushes lined the back part of Abby's property. Everything was perfect. The sky had a soft sun, but just enough clouds that we didn't feel the need to cover our eyes. The air was fresh with the springtime smell of the grass and flowers. A slight breeze just barely grazed our skin.

I walked inside the house through the large French doors on the back of Abby's patio. Julia was next to me, skipped over to a chair and plopped down on it. She put her doll on her lap and pulled up her purse, pulling out a couple of hair barrettes to fix her doll's tangled locks. She leaned back into the chair, preparing herself to wait. I walked up the steps to the second level of Abby's palace and down the long hallway to her master bedroom. I tapped lightly on the door.

"Is that you, Vi?" I heard Abby's muffled voice as she sounded as if she was in the back part of the room. I opened the door and slid inside as I answered.

"Yeah, it's me. How's it going? Almost ready?" I heard her moving around in her master closet as she leaned around the corner and peeped her head out.

"Oh, yeah. I'm so glad you're here now. I bought two pair of shoes and I want you to tell me which pair you think is best." I smiled wide and slowly sat down on the large high back chair close to the master closet feeling more tired than usual.

"Okay, bring them on down." Abby seemed to float out of her closet, which was larger than the average American's bedroom, and glided until she stood in front of me holding two shoes that were so opposite, but yet equally stunning.

"Oh, I don't know. I kind of like the sparkly silver one. But I also like the sleek high heel pump. What are you feeling?" Abby looked at both shoes carefully.

"I think it's a sparkle type of day, don't you?" My smile stretched wide as my heart was full of joy for my best friend. She nodded her head in agreement with her statement and set the beautiful Stuart Weitzman shoes on the table next to my chair. She put the other pair back in the closet before returning to look at herself in the mirror.

Abby looked stunning. Her classic and simple wedding dress was elegant, fitting her perfectly. Her skin was glowing with joy and she had an aura of vibrant happiness. Her hair was pulled back in a thick French twist as her bangs were side swept and a large white flower was on the side of her hair. Abby looked as if she belonged on the cover of a bridal magazine. Truth was she even looked better than the cover of any bride magazine.

"Are you nervous?" I asked this question mainly because I had not anticipated this event for Abby, not that I didn't *want* it for her, but simply for the fact that she had kept herself guarded for so many years, I had believed it might never happen. I was ecstatic when that turned out to be wrong.

"Actually, no, I'm not. It's kinda crazy though, right?" I stood up and took the floating pearl necklace out of her hands to help her put it on. She looked in the mirror at her own reflection and continued talking.

"I might have come to the whole matrimony party a little late, but they saved the best for last. I'm just crazy for Marcelo. He's the real deal, you know." I truthfully nodded in agreement with Abby.

Marcelo had a love for Abby that no other man could hold a torch to. It took Abby about a week to get her head out of the clouds and get past Marcelo's sexy appearance. And it only took Marcelo that week to fall head first in love with Abby. Anyone in a room with the two of them could easily tell their love was genuine and strong. Over the last year and a half, they had taken several trips to Brazil to spend time with his large family. Abby had finally become part of a large family that not only liked her, but also adored her tremendously. For the first time, in something that was unprecedented in Abby's dating experience, Marcelo insisted on paying for each trip entirely. He has an old fashion chivalrous charm in the way he treats Abby. All the chivalry without the sexist expectations of the female role. Their relationship was a perfect match.

"Hey, how did your mammo go? Everything still good?" Abby looked at me through the reflection in her mirror as she put her earrings in. The back of her dress laced up the back and had faint detailed work along the lace lines. It was still considered simple, with just a little something extra to it.

"Yeah, everything looks good." I picked up her sparkly shoe and held it in my hands as I thought about the whole scary experience. I was fortunate enough to catch it so early that treatment was not as extensive as I had feared it would be. I was fortunate to have both Abby and Kyle by my side. Kyle had stepped up in a way that I couldn't have even dreamed of. He never once made me go by myself. He took care of Julia without questions or complaints and always seemed to anticipate what I needed before I even had to ask. The memory of this started to bring a tear to my eye as I considered how much he really did for me.

"Are you okay? I'm just getting married! I'm not leaving you, Vi, please don't cry." I laughed a little and used my finger to wipe the single tear from my eye.

"No, I'm not crying because I'm sad you're getting married. I was just thinking about the whole cancer thing and all of that." Abby turned and gave me a sympathetic frown and I waved my hand in the air signaling that I was over my moment on memory lane.

"Oh, I got some good gossip for your wedding day." I gave her a mischievous smile, and in typical Abby fashion, her eyes lit up with anticipation.

"Ooh, spill. I love me some juicy news." I pretended to pause for a long moment as if I had forgotten what to tell her. She crossed her arms and let out a huff in frustration.

"Okay, soooo, guess who's getting another divorce?" Abby thought for less than a second before a look of confidence graced her face.

"You mean Miss Slutty Slutterson? *That's* a surprise." We both smiled and laughed at the same time. Olivia had left the office a year ago to go off to get married yet again. Her current divorce proceedings looked to possibly be lucrative for her. Either way, it wouldn't really matter since she had decided to move across the country with no signs of coming back. Good riddance to slutty trash like Abby had said when I told her.

There was a faint tapping on the door and Julia peeked her head through the opening. I waved her in and she walked with a bounce in her step until she stood next to the chair.

“Hi, sweet pea. You look very beautiful in your dress. Thank you for helping Auntie Abby out today.” Julia's face lit up and her tight lip smile stretched from ear to ear. Her little voice was full of excitement.

“You look beautiful, Abby. You look just like a princess, and Marky looks like a prince.” Julia had insisted on calling Marcelo “Marky” since their very first introduction. Both Abby and Marcelo thought it was so cute that Marky became his official and special nickname from Julia. Abby looked at the clock on her side table and sighed one last single gal sigh.

“Alright, ladies, let's get this party started.” She looked down at Julia and mockingly did a little dance that made Julia cover her mouth and giggle.

The backyard was decorated simply, but it still looked wonderful because Abby's backyard typically looked great every spring and summer anyway. Abby's large back patio had been furnished with three white cloth tents and hanging ball lights for the reception that was bound to go on long into the night. Even though Marcelo came from a large family, their wedding was relatively small. They had decided to have a small simple wedding for only their dearest friends and families.

I saw Marcelo standing by the arch, talking to his best friend and cousin. He glanced over and smiled warmly and I gave him a friendly wave. I turned to check out the cake when I saw Kyle walking toward me from the side of the house. He had a slight frown on his face and ping of worry came over me. Kyle stopped in front of me and dropped his arms to the side. He looked stunning in his white dress shirt and charcoal gray suit. His face was clean-shaven and his hair had just been trimmed. He was model picture perfect. He hunched forward and let out a little frown as he spoke.

"I'm sorry, Vi. I forgot to grab that dark purple ribbon from the house. I just remembered it as I was walking to the backyard. I'm sorry." He looked down as he apologized, probably feeling he had really messed something up by forgetting one piece of ribbon. I reached out and touched his arm.

"It's not a big deal. I think I'm going to take a flower and put it in her hair instead. Problem fixed." He gave me a half smile as if to say, you're such a genius. Kyle reached down, took my hand off his arm, and brought it up to his lips kissing the back of it. He then leaned in and kissed me, not having a care in the world that we were in public. I blushed and looked around but then realized that we were surrounded by romance.

"How are my three favorite girls doing?" He kissed me again on the cheek, putting his face only inches from mine.

"Julia is so excited and she looks so beautiful. I'm doing good.

I'm ready to get Abby married off." I laughed at my joke and Kyle smiled back before bending all the way down to kiss my stomach.

"I was referring to the favorite girl in here. How's the newest one doing?" He softly touched the small bump on my belly and then kissed it again before standing back up.

"I know you were talking about her. She's doing really good. She's been relaxed today, just moving a little, but not too bad." We had only known for three days that it was a girl, and for the last three days, Kyle had made the switch from calling the fetus the baby to her, she, and baby girl.

"That's good. I'm glad she's relaxed today." Kyle looked over at Marcelo and they waved at each other at the same time.

"I'm going to go say hey to Marc. I'll be right back. You should sit down for a second." He gave me a scolding but playful look, and then turned to go talk to Marcelo. I watched him walk away as the light cast a perfect hue around his body. It was almost reminiscent of the first time I had seen Paul in the classroom and the light had come into the window and outlined his body as well.

Paul had long vanished after Beth had him terminated. I wish I could say that what happened was a simple mistake and now I've forgotten all about it and life goes on, but that's not the case. I still on a rare occasion think of Paul. The thoughts are less often now than a year ago. Even though the thoughts are negative, and a reminder of my guilt and the humiliation that happened, I find that they come to me at the oddest of times and strangest of places. There are days when the love between Kyle and me is so strong that I can barely remember Paul, and can almost pretend it never even happened. Then there are other days where the smell of him and the memories haunt me like a horrible dream.

The truth was as if the whole experience put a stain on my soul. A stain that can never be fully removed or purged clean. I can only hope in time it might fade. Abby and I have had few, but deep conversations about the events of that fall and my decision to keep the knowledge of those events from Kyle. However selfish my decision may seem to some, I can't help but have the desire to protect him from the pain and torture of the truth. I know I could never even begin to ask him to forgive me if he knew, because I still can't, and most likely, never will forgive myself entirely.

I face the guilt and remorse for my betrayal alone and I try to hate myself a little less each day. Abby tells me often that time does heal all things. I am sure one day I will forgive myself.

I have come to learn to appreciate my side of the fence. I know I don't deserve the lawn that I have, but as it turns out, the grass really isn't greener on the other side.

Made in the USA
Middletown, DE
24 January 2018